#SURVIVING HIGHSCHOOL

#SURVIVING HIGHSCHOOL

Do It for the Vine

A NOVEL

Lele Pons

WITH MELISSA DE LA CRUZ

GALLERY BOOKS

NEW YORK   LONDON   TORONTO   SYDNEY   NEW DELHI

G ⫟

Gallery Books
An Imprint of Simon & Schuster, Inc.
1230 Avenue of the Americas
New York, NY 10020

First Gallery Books hardcover edition April 2016

GALLERY BOOKS and colophon are registered trademarks of Simon & Schuster, Inc.

For information about special discounts for bulk purchases, please contact Simon & Schuster Special Sales at 1-866-506-1949 or business@simonandschuster.com.

The Simon & Schuster Speakers Bureau can bring authors to your live event. For more information or to book an event contact the Simon & Schuster Speakers Bureau at 1-866-248-3049 or visit our website at www.simonspeakers.com.

Crying emoji created by Pham Thi Dieu Linh from Noun Project
Dancer emoji created by nikki rodriguez from Noun Project
Hourglass emoji created by Blaise Sewell from Noun Project
Wink emoji created by Arkthus from Noun Project
Devil emoji created by WARPAINT Media Inc. from Noun Project

Manufactured in the United States of America

10 9 8 7 6 5 4 3 2 1

Library of Congress Cataloging-in-Publication Data is available.

ISBN 978-1-5011-2053-4
ISBN 978-1-5011-2055-8 (ebook)

A Note About This Book

This is a novel, and the character "Lele Pons" is based on the real Lele Pons (but is not her, exactly), and the stories in this book were *inspired* by Lele's life and her Vines (but the story is made up).

This is not a memoir.

It's a fictional memoir, if such a thing can exist.

Why not?

—Lele Pons and Melissa de la Cruz

Lele:

For my fans

Melissa:

For Mike and Mattie, always

#HIGHSCHOOLZERO

September to December

PROLOGUE

𝒯o my lovely and beautiful readers. Before I tell you the story of how I vowed to survive high school, I'd like to talk about something near and dear to my heart.

See, every human being (and most animals, I find) have their own unique essence, an essence comprised of deeply rooted qualities that make them who they are. Ancient Greek philosophers would refer to this as the "soul"—but I am not an ancient Greek philosopher, I am a teenage girl, and so I will call it Lele-ness. Of course, you wouldn't call it Lele-ness, you would call it Sara-ness or Jason-ness, or whatever your name might be.

My point is: I believe that YOU-ness is something very special, no matter who you are, and it ought to be celebrated. So I shall now tell you how I came to be truly Lele, a person I love for better or for worse.

Of course, part of your essence comes into this world with you at birth, but it's really what happens next that starts to shape you into *you*. I was born in Caracas, a major city in Venezuela, but quickly moved to the countryside where I—get this—lived in a barn. I mean, can you even? Picture this: baby Lele running barefoot through cornfields miles and miles away from civilization.

I didn't have dogs or cats as pets, instead I had baby tigers and monkeys as close friends. My whole childhood I knew nothing of shopping malls or (gasp!) the internet. For entertainment I had only nature—bird-watching and berry picking and, best of all, stargazing.

For as long as I can remember, language has been a struggle for me. Words didn't come to me as a child, so I used my body to communicate. It felt so much more natural to express my-self that way. I felt comfortable drawing out my thoughts and feelings, instead of verbalizing them, so I'd often draw out storyboards—sometimes eight pages long—to explain to my parents or teachers what it was that I wanted. Everyone has their strengths and their weaknesses: for me, artwork and move-ment were strengths, while speaking to others using words was a weakness.

Now take all of that and add immigrating to the United States, and you have a potential disaster on your hands. I knew nothing about American culture, and my differences paralyzed me with anxiety. For comfort and peace of mind, I turned to entertain-ment. I found I was embraced by my peers for being physically dramatic and, well, funny. I found that I knew how to make people laugh, and so I held on to that as a life raft in the sea of the most confusing and alienating time in my life.

I believe it was my wild upbringing plus my verbal disadvantages that led me to be the performer and one-of-a-kind weirdo with a heart of gold that I am today. It's not always easy being Lele, but every morning when I wake up I say, "Bring it on," and that attitude is what has taken me on this incredible journey.

I encourage you to think about the life events and circumstances that have made you truly YOU, and to celebrate every single part of yourself—the strong, the weak, the good, the bad, and the ugly—because each part contributes to making you special and AMAZ-ING. Trust me.

So that is the story of how I developed my Lele essence. What follows is the story of how I survived my first year at Miami High and how I got to share my message with almost ten million followers. I hope you enjoy it!

XO Lele

1

Aaar, That's Quite a Black Eye, Matey

(O FOLLOWERS)

The first thing you need to know about me is that I wasn't always the gorgeous, sexy, cool, breezy blonde you know today. I know, I know, it's shocking. The truth is, it wasn't so long ago that I was an awkward outcast wearing braces and last season's clothes two sizes too big. "No!" I can hear you disagreeing. "Lele has always been *perfect.*" Well, you're right, I have always been perfect, but that's another story for another time. Let me take you back to the dark days so you can see that once upon a time my struggle was deep and my struggle was real:

I'm sixteen and it's my first day at Miami High. The hallways are long and the student body is . . . intimidating. See, my last school (St. Anne's School for Girls) was small—you might even say cozy, intimate. Oh, right, and Catholic. I come from a small Catholic school and a sheltered Catholic family; until today all I've known are the sweet, familiar faces of the same twenty kids I grew up with, plus everything that's ever happened on the Disney Channel (#TBT Zenon: The Zequel #NeverForget).

My parents, Anna and Luis Pons, decided, abruptly and unjustly, that I should move to a bigger school so I could meet more people, broaden my horizons, blah blah blah, before I go to college. Didn't anyone tell them you can get into college from any old high school just as long as you have a dope internet presence? Welcome to the twenty-first century, Mom and Dad, please take a seat.

Okay, I didn't mean that, sometimes I let sassiness get the better of me. Obviously college is a good and important thing—but is it for me? I'm super eager to become an actress and would get so impatient having to put that off for an extra four years, so I don't know. I'm ready to put on a show for the world; I'm ready to seize life by the horns and make jazz hands.

Anyway, I'm a good Catholic girl and I respect my parents' wishes (look, I do my best, okay?), which is how I got here, day one at Miami High, epicenter of pretty girls and some of the most unrealistically good-looking guys you will ever see.

I wake up late (typical) and fail to get my first-day outfit down the way I had envisioned. The frilly white blouse, black pants, and knee-high boots that Rihanna had pulled off so effortlessly have me looking less like a pop star and more like a pirate. But I figure, hey, YOLO, right? And head out to Hot-Guy High in disguise as Captain Jack Sparrow. (I know YOLO is dated, but come on, you only live once! Heh.)

First things first: my schedule. A lady who looks like an old potato with glasses and unevenly applied lipstick hands it to me at the front desk.

"Welcome to Miami High," she says, like she'd rather kill herself than even open her mouth to speak these words. She smells like strawberry candy and cloves, and it's a little too much to handle first thing in the morning to be *quite* honest. Anyway, here it is, my educational fate for the next ten months:

1st period: English
2nd period: World History
3rd period: Calculus
4th period: Gym

5th period: Marine Biology
6th period: Spanish

Right away, I stand out like a sore thumb. And yes, I get the looks. You know what I'm talking about: those evil stares kids love to give that say "Ew, who the F is she?" In first period, English, a boy with spiky blue hair throws a crumpled ball of paper that bounces off my head. During second period, world history, a kid with a backward baseball cap calls out, "Hey, why do you talk so weird?" When I explain to him that I have a Venezuelan accent, he calls back, "I dunno, it sounds like you just don't know how to talk."

"You mean speak," I say.

"Huh?"

"You mean to tell me that I don't know how to speak. Grammatically, I mean. It's speak, not talk. In this context."

"Oh my God, what a freak," the boy mutters to a cluster of equally jaded, pimple-faced boys who laugh and nod their heads.

In third period, calculus, a redheaded girl with glasses approaches me to say, "Everyone here dresses kind of more . . . subtle. Just so you know. For tomorrow." Then she scuttles away to join her gaggle. Everyone has a gaggle. Except me. Lele Pons, lost and friendless, small fish in a big pond. Sigh. *Here we go, junior year,* I think to myself, then drown my woes in an ice-cold Pepsi.

After third period comes lunch. Now, reader, I don't know how long it's been since the last time you were in a public school cafeteria, but let me tell you: it is one of the single most frightening places in the world. Literally, high school cafeterias deserve their own season of *American Horror Story.* Reader, please let me have the honor of describing the diverse array of atrocities within the Miami High cafeteria:

- **Lunch ladies:** Mean, scowling women who seem to hate their lives and hate us just for being who we are. One with a name tag that reads "Iris" yells at me for not having my money ready in time. Then yells at me more for not having my money transferred onto a One Card (which apparently is like a debit card specifically for gross high school cafeterias?)

- **Hairnets:** The lunch ladies wear hairnets that get sweaty and oily and make me think of nets used to catch fish—I can't look at their heads without imagining fish out of water flapping around desperately for their lives. Appetite = gone.

- **Inedible food:** This food is practically criminal. I honestly, *honestly* don't know what it is. It looks like a mound of Styrofoam covered in gravy and topped with cubes of something that could or could not be chicken. It comes with a side of "tangerines" that are actually just shreds of tangerine floating in corn syrup.

- **Atmosphere:** It smells bad; it's loud; there isn't a fair amount of oxygen to go around.

- **High school kids:** Never will you see as many high school kids packed into one place as in a cafeteria. If you've seen *Mean Girls,* then you know about the clique labels (sexually active band geeks, preps, girls who eat their feelings, hot Asians, etc.), but at Miami High there's none of this. At Miami High, nothing is simple. Everyone is clumped together, each clique infringing on the personal space of the one next to it, so that you can't tell where the jocks end and the nerds begin. School administrations won't ever be able to abolish cliques, but they can force them to sit together, and this nightmare is the result. Unlike in *Mean Girls* and also Every High School Movie Ever Made Ever, where the main character and often new girl doesn't know where to sit because none of the cliques will welcome her, I don't know where to sit because there are literally *no places to sit.* Even if a clique were to welcome me,

I would have to sit on someone's lap. Dear God, this place is a zoo.

With nowhere to sit and no desire to eat my food, I toss my cardboard tray in the trash and hurry outside to get some air before I have a panic attack or accidentally stab someone out of fear and confusion. I sit down outside with my back against the wall and count down the minutes until this weirdness is over. But of course a watched pot never boils, and there's no rest for the weary. A very professional woman in a blue blazer and patent-leather heels and a Hillary Clinton–type haircut clicks by clutching a walkie-talkie like she's headed to diffuse a bomb. When she sees me, she comes to a startling halt.

"Excuse me, why are we outside?" She sounds vengeful and thirsty, like she wants to suck my blood.

"Ermm . . . I don't know why *you* are. I am outside because I couldn't breathe in there."

"That doesn't matter; you know the rules. No students allowed outside the cafeteria during lunch hour."

"Oh, see, this is my first day. I didn't know."

"Well, now you know. Get back in there so I don't have to write you up."

"Write me up? Like in jail? I really don't want to go back in."

"Listen, I don't know how they did things at your old school, but we don't make exceptions for Miami High students. If I treated you like a princess, I'd have to treat everyone like a princess. You're just going to have to eat inside like everyone else."

"Because I want fresh air I'm asking to be treated like a princess?"

"Please don't take an attitude with me, I haven't written up anyone today and I don't want to start now."

"Good Lord." I'm practically laughing at this point, the absurdity of this woman and the situation is too much to handle. "I guess I'll have to start a rebellion."

"No need to be so dramatic. Stop by the main desk after school to pick up an off-campus form. Have your parents sign it and you'll receive off-campus privileges during lunch. You don't have to eat in the cafeteria, but you can't be on campus. It's for safety reasons."

"*Thank* you. I'm so glad I didn't have to turn this into something dramatic."

She huffs and clicks away, her head leading her body so that she was practically a diagonal line. Gotta admire that delusional determination.

The bell rings and I've never been so excited to get back to class. I notice a kind-looking African American girl walking back on campus with impeccably braided hair and indisputably nerdy glasses.

"Hey," I call to her, "do you go off campus for lunch?"

"Oh, yeah, there's no way I could survive going in there every day." She gestures to the cafeteria.

"It's disgusting, right? I thought maybe it was just my imagination."

"No, girl, you're right on track."

"For the first time in my life, maybe. I'm Lele Pons."

"I'm Darcy Smith. Nice to meet you. Make sure you get an off-campus pass ASAP, you seem nice and I would hate to lose you to that place."

Note to self: get an off-campus pass or perish.

Note to self: I don't like this school.

Note to self: But I sort of like Darcy.

Fourth period is gym. Coach Washington is this boxy-shaped woman with a bowl haircut and two silver teeth. Oh, and she's missing the pinkie finger on her left hand. She passes out these ugly neon uniforms and then marches us to the locker room where we are actually supposed to get naked in front of each other. Ew. Being a Catholic, I'm modest, and I try to be as discreet as possible—I don't even know these girls' names yet, and I don't want their very first impression of me to be this beige Nike sports bra. But it's too late. A slender-though-curvy brunette with big, bright brown-green eyes and fluttery eyelashes spots me in the crowd and, sensing my weakness, pounces.

"Hey, new girl." She smirks. "I think my grandma has that same bra."

"Congratulations on knowing so much about your grandma's underwear," I say right back, without thinking. The room goes silent and Bright Eyes raises her eyebrows at me in a way that, I have to admit, freaks me out a little. Have I messed with the wrong chica? She shuts her locker door slowly and deliberately, as if sending me some kind of warning sign, then flips her hair and turns to leave. "Yo' mama wore this bra last night," I mutter to myself and whoever is still listening. Great one, Lele, great one.

Out on the field, Coach Washington takes roll and I learn that Bright Eyes actually goes by the name Yvette Amparo. Washington pronounces my name like "Lee Lee" and I just absolutely have to correct her. That's the second thing you need to know about me: I can really lose it when bitches call me Lee Lee. Some dimwits even call me Ley Ley or Lilly. Does nobody know how to read? It's Lele . . . like, Leh Leh, or like "you can stand under my umbrella ella ella eh eh eh," except if you add some L's: "You can stand under my umbrella ella ella Lele Lele." That's how you can remember it whenever you're struggling. Leh, like heh. I try to explain this all to Coach Washington, but she loses patience quickly and moves on.

I gotta tell you, tackle football seems a little intense for a first-day sport. Couldn't we just stick to something safe, like jumping jacks? Apparently not. Apparently gym teachers in large public schools enjoy torturing their students. As soon as Coach Washington puts Yvette and me on opposite teams, I know I'm going to have to take her down. That's the third thing you need to know about me: I'm a physical person. I'm not saying I'm not smart, I'm just saying

I prefer to use my body to work out issues. You know, go on a run, have a solo dance party, punch someone if necessary. I've seen the way boys resolve their discrepancies: a little roughhousing and it's all in the past. They're like lions in the wild. But us girls, for whatever reason, we're expected to talk it out like little ladies. Gah!

Anyway, so we get out on the field and I'm all in. Suddenly it's like if I don't win this game for my team, I will have officially failed my first day. If I win, however, I'll be my own personal hero and will triumph over the brutal awkwardness leading up to this moment. As soon as Washington blows her whistle I'm running and jumping and diving and clawing my way through the field with so much enthusiasm that I forget I don't actually know the first thing about tackle football. Oops. Through my veil of adrenaline I can see someone toss Yvette the ball, and I go for it. Maybe I shouldn't, maybe it's wrong, but I throw my body on top of her, tackling poor skinny Yvette to the ground. But she doesn't go down easily. She puts up a fight, thrashing her head all around until CLONK, her skull knocks into my face with the weight of a bowling ball. I bite my lip, trying not to scream. Stars spin around my head cartoon-style and Coach is blowing on that stupid, shrill whistle.

"Okay, okay, time out. What's going on here?" she says, ramming her hands together perpendicularly in the "time out" gesture.

"*Lee Lee* attacked me." Ugh.

"I didn't attack you; I tackled you. Like how you do sometimes in tackle football. Which we are currently playing." I put my hand to my right eye, which already feels bruised. Yvette gets all huffy and Coach makes me sit down, and then I get huffy all by myself in a corner, mad at Yvette and Coach Washington and the kid who threw a paper ball at my head earlier and my stupid parents for making me come to this evil, awful place.

By the time I'm changed back into my regular (a.k.a. pirate) clothes, my right eye is completely swollen shut. Bitch gave me a black eye!

"You know you look like a pirate, right?" Yvette snarls, sauntering out of the gym.

"Arrrrr!" I holler after her. I want to make her walk the plank.

At home my parents ask me that awful question every kid dreads hearing, the question that sounds like nails on a chalkboard: "How was your day?"

"Fine," I say. Then I change my mind, suddenly inhabited by the spirit of honesty. "Actually, it was terrible. The place is ginormous and everyone thinks they're so cool."

"Oh, Lele"—my mom says my name perfectly, always a comfort, albeit slight—"I'm sure none of them are as cool as you."

"Thanks, Mom, I'll make sure to tell them my mom thinks I'm super cool."

I go to my room and collapse onto my bed, groan into the pillow, kick my feet a little bit for dramatic effect. After my self-pity party I decide I've suffered enough for one day. It's time to shake it off like Taylor Swift, time to let it go like Elsa.

It's time to go to my happy place: Vine. In *Breakfast at Tiffany's*, Audrey Hepburn says that nothing very bad can happen at Tiffany's, and that's exactly how I feel about Vine. Nothing very bad can happen on Vine, at least not to me. Vine is the one place I feel untouchable. I sign into my account and type in the title of tonight's Vine: "The Advantages of Being a Boy."

2

The Advantages of Being a Boy

(2,000 FOLLOWERS)

*A*llow me to back up. What is this Vine, you might ask? Well, maybe no one would ask that. But the truth of the matter is, I once did have to ask that. Not only did I used to be "uncool" but I also used to be a social media virgin, long past the time it was normal. Meaning, it was 2011 and I still didn't have Facebook. Or a phone. At my core I was *not* a city girl. Sometimes I felt like I wasn't even a Planet Earth girl. Sometimes I still do feel that way, actually. But back to social media: it never made sense to me. It just didn't seem appealing to collect fake friends like Pokémon cards and listen to everyone brag about the cool things they did over the weekend.

I mean, am I crazy or might there be more to life than that?

Anyway, when Lucy, a BFF from St. Anne's, showed me her Vine account, I felt an instant connection. It was the first social media platform I had ever encountered that seemed to be about genuine self-expression versus only the blind desperation for social valida-tion. But I mean, it was more than that.

Vine wasn't just a way to express myself, it was the outlet I had been waiting for my whole life. For as long as I can remember, whenever I struggled with words, I used images to tell a story. I used physical communication. When I discovered Vine, I found the medium through which I would finally be able to communicate fully with the world around me, to share my thoughts and concerns with anyone who might want to listen. I finally had a voice, and I was hooked.

I wasn't looking to gain a following. Really, I wasn't! But the girls at St. Anne's thought my videos were funny and were really supportive about it right away. I quickly became "Vine famous" within my tiny private school, which means basically I went to school with one thousand kids and all of them followed me! People ask me how this happened, and I want to be clear that it was really never anything fancy at all: people want honesty, and I was not afraid to give it to them. It's as simple as that.

Cut back to: I'm at Miami High and nobody knows who I am—nobody appreciates my humor and honesty and uniqueness, because I've been quickly dismissed as a freak. Would I be so ostracized, so quickly judged, if I were a boy instead?

Don't get me wrong, I like being a girl. I like my long, thick blond hair and wearing a glamorous dress for a fabulous occasion. But being a girl comes with a price. Well, lots of prices. Being a girl means having to put energy into your looks, having to wear a bra (so uncomfortable), having to pee sitting down (so inconvenient), and ultimately, it means one day having to push a bowling-ball-sized human out of you and call it the miracle of life—if that's your thing. Miracle shmiracle, that sounds like a straight-up nightmare.

For me, on morning number two as a Miami High outcast, being a girl means having to wake up three hours early to get my look on fleek. In case you don't speak my language, "on fleek" means "on point." And "on point" means, like . . . fabulous. So anyway, I set my alarm for five in the morning (brutal!) but I manage to hit snooze a couple hundred times and end up sleeping until about seven thirty, which means I only have thirty minutes to get on fleek *and* get to school. If you know anything about being on fleek you know that thirty minutes will not do the trick. Or the fleek. Heh.

I slip into my jeans and navy-blue polo shirt hoping to glide through the day unnoticed. A simple pair of white Converse, I figure, are sure to keep me under the radar. Getting dressed goes smoothly enough, but here's where I run into trouble, here's where the day first goes off the rails (7:45 a.m. is as good a time as any for the madness to begin): it's my hair. Oh God, my hair. My hair is long, long, long, long. If it were any longer I would be Rapunzel, I swear. And sure, long blond hair sounds nice, it might even sound enviable, but I am telling you, it is the hair from hell. No matter what I do, I wake up with it in complete disarray, knots and tangles and kinks and frizz. It's a daily battle, a struggle of good versus evil, me in the bathroom using a comb to wrestle my hair like a dragon (do dragons wrestle? I don't know). As soon as I get my thousands of hair strands untangled and smoothed out, a bunch of them start popping up again, refusing to stay in place, rejecting the status quo of hair, rebelling against their oppressor, going against the grain like a bunch of whiny hippies. Sometimes I think I should just shave it all off.

Boys don't have this problem. Boys run one hand through their hair and they're good to go. That's why they're the enemy. Their life is *way* too easy.

Downstairs Mom and Dad have made me my favorite breakfast: Eggo waffles and Vermont natural maple syrup. Okay, so it sounds basic, but I don't even care, there's really nothing better. I know I complain about my parents, but the truth is they're not the worst. How bad could they be, when they've been consistently making me Eggo waffles every morning since I was five? Legend has it, when we first moved from Venezuela I was so homesick that all that could cheer me up were these frozen waffles, so it became a daily morning tradition. Okay, so it's not the most interesting legend in the world, but it's mine, so leave me alone.

"You look different today, sweetheart," Dad says as I sit down and take a bite of my syrup-drenched Eggo.

"I'm not dressed like a pirate today," I say, mouth half full.

"Oh, maybe that's it."

"You look lovely," Mom says, filling my glass with orange juice.

"I liked your outfit yesterday," Dad interjects rather uselessly. "It was creative. Unique. I hope you're not going to let this new school squash your individuality."

"Well, if it does squash my individuality it will be your fault, as you are the one who sent me there."

They give each other the famous look that says, "Well, that's our Lele," and that is the end of that.

A miracle in first-period English: Mr. Contreras presents us with Alexei Kuyper, transfer student. There's really only one way to say this: Alexei is *hot*. Blue eyes, blond hair pushed playfully off his brilliant forehead, abs loosely defined behind his white T-shirt. He's James Dean for the modern schoolgirl. A dream. Mr. Contreras asks him to tell us about himself, just like I had to on the first day, and he does so effortlessly, unlike me, who, um, just stood there turning red.

"Hi, I'm Alexei, I just moved with my family to Florida."

"Where are you from, Alexei?" someone asks eagerly.

"I'm from Belgium. We moved a few weeks ago. I'm happy to be here. Any other questions?" The class laughs with him, he's won them over. Lucky bastard. His smile is winning. Swoon!

"Lele is also new," Mr. Contreras says, and my ears get instantly hot. "You can sit next to her. Lele, raise your hand please for Mr. Kuyper." I raise my hand, certain I look like an outright baboon, and gorgeous Alexei finds me right away. He must be super smart.

"Hey," I say, "nice to meet you."

"You too."

"Are the waffles really good?" I ask.

"What?" He doesn't get it. Oh God, oh God.

"In Belgium. You know, Belgian waffles? Aren't the waffles supposed to be really good there? I'm really into waffles." *I'm really into waffles?* Oh, Lele.

"Yeah, actually"—he laughs, flashes that winning grin—"they're supposed to be the best, but I don't really get waffles, to be honest. I'm more of a pancake guy."

"You don't get waffles? Are you psycho?"

"Are YOU psycho?"

"A little."

"Me too," he says, and then you'll never guess what happened: HE WINKED AT ME! We both smile and my heart feels like it's going to jump out through my throat.

Leaving class, I trip over a backpack and crash straight into him, bumping my lip on his shoulder. His T-shirt gets caught in my braces and untangling it becomes this whole thing. So much for that romantic and flirty moment. He's nice about it, helps me get to my feet and all, but not soon enough to prevent everyone from noticing.

"L-O-L," one girl says to another. "That new girl is sooooo clumsy."

"Oh, I know," says the second girl. "Awk-ward."

When I arrive at my locker after school I find that it has been spray-painted with red letters that spell out: FRESH MEAT.

"Are you kidding me?" I say out loud to no one in particular. I'm so shocked, I don't know whether to be scared or to laugh. This sort of thing gets people suspended now. We've all seen the It Gets Better ads, right? Out of the corner of my eye I can see a group of guys and girls snickering and pointing.

"Welcome to Miami High, fresh meat!" one girl with buoyantly curly hair calls out with a mean-intentioned laugh. The way she says it makes it sound like a warning, like this won't be the last of my metaphorical beating. Like I better watch out. Who the hell are these kids and why don't they have anything better to do? I guess I always thought high school bullying was a fiction created for 1980s rom coms, I didn't realize kids could actually be that petty in real life. Sure, kids at St. Anne's weren't perfect, but they weren't ever this outwardly mean. Normally I'm a big fan of crying, but I can't let these idiots see that they've gotten to me, so I fight back the tears and frustration, and stand up extra tall like I can't see or hear them.

Alexei walks up as I'm struggling to cram all my books into my vandalized locker. One falls out and he grabs it for me. What a gentleman.

"Thanks," I say. "Hey, did they do this to you too?" I show him the front of the locker.

"Um, no, that's pretty brutal."

"I don't get it! You're new too, why aren't you getting picked on?"

"I'm normal; I fit in. Kids are insecure and they lash out at who-ever is the most different." He shrugs.

"It's not fair."

"Are you saying you prefer that I get picked on?"

"No—I just don't know what it is about me. I guess I never thought of myself as *that* different. And I guess I'd prefer not to go through it alone."

"You're not that different; you're just a free spirit. You don't care as much about what people think, and that makes them nervous. And you're not going through it alone; I'm here. I got your back."

"Oh." I try to keep from blushing but I can't help it. "Thank you."

"Where do you live?" he asks. "I was thinking I could walk you home." What is this, 1952? Romance central? Where am I? Who am I? Why can't I feel my face? (But I love it!)

"On Romero Street, it would be like a twenty-minute walk."

"I could use a bit of a tour—we just moved here." His voice is husky and exotic; it has the sound of a tropical breeze, you know, if tropical breezes had a sound. He can speak English perfectly but he's got that offbeat rhythm that comes from being foreign, that hint of insecurity that comes off as sexy.

"Yes, you definitely need a tour. We can walk, you seem like you're in good enough shape. I mean good shape. I mean, you look like a twenty-minute walk wouldn't kill you. I didn't mean to say that you're hot." I once read an article in *Cosmopolitan* about how to flirt; somehow I don't think I've mastered the art.

"So you don't think I'm hot?" he asked.

Uh-oh.

"Um, no, it's not that I don't think you're hot. I think you're . . . I mean, are you nice-looking? Sure. You don't look bad. I mean—"

"I'm just messing with you, weirdo. Let's go, yeah?" He smiled. *Weirdo.* He already has a pet name for me! Heart-eyes emoji, heart-eyes emoji.

Is this really happening? I am being walked home by a boy. On my second day of school. Maybe I'm not such a loser after all. I bet stupid Yvette Amparo didn't get walked home by a boy today.

We have the best conversation on the way home, him with his sexy foreign accent and me with my garbled Venezuelan undertones. We talk about really deep stuff, like last week's episode of *So You Think You Can Dance* and the Red Wedding on *Game of Thrones.* He so obviously gets me. He asks me about my hopes and dreams, and I tell him all about how I want to be a famous actress but the idea of auditioning in front of producers gives me panic attacks. I ask him about his hopes and dreams, and he tells me about how he wants to be a model or professional surfer, and maybe an actor too, but if that doesn't work out then maybe a doctor.

The whole thing is beyond perfect except: I have to pee *so* badly. Why did I drink that liter of Coke during sixth period? Every caffeine rush has its price to pay, lesson learned. *Ten minutes until I'm home, only ten minutes. You can do it, Lele, you're almost there.* I try to tell myself these things but I can feel my bladder stretching like a water balloon. Alexei is talking about how much he misses Belgium, and how he wonders if he'll ever get to go back, but all I can think of is getting to a toilet, so I'm just nodding and saying mhm-mhm like a moron. He probably thinks I'm a total idiot. Or a bitch. I keep smiling and fluttering my eyelids like the *Cosmo* article said to do, but I think I just ended up looking deranged. Deranged and agonized. Not sexy.

Did it just get hotter? Yes, it definitely did. A cloud has shifted and the sun is now beating down on us. I can feel beads of sweat gathering under my bra, I worry my boobs might be in danger of drowning.

"Wow, it's hot out today," Alexei says.

"Oh, is it? Yeah, I guess so." I shrug, easy breezy, all the while inside I am dying. Then, because this Belgian boy is evil and wants to torture me, he actually takes off his shirt. This is cruel for two reasons: (1) I am about to die of heatstroke and can't do anything about it, and (2) his abs are so marvelously defined he could be a statue. A bronze, brilliantly beautiful statue. I try not to look directly at them, for fear they might blind me. To add insult to injury, Alexei taps my shoulder and says, "Be right back, I have to pee," then saunters off behind a nearby tree to relieve himself.

First of all, rude. Doesn't he know he's in the presence of a premium woman? Second of all, not fair! I'm honestly seconds away from bursting and this guy can pee as soon as he feels the urge. This is what I'm talking about with boys. They have it so much easier. They'll never know the true meaning of discomfort; they'll never know how we suffer.

When he comes back all shirtless and relieved, practically glowing, the guy has the nerve to try and give me a high five! What do I do? Well, I'll tell you. I punched him in the balls like he deserved!

Just kidding, I didn't leave him hanging. After all, his greatest crime is also part of why I already like him so much: he's a boy.

3

That Person Who Always Catches You at Your Worst Moments

(2,500 FOLLOWERS)

*D*ay three and I'm already a Miami High Master. I've met a boy and I have a lay-low plan ready to be put into play: dress inconspicuously, blend in, avoid Yvette Amparo, stay quiet in class, slip off campus for lunch, and always watch where I'm walking. Easy enough. In other words, I have conquered one of the biggest feats of all time: surviving high school. Okay, fine, so I have about six hundred more days of this madness until I can properly say I've survived, but still, I'm on my way, all right?

This is how I went into the day: confident, glowing, *West Side Story*'s "I Feel Pretty" jogging through my head on repeat. In English class, Alexei passed me a note that reads, "Hey, cutie." WITH A WINKY FACE! He could have just sent me a text, but he's the old-fashioned type. Swoon, double swoon. I'm telling you, I was on top of the world.

It's second period world history when things start to crash and burn. I walk into the empty class like I'm this invincible goddess, five minutes early, head held high. And because my head is held so high—in the clouds like a total moron—I'm not looking where I should be, i.e., at the *floor*. My foot gets caught on a chair leg and I go flying. I mean, literally, I'm in the air soaring headfirst into a nearby desk.

It's okay, Lele, I tell myself, collecting my books, which have scattered uncontrollably like marbles every which way. *No one is here yet, you're good, bb, you got this.* At which point I stand up and, to my absolute horror, see Darcy Smith sitting on the other side of the class, watching me with quiet, judging eyes. Darcy is a pretty girl, but from what I can tell is an outcast too. She has dark, smooth skin and a smart-looking smile.

"You didn't see that, Darcy," I say. She just stares, blinking, then looks away. All I can do is hope she gets the picture: Dead girls tell no tales.

Was that the worst of my day? Not even close. During gym, I got hit in the head by a basketball. I don't know who threw the ball so unprofessionally, but my money is on Yvette Amparo. And guess what?! There was Darcy, who doesn't even have gym fourth period, giving me that silent stare. What is she, stalking me? I put my finger to my lips and said, "Shhh." She shook her head and smiled.

Small potatoes, I figured, it's not like anyone important has seen me act a fool. And by "anyone important" I mean Alexei. I shouldn't have even let those thoughts anywhere near my head, because just by thinking them I bestowed a curse upon myself. Here's how it goes down:

It's lunch and the cafeteria is serving up my favorite (spaghetti and meatballs), except it's watery and smells like a barn. Lovely. My plan to sneak off campus didn't quite happen. Oh well. I set the sad excuse for food down on one of these Day-Glo orange tables across from Alexei, a.k.a. Bae, a.k.a. Sex God.

"How's your day been, Lele?" He says my name more perfectly than perfect. Never has a name sounded so magical.

"Oh, you know"—I flip my hair and slide as gracefully as possible into the seat—"it's been another regular day in paradise." I flash him the most genuine smile I can muster.

"Anything interesting happen so far?" Just as he says this, I set my elbow down on the corner of my food tray, creating a *Titanic*-like tip. Only this tragedy is *much* worse. Spaghetti *everywhere,* pasta sauce splattered across my white polo: I look like a murder scene.

"Oh my God, what a freak!" A voice rises up from the cafeteria crowd and suddenly everyone is pointing at me. iPhones raise and the room fills with the *chk-chk-chk* sound of photos being snapped. I could die. I should die. Instead, I scream.

"MOTHERF**KER, WHAT THE F**CK, STUPID F**CK-ING SPAGHETTI! I SWEAR TO GOD IF THIS DAY GETS ANY WORSE—"

"Lele." Alexei grabs my arm. "It's okay. It's okay. It's just pasta. I'll help you clean it up. This stuff happens." Isn't he the best? Alexei, Bae, Sex God, Hero. He likes me despite my being a total space cadet; he sees through the madness to the real me, my awesome sexy self. I know it. I can feel it. Okay, so maybe it's a little early, and I'm projecting. But maybe I won't end up alone forever after all. He runs to get some napkins. I sigh a deep sigh of relief: everything is good in the world; it doesn't matter that I'm a hot mess—I was born this way, baby. That's when I look up and see Darcy Smith, calmly eating alone in the far corner of the room, and this time she is outright *laughing* at me.

Waiting for Alexei after school, I see Darcy walk past my locker. She's wearing the same white polo as me, only hers isn't spaghetti-stained.

"Hey," I call after her, and she turns around. "It's Darcy, right?"

"Yeah, and you're Lele?"

"Lele the Miami High hot mess. That's the full name, actually."

"Nothing wrong with a hot mess," she says. Fireworks go off in my head; an orchestra plays.

"Yes, thank you! That's what I always say!"

"Great minds think alike."

"You," I say, "I knew you were smart. You know what you are?"

"Besides smart and pretty and a representative of the black minority at Miami High?"

"Yes, besides that. You're that person who always catches me at my worst moments. Everyone has one."

"Really? I don't think I have one of those."

"Well, now it can be me!"

"Yikes, I'll make sure to be on my best behavior whenever you're around."

"No, you have to be on your worst! Hey, do you wanna come over? I'm in the mood to postpone homework for a few hundred hours."

"Wow, great minds do really think alike."

We're days away from having a secret handshake, I can feel it.

I let Alexei tag along for homework procrastination too, mostly because he's so nice to look at. At home, I make sure my parents are locked safely in their rooms (Lord knows I've had enough embarrassment for one day) and then get to work on my latest masterpiece. Alexei films while Darcy and I act out tonight's Vine: "That Person Who Always Catches You at Your Worst Moments."

4

Bully Target / Sometimes I Feel Invisible

(2,543 FOLLOWERS)

*I*t's an extra-sunny Friday and we're walking to third-period calculus. We're halfway across the grated bridge connecting the history
building to the math building when Darcy says she knows some
people who are having a party.

"Wait a second," I say, stopping us in our tracks. "Am I not your
only friend? Have you been hiding your other friends from me because you think I'm not cool enough to hang with them? Or worse,
are you hiding ME from your other friends because you're worried
I'll embarrass you?!" I miss my Catholic-school friends and find
myself resenting their extra-busy extracurricular activities, miss
knowing where I stand at all times, miss knowing that my friends
are proud to know me, the security that comes with lifelong loyalty. At Miami High it feels like that rug has been pulled out from
under me.

"Whoa." She looks at me like I'm psycho. Psycho but lovable . . .
a lovable psycho, if you will. "First of all, I wouldn't really call Becca
Cartwright and Yvette Amparo my friends, more like acquaintances.
Second of all—"

"Hold on, this is Yvette Amparo's party?"

"Yeah, do you know her?"

"Know her? She's only ruined my life about seven hundred times." I breathe out my nose like an agitated dragon.

"Anyone ever tell you you're a tad dramatic?"

"Maybe." I do a cinematic, movie-star hair flip for effect. "But anyone in their right mind would agree that Yvette is a real see-you-next-Tuesday."

"Nice, Lele, very mature," says Darcy.

I've barely been friends with this girl for three days and she's already scolding me. I admire her boldness. "Whatever, I'm not going. I honestly can't stand that girl. She's a bully."

"You don't have to talk to her, but I think it would be good for you to go. You could use some socializing, you know, get to know your classmates. All the cool kids are going to be there," says Darcy.

"I'm sorry, did you just say cool kids?! What is this, *High School Musical*?"

"What? What does that even mean?"

"I'm not sure," I have to admit. In *HSM,* was Sharpay the cool kid? Can anyone named Sharpay be cool?

"Look, you don't have to go. I just think we'll have fun. I mean, what else are we going to do on a Friday night?"

As it turns out, Alexei has plans to party with the enemy as well (et tu Brute?!).

"It'll be a good opportunity for you to show her that she doesn't scare you," he says. "I'll see you there."

"No one scares me," I say. "I'm unscareable."

"Boo!" Darcy hollers in my face, and I practically faint from fear.

"Do I have to dress up for this?" I ask from a comfy place on the floor slumped against my bed. Darcy is applying red-brown lip gloss in my vanity mirror, and already looks super gorgeous. She turns to me, scans me up and down.

"Um, you don't have to dress up necessarily, but I would advise you to not wear pink pajamas."

"Aw man, but I love these! They're so cozy. And they fit me so well." I wrap my arms around myself, grinning cheek to cheek.

"That's great, Lele, but this is a party. People do tend to put at least a low amount of effort in."

"Ugh, everything's always so hard." I use the bed frame to pull myself up and begrudgingly head to my closet. Pants, pants, pants, T-shirts, T-shirts, T-shirts . . . hmm, I don't have the most diverse closet in the world. Ah, a dress! At last! Just behind a row of polo shirts is a flowy, flowery white sundress that I think I wore once to a family picnic two years ago, and luckily it still fits like a glove. A slightly tight glove, but a glove nonetheless.

"Cutie!" Darcy exclaims. "Now let's figure out shoes."

"I don't have a lot. I don't think I really get shoes, you know?"

"No, I do not know. Shoes are very important. Everyone knows that."

"Really? I thought clean water and oxygen were really important but okay, I see, it's shoes. You learn something new every day."

"Don't be such a smart-ass. Pick out something strappy and san-dally."

"Jeez, since when are you the fashion police? Look out, world, Miss Bookworm has a whole other side. Well, I hate to disappoint you, but these are our only options." I go into my closet and bring out a pair of white Converse and orange jelly sandals.

"Oh dear," Darcy despairs. "These are your only shoes?"

"Yep."

"How is that possible?"

"I dunno." I shrug. "My old school had uniforms and it just didn't really matter what we wore. It was kinda cool."

Darcy sighs, glances back and forth between the two pairs of shoes, then back and forth again, taking her sweet time as if some-body's life depends on this. Finally, she makes her decision and we head out of my room: Darcy in black Steve Madden flats and me in orange jelly sandals, the official shoe of the five-year-old.

"Um, excuse me?" Mom stops us just as we're about to walk out the front door.

"Yeah, hey, what's up?" I try to keep it cool, confident—nothing to see here, Mom, just a grown-up lady heading out to a party same as always.

"Where do you think you're going?"

"A girl from school is having a party."

"And you were just going to go without asking?"

"I didn't think it would be a big deal," I lie. "It's just a party. Nothing crazy." Darcy stands in the doorway awkwardly chewing a lock of hair.

"Lele, you know the rules, if you're going to a party I need to have the parents' phone number. Will there even be adult supervision?"

"Mom, come on, that's embarrassing. I'm old enough now to use my own judgment, don't you think?"

"No, I do not think. You've already demonstrated bad judgment by choosing to not ask permission."

"Fine." I don't feel up for an argument. "I didn't even really want to go; I don't like these kids anyway. Darcy, go ahead, I'll talk to you after."

Mom eyes me suspiciously.

"What? You're giving in that easily? Lele, this is not like you, what's going on? Are you still not getting along with kids at school?"

"That is correct. Darcy is my only friend." Darcy waves uneasily.

"You know what, just go. Go make friends, be social," says Mom.

"Really?"

"Yeah, you're only young once. And plus, I don't want to be part of the reason you don't have friends."

"Hey, I have friends. Remember Darcy?"

"Just go before I change my mind."

"Hey, what's goin' on here?" My dad has appeared behind Mom, eating off a tray of french fries. He's always had a youthful presence that made him an amazing guy to grow up with as a dad—always up for adventures and practical jokes.

"Lele's going to a party," Mom says. My mom is youthful too, but in a more glamorous way—she curls her ink-black hair and wears oversize, almost cartoonish sunglasses both outside the house and in. They're the type of sunglasses I imagine I'll wear when I'm a movie star. She's my biggest role model. Both of them are, actually.

"Have fun!" Dad calls as I pull Darcy down the driveway toward the Uber. "Don't do drugs!"

"You know I never would!" I call back, pretending to be insulted that he'd even have to say it. Secretly, I like when they act protective of me.

I don't know what it is about Darcy and Alexei, who arrives just as we do, but they both fit right in at the party. Maybe it's because they're hot enough to be models and nod along with whatever anyone says. Psh. We're there for mere minutes before I'm standing alone, in a corner, like a middle school dance cliché. I'm deep in an ocean of kids, and everyone just swims on by like I'm not even there. Sometimes I feel invisible.

And it's not that I'm shy. I'm outgoing, I'm a genuine bundle of fun, let me tell ya, so how is it that I'm so easy to ignore? Hello?! Does anyone see me? I wave my hands but I get nothing. Just like I thought, invisible. This new school is creepy, kind of Stepford wives-y. Everyone, even Alexei and Darcy, seems to be standing on the opposite side of a pane of glass where all have been brainwashed into giving up their individuality.

Yvette Amparo's house is gigantic. Big marble columns and

rounded porticos, a chandelier that would crush somebody to death if it fell. I climb a red-carpeted spiral staircase up to the second floor, figuring if no one wants to talk to me I don't need them anyway. Their loss. I stand out on one of the house's many balconies, looking over the pool below. If I jumped, would anyone notice? What if I tripped and fell, screamed for help as I hung on to the balcony for dear life? I bet they'd still ignore me. Even Alexei, the grand betrayer. He hasn't even introduced me to anyone as his girlfriend yet! That's how it's supposed to work, right? When a boy walks you home it means he's claimed you as his girlfriend? I've never had a boyfriend before, you gotta help me out!

Down below I can see everyone getting into the pool. Alexei is topless, as he apparently loves to be, surrounded by YES, YOU GUESSED IT: GIRLS. Oh, the girls just love a topless guy with model potential. What a bunch of basic bitches!

Yvette brings out a tray of strawberries and graham crackers with a gigantic jar of Nutella in the middle. From my Grinch-like pedestal I watch everyone get ultra-mega excited over this as if the Nutella is actual crack-cocaine, which I assure you it is not, the main difference being that eating a jar of Nutella will make you fatter than a Christmas ham. But not for these hotties, apparently. Nooo, nothing stands in the way of Miami High kids and their hot bods. Not even Fatella. Yvette and the other girls down below, Becca and Maddie and Cynthia and Emily, gorge themselves without sacrificing their anorexic mermaid physiques. Well, Maddie is actually quite voluptuous, but just as pristinely stunning as the rest. Alexei takes a bite and I swear his abs actually get *more* defined. Oh, those abs. I'm glad no one is calling me down to join the chocolate-hazelnut festivities; whenever I so much as go near desserts I blow up like a puffer fish. They'd have to roll me out of here. Not cute.

Well, that's it: no one is coming to look for me. I could be dead and no one would ever notice. Somewhere down the line, maybe at a high school reunion, someone will say, "Remember that weirdo who came to Miami High for, like, a week and then just disappeared?" and someone else will say, "OMG, if you hadn't mentioned that right now I literally never would have thought of her again. What was her name again? Lee Lee?"

"No," the first person will reply, "I think it was like . . . Lay Lay, or something like that."

"La La?"

"Lie Lie?"

"Oh, it doesn't matter."

Playing this out in my head gets me feeling really sorry for myself; I get all blue with self-indulgent melancholy and storm downstairs, out the front door, past the Nutella eaters, who of course do *not* acknowledge me, and onto the street. I'm a girl of the streets now, an unwanted. I walk along the road with my head down, melancholy Charlie Brown–esque music playing in my head, watching my sad reflection in the ample puddles that fill the gutters. That's when—*WHOOOOOSH*—a car races by out of nowhere and—*SPLSHHHH*—a puddle becomes a tidal wave that crashes over me, drenching me to my poor, sad soul.

"Sorry, didn't see you there!" the woman calls from her car as she speeds away, like it's no big deal. Oh yeah, sure, no problem, I'm not really a person anyway; I'm just an empty void for people to walk through.

I decide I should at least say good-bye before leaving the party from hell and go back inside. "Alexei," I say very sweetly through gritted teeth, "I am leaving now. Good-bye."

"Lele, wait! Where have you been? And what happened to you? I've been looking everywhere!"

"I got splashed by a car," I say, smoothing out my dress that is now wrinkled and sticking to my thighs. "But it's not a big deal, I will be fine, thank you and good day, sir."

"Lele, why are you being weird?"

"Am I being weird, am I?"

"Well, yes, you are."

Poor guy, I can be quite a handful.

"Ewwww," Yvette Amparo shrieks. "Lele looks like a sewer rat!"

"Yes," I say. "I got splashed, I don't look cute. Whatever, Yvette, what's your problem with me?"

"My problem with you is that you're a freak and you don't belong here. I don't like when girls like you come around thinking you're special and can just be whoever you want to be."

"But I *can* be whoever I want to be. That doesn't mean I'm special, that means I'm human. Anyone can be whoever they want to be. It's just that not everyone realizes it."

"Sounds exactly like what a freak would say." Yvette laughs, and some of her minions laugh quietly along until she stares them down.

"She's not a freak," Alexei says. "She's cool. And so what if she's a little weird, that's what makes her so incredible."

"Yeah," I say. "What he said." My heart nearly bursts behind my chest. I want to call out "You're my hero" like Megara does in *Hercules* (Disney rendition, obviously), but then I remember how Mom always said that wasn't very feminist of her, and that girls should learn how to be their own heroes. Still, total swoon.

"Come on, Lele, let's get you dry." Alexei grabs his jacket and drapes it over my shoulders, while Darcy ushers us out, shooting Yvette dirty looks as we go. The gate slams behind us and I can hear Becca Cartwright saying, "Okay, people, show's over."

On the Uber ride home Darcy turns to me and says, "Um, you did kind of look like a sewer rat," and the three of us burst out laughing.

Darcy has to pee the whole ride home, so when the car drops us off back at my house she darts inside, leaving Alexei and me alone at the front door.

"Hey, thanks for standing up for me," I say. "That was very . . . gentlemanly."

"I just couldn't stand her talking to you like that. I mean, who does she think she is, anyway?"

"I know, right?!"

"You have a great attitude though," he says. "I admire your positivity. I like it. I mean . . . " AND THEN IT HAPPENS.

THE MOMENT I'VE BEEN WAITING FOR ALL MY LIFE.

He kisses me.

No.

He doesn't.

I thought he was going to, but instead he says . . .

"I like you. I like you a lot, Lele."

I'm sitting there with my lips puckered and it's all I can do to say, "Yeah, I like you too, I guess."

So I didn't get a kiss from Alexei, but it's okay, all's well that ends well.

And this night certainly did end well. We film "Sometimes I Feel Invisible" and upload it to Vine, where I receive a very pleasant surprise: Wednesday's Vine, "That Person Who Always Catches You at Your Worst Moments," has received over five thousand loops! Take that Yvette Amparo! Take that Miami High!

5

The Problems of Living in Florida / Mama's Girl

Oh, Miami, my one true love. Miami, city of crystal beaches, babes, and booze; city of neon and palm trees, white sand, and tropical breezes; city of senior citizens, humidity, and Ray-Ban aviators with reflected lenses. City of 2.6 million people. I can't believe I have to share this place with so many basic losers! Like any good city, Miami is both elegant and filthy, a juxtaposition of lush history and trashy tourists with fat, exposed bellies and bad sunburns. But I love them as well, since they are part of what makes Miami home.

I wake up early on Saturday, high off my five thousand views on Vine. The sun is out and it's the perfect day for a nice swim. We have a pool in our backyard, but not the extravagant kind that the evil Amparos have. Ours is modest, a simple rectangle, the floor painted dark blue and the rim lined with dark blue tiles. A warm breeze blows through my hair as I step outside and see that Dad has beat me to it. He's sprawled out on a towel like a corpse, soaking in the rays.

"Good morning, pumpkin!" he says, not noticing the two baby alligators the size of large lizards, about nine inches each, waddling silently toward him. Miami, also the city of two point six million alligators (okay, maybe not, but there are a ton of them here). I choose not to warn him; it will be more fun this way.

"Morning, Dad. Just going to go for a little swim."

"Sounds good, sweet pea." He likes to use as many American terms of endearment as is humanly possible. Oh, my immigrant dad.

I dive in headfirst; the cool, silky water feels amazingly soothing against my sizzling skin. I swim two laps back and forth before I hear the terror.

"Lele!" my dad is screaming. "Lele!!!!!" I pop my head up and see the alligator babies crawling across his bare chest. He's paralyzed with fear.

"What's up, Dad?" I chirp.

"Lele, please dear God get these monsters off me!"

"Dad, chill." I hoist myself up out of the pool. "We've gone over this. They're babies, they're not going to hurt you."

"Just get them off, get them off of me!"

"Okay, okay." I lift them gently; they're light like puppies. "Why am I the only one in this family who isn't afraid of these guys? They're so harmless."

"Jesus Christ." He sighs a deep sigh of relief. "That was a close one. This place is a battlefield! No one is safe!"

"Ugh. Everyone is safe. These babies just want to cuddle." I hold one up to my face and nuzzle it. I must look so cool holding them like they're my own children. I'm like Daenerys Targaryen, but with alligators instead of dragons. Mental note: turn this into a Vine, because reptiles are a great look for me.

"It's not the babies I'm worried about, it's their mother, who is most likely nearby ready to destroy whoever messes with her babies!"

"But we're not messing with her babies, they're messing with us."

"She's an alligator, Lele, she doesn't know that."

"Hm. I see your point, I see your point. But don't you think if there was an adult-size alligator nearby we would notice it?"

"Not necessarily, they're very quiet. And surprisingly swift."

I imagine my dad and me being consumed in mere seconds by an angry mother alligator. Blood and flesh flying everywhere. Yikes. Note to self: when filming Vines with alligators have someone on mother-watch duty. I kiss the babies on the head before returning them to the wild (a cluster of palm trees and pink hibiscus plants just outside our property), then slink back inside before anyone gets the idea to devour me. I haven't done much meditating on how I intend to die, but I know I'd prefer to avoid death by alligator.

My mom cooks lunch, which is a very nice and motherly thing to do. (Not as nice and motherly as an alligator that would dismember anyone who tries to mess with her babies, but nice enough). Today it's pasticho Venezolano, a Venezuelan creamy lasagna, because apparently my parents are trying to fatten me up before sacrificing me to the devil. Or the alligators. Okay, so I can get a little paranoid from time to time, but hey, you would too if the whole world were against you!

Mom sits down at the table, wearing a green face mask and her hair in curlers—that's the coolest thing about my mom: she doesn't give a f**k. Dad doesn't really either, even though he's a wimp about baby alligators who don't even have their teeth in yet. He's wearing his aviator sunglasses with reflective green lenses and with *no shirt on.* Ever since he got that Bowflex he's been strutting around like he's real hot stuff, even if he's in his fifties. What is with Miami men wanting to be topless all the time?

"Ugh, Dad. Put your shirt on, no one wants to see that," I say. He just scowls at me. I roll my eyes. It's all very *The Breakfast Club* (you know, when they're all with their obnoxious parents in the beginning, before they get to detention . . .).

"Lele, don't roll your eyes at your father," Mom says from behind her green mask. She looks like an alien, and not the cute kind.

"Why not?" I say. "You always do." At this, she laughs and raises her hand for a high five. I swear sometimes I think my parents are about eleven years old.

"Very funny, make fun of your old man, go ahead, I don't care." He raises his eyebrows like he's about to say something really clever. "I'm rubber, you're glue." See? Eleven. Years. Old. For sure.

"What's on the agenda for today, Lele?" Mom asks.

"Well it's Saturday, so I guess I'll do nothing by myself while everyone who has friends hangs out on the beach and takes shots out of each other's belly buttons."

"People you know do that?" Dad is intrigued.

"You have friends, honey," Mom says. "What are their names again?"

"Darcy and Alexei. They're okay. But they're also traitors."

"That sounds a little dramatic."

"Well, it IS dramatic, Mom. They are friendly with my worst enemy."

"You have an enemy?" Dad is concerned.

"Duh. Yvette Amparo."

"Impossible," Mom protests. "How could anyone not love my baby?"

"I don't know, Mom, I'm just as shocked as you."

"Not everyone can handle the Lele magic," Dad says, ruffling my hair. Oh boy. I grimace, imagining the hours I'll need to fix the mess he's created.

"Thanks, Dad."

"I know! You should have a party. Invite anyone you want from your new school," Mom suggests. "We'll get out of your way and you can show everyone a good old-fashioned fun time."

"With belly-button shots!" Dad adds. Grimace, double grimace.

My parents are the most incredible parents any girl could

possibly ask for—don't get me wrong. It's just that, as of the past few years, they seem to understand me less and less. As I understand it, this is a pretty common phenomenon: as kids grow up, their parents become increasingly intolerable, despite their best intentions. It's extra weird for me though, because I'm an only child, so my parents have always been basically obsessed with me. And I used to be obsessed with them too (like I said, they are dope parents)! You've heard of a daddy's girl or a mama's girl? Well, I was both. Trips to the zoo, family movie night, road trips, bedtime cuddles: my childhood was a picture-perfect portrait of baby-makes-three bliss.

6

That One Person Who Is Super Hyper in the Morning

(3,012 FOLLOWERS)

*C*UT TO: Monday morning, current day.

"Lele!!!!!!!" Mom's voice screeches like a fire truck. I'm brushing my teeth, half awake.

"Whaaa????!!!!!" I scream back, mouth full of toothpaste.

"You're late for school!!!!!"

"Aaagggghhh!!!!!"

"Aaaaaaaaaagggggghhhhhhh!!!!"

"Aaaaaaaaaaaaaaaaaggggggggghhhhhhh!!!!"

At this, she opens the bathroom door and throws a backpack at my head. That shuts me right up.

Okay, so I started my day by being knocked out by a backpack, big deal. So Alexei hasn't kissed me yet. So my enemy Yvette Amparo is wearing super fancy jeans from Rag & Bone and a Proenza Schouler handbag while I might as well be wearing a potato sack. None of this matters, because I am Lele Pons and nothing can keep me down. I am invincible! The invincible invisible girl, that's me.

I bounce into first-period English with a literal spring in my step and a jack-o'-lantern smile plastered across my face. If you want success you have to project an image of success! I read that somewhere. Or saw it in a movie. Or made it up. It doesn't matter, what matters is that I'm going to dominate this day! I am the queen of this day! I am a Monday Morning Murderer, a Miami High Master! Oooh boy, did I drink too much coffee? Maybe just a tad.

As it turns out, no one is in the mood for my good mood. They're jealous is what it is—jealous that they can't get on my level. Even Mr. Contreras is glaring at me like I'm the Antichrist. Has no one here heard of a little place called Starbucks? Look it up. I try to turn down but I can't! I'm a turnt-up whirlwind of enthusiasm and caffeine!

"Don't mind me," I say to the class. "Just gonna sit down over here at my desk and get to work like everyone else. Nothing to see over here. Sorry I have so much energy. I think I had about four and a half cups of coffee. Venezuelans love coffee. That's where I'm from originally. No one asked me that on my first day, even though you guys asked Alexei where he was from and he only started school one day after me but whatever, that's okay, I'm over it, I forgive everyone." *Whoa, Lele.* Sometimes I get to talking and just can't stop. If people weren't staring before they certainly are now. Especially Alexei. Oops.

"Well, uh, anywayyyy," Mr. Contreras says, "can everyone take out their copies of *The Great Gatsby* and turn to chapter two?" There is a great shuffle of backpacks and books all around me. *The Great Gatsby*?! Since when are we reading *The Great Gatsby*? Did anyone care to tell me this? I mean, I know it was on my homework and supplies list, but I guess I forgot. I may have a daydreaming problem. And a coffee problem. Well, I'm just on a fast track to rehab, aren't I? Suddenly I'm surrounded by a sea of *Great Gatsbys*—where does one buy books these days, anyway? I close my eyes and imagine Mr. Contreras ordering everyone to hurl their books at my head. I'm under siege, attacked by hardcover corners and Dr. T. J. Eckleburg's big looming spectacles (yeah, that's right, I've read the book already, so there).

Note to self: a Vine where teacher orders class to throw books at my head, a punishment for being too hyper. Note to self: nothing wrong with a little daydreaming.

After class I try to slip out undetected as to avoid being bombarded by a mob of angry readers, but Alexei catches me at the door.

"Where were you all weekend?" he asks. "I was hoping we could hang out." Grrr. *Well, you failed to introduce me as your girlfriend, so now you're dead to me! I am a very temperamental Venezuelan girl!* is what I want to say. Instead, I say, "Oh, did you try texting?"

"Yeah." He's right, he did. I ignored him as an attempt to seem cool. And it worked! Muahaha.

"Sorry, must have missed it. We'll hang next weekend!" Super casual.

"That would be great," he says. "Hey, I've been watching some of your Vines. They're really awesome."

"Really?"

"Yeah, and a lot of people seem to like them, they're getting pretty popular."

"I guess." I shrug modestly. (TEN THOUSAND LOOPS, HELLO!)

"I was thinking I could be in one with you next time? I used to model a little bit back in Belgium, and I'm trying to get my acting career started sort of. I just started my own Vine account, but I thought it would be fun to make one together." His acting career? I make fun of him in my head for one second, and then move on to being beyond flattered and beyond thrilled.

"Of course, yeah!" I can forgive him for ignoring me at Yvette's party, and he did stand up for me. The past is the past, right?

"Yeah?"

"It would be totally fun."

"That's awesome, I wasn't sure if you'd be down. I'll catch up with you later and we can make a plan."

"Sounds good. Catch up with you later." Blech, that sounded dumb. So what, he sounded dumb first. Shake it off, Lele, your crush wants to collaborate with you, we are pwning this day.

7

When You're the Ugly One in the Group

(3,055 FOLLOWERS)

*I*t's nice that Alexei wants to work with me, but he obviously doesn't like me like me, otherwise he would have asked me out by now. Anyway, this just serves as evidence to prove what I always suspected: I'm just not pretty enough.

I'm a pretty girl, no doubt, but I'm not pretty ENOUGH. If you don't live in girl world, you might not know what that means. You might say, "Pretty enough? If you have blond hair and big boobs you're pretty enough. Stop making things so complicated, woman!" To which I say, be quiet, you sexist pig, and let me talk. Then I would say here, listen to this:

WHAT IT MEANS TO NOT BE PRETTY ENOUGH, EXPLAINED BY THE ONE AND ONLY LELE PONS

When you're a girl, you are constantly surrounded by other girls, and are therefore going to notice all the pretty features they have that you just do not have. Boys don't compare themselves to other boys, because that isn't how they're wired. As I've said before, boys are programmed to battle out any competition with their fists and aren't so in their heads about it all. A boy sees another boy with nicer hair or, like, bigger muscles (in the gym, let's say), and all he thinks is *I could beat him up if I wanted to,* then moves on. Any emotions or feelings of inferiority are neatly and conveniently suppressed.

Girls are different. We see a girl who has something we think is prettier or better than what we have and instantly interpret that information as evidence that we are lacking in the value department. Writing it out makes me realize how ridiculous it actually is: my smile is less pretty than that girl's, therefore I am less valuable as a human or less desirable as a girlfriend. It's not logical. But anyway, even if you're nice-looking, there are all these girls around you who are going to be prettier, at least in your own opinion, and you'll compare yourself to them over and over and realize your beauty is dwarfed by their beauty.

I *think* this is what it's like to be a girl, but maybe it's just what it means to be Lele.

For me, not being pretty enough means that my hair is lovely and my breasts are big and my lips are plump and pouty, but my nose doesn't match my face and my skin is on a mission to ruin my life. And, in case you didn't know, nose and skin are pretty bad items on your face to have off point. For example, if your ears are your biggest problem, then you're in good shape. A bad chin can be easily overcome as well—plenty of girls with butt chins are still perfectly gorgeous. It's the midface features that really matter, and the very middlest feature that matters most, which is the nose. I came up with that theory this very second and I think it really holds up.

In addition, your skin is the backdrop of your whole face, and if it isn't smooth and clear and silky how is the rest supposed to look good?! Think of a beautiful painting . . . if the canvas is all bumpy and red, the beauty of that painting is canceled out. My goodness, in this analogy my face is practically a Picasso. A Picasso with braces. Yikes.

My insecurities have been with me for a long time (whoa, getting kinda real right now!). I was a mega-confident kid up until I turned twelve and went to summer camp, which is where I was when my body decided to stop metabolizing calories at the speed of lightning. I kept on my steady "no parents, no rules" diet of 3 Musketeers, Red Vines, and Sprite, not realizing that now food came with consequences. I gained about twenty-five pounds that summer and have never quite recovered from the image I saw in the mirror upon returning home. I exercised, I got taller, and was back to my thin self, but it was too late: the hormones had kicked in and I was anchored in a state of constantly feeling just a little bit bad about myself. (Welcome to girl world, sigh.)

Anyway, on Tuesday after classes, I finally meet up with some friends from my old school. Lucy, Arianna, and Mara. They've all been so busy lately, and their stupid school is on the other side of town and after school I'm just too lazy to travel the distance.

These girls have been my friends for almost five years, and I love them, but I am without a doubt the ugly one in the group. Lucy is the athletic beach babe, Arianna pulls off the sexy-bookworm look, and Mara is . . . well, she's the most beautiful girl most people have ever seen. Beautiful but approachable in a girl-next-door kind of way, that's what everyone is always saying. Plus she's the sweetest person and an amazing friend, so I can't hate her for it, which makes it even worse.

"Lele," Lucy says, "you have to tell us about your new school! We feel like we haven't seen you in forever." We're eating frozen yogurt in the food court right by some skater boys with studded belts and backward baseball hats. You know the look.

"Ah, yeah, well, I've been so busy making a fool out of myself that it's been hard to find time for friends."

"Has it been that bad?" asks Lucy. "Are people being mean to you, Lele? You know I'll beat them up."

"Thanks, Luce. People have been . . . less than welcoming.

Public school kids have some anger issues. Especially this girl Yvette."

"What's her last name?" Arianna is pulling up the Facebook app on her new iPhone.

"Amparo."

"Is this her?"

"Whoa, that was fast." I look at the page, Yvette's sleek hair pouring over her shoulders like a waterfall of ink while she poses on that balcony overlooking the pool. My balcony of shame and self-loathing. "Yeah, that's her."

"Oh, you're so much prettier," Mara says, getting a peek. I don't think so, and Mara probably doesn't either, but that is exactly what good friends are supposed to do: lie to each other about how pretty they are.

"You're an angel from heaven," I tell her, kissing her on the cheek. "Why can't you guys be with me at Miami High? I miss you so much!"

"We miss you too! Things are so boring since you've been gone," says Lucy.

"Like really," the others agree. These are my girls, the people who appreciate me. I want to shrink them down to pocket size and carry them around with me all day so I'm never alone. #SquadGoals. I'm about to tell them this, but then I hear how it might sound creepy if said out loud.

"You are the best friends and human beings," I say, then excuse myself to ask for more sprinkles for my frozen yogurt.

Over by the yogurt stand, I can see Skater Boys checking out my friends.

"Hey, girls," one of them says, and puts his hand up in one of those motionless waves. Mara waves back at him, then expertly turns her attention back to the yogurt. Way to leave 'em hanging, bb. This aloof attitude makes the guys stare even more. They like what they see and they want attention from these girls who are so clearly out of their league.

"Hi, guys!" I say, plopping back down next to my girls. "What's up?"

The skater boys might as well have visibly recoiled in disgust. They exchange awkward glances with each other and then one, clearly the ringleader, the Mara of the group, says, "Uhh, we were just heading out. See ya." Their faces are graced with looks of sheer horror and disgust.

See? What did I tell you? I'm the ugly one. Plus, no one likes a girl with braces.

"Oh, Lele, don't let them get to you," Mara says. "Guys are intimidated by confidence."

Me? Confident? Nah. This is everyone's way of saying, "Guys prefer mild-mannered ladies with easy faces to look at who will cook them dinner and tie their shoes." Well I won't have it! I can be me and still be desirable, right? I can be a beauty queen with just a little extra work; I can slay the hearts of men everywhere and influence girls to respect and honor me, even fear me. In other words, I can become popular without sacrificing my individuality, I know I can, all I have to do is tell the world (Miami High) that I am here and I am taking over, no more Miss Nice Guy, no more target of ridicule!

I may not be the prettiest girl at Miami High, but when I put my mind to something, I tend to get what I want.

And that, my friends, is called confidence.

At home I take a bag of Rolos from the fridge (candy is always better cold, duh) and devour them in front of my computer while I upload "When You're the Ugly One in the Group" and watch the likes start to pour in. Ah, the reliable comfort of validation from others. Then I have to spend twenty minutes cleaning Rolos out of my braces. It is not cute. Note to self: get these things off. IMMEDIATELY.

8

When Your Friend Wears Your Clothing Better Than You

(3,827 FOLLOWERS)

*D*arcy's house is my new favorite house. It's charming and warm, with an old-fashioned beach house vibe, decorated with seashells that look actually from the ocean and not from Pottery Barn. I'm very into the authenticity, it reflects well on Darcy and her fam. I asked her mom if I could move in but she said no. Typical.

"I'm turning over a new leaf," I tell Darcy. We're reading *Seventeen* on her bed, the ceiling fan whirring above us.

"Oh yeah? What kind of leaf?"

"I've decided to stop feeling bad for myself. I'm going to get a makeover and prove to everyone that I can be the cool girl. BUT, I'm not going to stop being myself."

"But you're going to stop looking like yourself."

"No, I'm still going to look like myself, but now I'm going to be a better version. Lele 2.0, if you will."

"All right, so what's going to change?"

"Well, to start with, I'm getting my braces off next week!"

"Oh my God, you're going to be so much happier without those. When I got mine off, I'm telling you, it was like being reborn." She flashes her impeccable teeth at me like she's in a frickin' Trident commercial.

"Yes, Darcy, you're very attractive. But back to me now, this is my life transformation story."

She rolls her eyes but gestures for me to go on. Darcy has her shortcomings, like everyone in this world, but she's a great friend. I think she really gets me. She gets that I have a heart of gold despite being a bit difficult as a human being.

"I'm thinking I'll get a haircut, something with shape, maybe even some highlights," I say.

"What color highlights? Your hair is already extremely blond."

"Like extra blond-platinum highlights, just to add a sense of complexity and sophistication."

"It sounds like you really know what you're talking about."

"That's good, but I don't. I'm making this all up on the spot."

"You're really something else, Lele."

"*Merci, mon ami,*" I say, thinking maybe little spots of French will be a part of Lele 2.0. "I've also lost, like, five pounds over the stress of being a fundamentally unlovable social outcast, which is very exciting for my new look."

"You're not fundamentally unlovable, you weirdo. Put that outfit on that you bought today."

"Oooh! Fashion show!"

I find the shopping bag and remove a black crop top and gray shorts covered in an abstract snakeskin print. *Yes!* Complexity and sophistication, this is exactly what I was talking about.

I hop up and slip into the outfit, check myself out in the full-length mirror. I'm not going to lie, I look amazing.

"Soooooo pretty, Lele." Darcy smiles. "You look amazing."

"Thank you! I kind of do, don't I?"

"Mhm. Can I try it?"

"Yeah, why not?" I shrug. I take it off and hand it over, then get back into my mundane, pedestrian attire. Not complex or sophisticated at all.

Darcy puts on the outfit and I can practically hear "Get Busy" by Sean Paul start playing. "Shake that thing, Miss Kana Kana / Shake that thing, Miss Annabella . . ." Aggh seventh grade post-traumatic stress flashbacks! What I'm saying is, she looks goooooooood. Better-than-me kind of good. I had no idea she was in such great shape—her legs and abs are the perfect amount of defined, and her mocha skin is smooth and even-colored all over. Her hair, newly blown out, shimmers as it cascades off her shoulders. She's like a mermaid, a complex and sophisticated mermaid. Dammit. I think my mouth might be hanging open.

"Do you like it?" she asks.

"Nah." I shake my head and quickly divert my eyes back to *Seventeen*. Great, tons of hot babes in here too, they're everywhere I look!

"Come on, Lele, don't be like that," she says. "It looks great on you too."

"It looks so much better on you, you have no idea. You should wear it. I never knew you worked out!"

"I don't."

Grrrr.

"You evil, sexy sorcerer of black magic!"

"Racist," Darcy jokes.

I push her into the closet. "Get out of here."

"Listen to me, Lele. You're almost there, you just need to try a little bit harder and you can be the hottest girl in school, if you cared about that sort of thing. Well, one of the hottest girls in school." She flips her hair and winks.

I try to wink back but fail epically. I probably look like I'm having a seizure.

Maybe she's right. Maybe I'm almost to my dream goal of

hotness and popularity, maybe the end of social outcast-hood is just within reach. Does this mean I have to start wearing makeup? Does this mean I have to start working out? Oh my God, does this mean I have to stop eating chocolate?! I'll die, I'll just die. Get it together, Lele, one must make sacrifices when planning to take over the world. Cue evil laughter.

9

When You Go to Get a New Haircut

(3,998 FOLLOWERS)

*M*om lets me get a haircut because she is the best. Well, I may have told her that if she didn't give me her blessing and a couple of Benjamins then I would be forced to take matters (and scissors) into my own hands.

"Baby, but your hair is so beautiful." She winces and then presses my cheeks together between her hands.

"Calm down, calm down." I manage to wriggle out of her clutches. "It's just a minor cut and some highlights. The change will be subtle, I swear."

"Ay, fine, I'll take you to Juan."

"Who is Juan?"

"My stylist. I've been going to him for years."

"But you don't do anything to your hair."

She laughs, half snorts. Charming.

"If I didn't do anything to my hair it'd be gray as a bat," Mom says.

"Is that an expression? I thought bats were black?"

"I dunno." She shrugs, runs one hand through her ink-black locks. How did I turn out blond? Maybe I'm adopted.

She drives me to Gianini's, a hair salon on Española Way. I can't believe my mom has been coming here for years and hasn't been taking me! It's basically heaven in hair salon form. Big porcelain tubs and polished granite floors, the soothing smells of lavender and honeysuckle drifting through the air. White cherub figurines pose with their heads resting on pedestals. I think I could live here.

"Hola, hola!" A tall, effeminate man with a flawless, slicked-back head of hair struts out from behind a black curtain, wearing an apron equipped with every hair-cutting tool you could possibly imagine, all silver and resplendent. This must be Juan.

"Juan, darling!" Mom says, as he pulls her in for double-cheek kisses.

"So good to see you, Anna. And who is this?"

"This is my daughter, Lele. She's looking for a new, updated look. I told her she had to go to Juan, of course."

"Well of course, who else is there?" They laugh like old friends. "Lele, tell me, what are you thinking? What's the look you're going for?"

"Complex and sophisticated," I mumble. He gasps, claps his hands together.

"Say no more! I've got it!"

He whisks me into a chair and gets to work. I relax into his care as he washes and snips and foils, ease into a Zen-like trance knowing I will soon be Lele 2.0.

"Okay, what do you think?" he asks after what seems like only seconds. He spins me around to look in the mirror and to my profound, bloodcurdling horror, I am bald.

"Aaaaaaaaaaaaaaaaaaaaaaaaaaaaaaaaaaaaaaaaaaaaaaaaaaaaa aaaaaaaaaaaaaaaaaaaaaaaaaaaaaaaaaaaaaaaaaaaaaaaaaaaaaaaa aaaaaaaaaaaaaaaaaaaaaaaaaaaaaaaaaaaaaaaaaaaaaaaaaaaaaaaa aaaaaaaaaaaaaaaaaaaaaaaaaaaaaaaaaaaaaaaaaaaaaaaaaaaaaaaa aaaaaaaaaaaaaaaaaaaaaaaaaaaaaaaaaaaaaaaaaaaaaaaaaaaaaaaa aaaaaaaaaaaaaaaaaaaaaaaaaaaaaaaaaggggggggggggggggggggggg ggg!!!"

I wake up screaming, drenched in sweat, my heart pounding like a stampede of frightened wildlife.

Oh my God, it was just a dream. I touch my face, pat down my blankets, clutch my long, luscious hair. Is this real? Okay, this is real; we're safe now. What a nightmare!

"Poor babies!" I cry, and bring my strands of hair to my lips so I can kiss them.

Hmm, maybe I don't need a haircut. Wouldn't want to risk actually going bald! But I'm going to change, I'm going to show everyone that I can be charming, I can be pretty, I can be popular. I am human and I need to be loved, just like everybody else does. Am I right, Morrissey, or am I right?

Neon green numbers on my nightstand flash 3:00 a.m. Typical. I hate 3:00 a.m., it is my least favorite time. Of all the twenty-four hours, it is by far the worst, which is normally all right because normally you sleep right through it. Tonight, no such luck. In ninth grade we read *Something Wicked This Way Comes* by Ray Bradbury, and there was this one line that says something like three in the morning is the time when your body has slowed down so much that it is as close to death as it ever will be while you're alive. I'm probably messing it up majorly, but the point is, that info really traumatized me. Now, 3:00 a.m. seems like a twisted, haunted hour that no one should have to deal with. The shadows and total stillness, it all just gives me the creeps.

Note to self: from now on, don't ever be awake at 3:00 a.m.

To distract myself from the creepiness of 3:00 a.m. and the sheer horror of going bald, I get up and start doing sit-ups on my floor. Oh man, if I could have abs as flat as Darcy's I would be one happy Lele 2.0. Okay, let's start with some basic crunches. One, two, three, four, five, oh boy this burns, six, seven, eight, dear Lord I'm on fire, nine, and ten agggghhhhhhhhhhhh never again, never again. Too. Hard. Too. Tired. To. Keep. Going. I lift my shirt and check to see if I've made any progress.

None.

Okay, so this is going to be like a process or whatever, I get it.

I force myself to do two more sets of these torture crunches and then spend the next two hours browsing the internet for new makeup. It turns out there are all these YouTube videos of girls—Bethany Mota and Ingrid Nilsen are particularly helpful—showing you how to apply makeup properly.

This is exactly what I need! I spend the next hour learning about cat eyes and smoky eyes and pouty lips and how to create the illusion of high cheekbones, and then use my mom's credit card numbers (memorized) to order everything I need for Operation Makeover. Do *not* try this at home.

By the time the sun comes up my eyelids are heavy as a zombie's and I'm mumbling "Maybe it's Maybelline" over and over, unable to stop myself. In other words, I am delirious.

"Whoa, bad night?" Alexei says when he sees me in English that morning. I check my compact mirror and see that I have massive dark circles under my eyes and my cheeks are all puffy. The release of Lele 2.0 is going to have to be postponed for some time after I've had my beauty rest.

"I had a nightmare."

"Oh no! I hate that."

"Mmmnnnnnnnn," is all I can manage to say. I want to let my head fall onto the desk and block out the world. I'm too tired to care that Alexei is looking at me with this concerned and vaguely nervous glance.

"So anyway," he says, "did you see that last Vine you did got twenty thousand loops?"

"Twenty thousand?!" I'm jolted awake.

"Yeah. 'When Your Friend Wears Your Clothing Better Than You.' Twenty thousand loops."

"Whaaaaaaa?" I'm speechless. I stare into the empty space behind Alexei's beautiful blond head, too tired and now shocked to organize my thoughts.

Alexei laughs. "You look like you're having a stroke."

"Yes," I say. "That is very normal for me."

"I meant what I said before, about wanting to do it with you."

"I'm sorry, do what with me?" Did he just say he wants to "do it with me"!? Wow, European guys are really forward!

"To be in a Vine with you? Remember?" he says, so innocently.

Right. A Vine. Not *it*. Okay then! I can do that! "Ohhhh, yes. Yes, I remember. I'll think of some ideas and then I'll let you know."

"Perfect! Thanks, Lele, that's really cool of you."

I just nod along, smile lazily. After first period I walk out onto the track field and fall asleep behind a tree. Ahh, the good life.

10

Parents' Idea of "Cool"

(4,004 FOLLOWERS)

I've taken my mom up on her offer to let me have a party. So far Alexei and Darcy are my only Miami High friends, but I spent Friday inviting anyone who seemed like a particularly nice person, and I told Darcy to do the same. We even made invitations out of some Lisa Frank stationery I found under my bed—technicolor dolphins frolicking through a flurry of hearts in a neon rainbow ocean. Lisa Frank stuff is timeless, in my humble opinion, don't you think?

It's Saturday night and I'm applying cat-eye makeup step-by-step, following the instructions from a YouTube tutorial by a girl whose voice has the poise of a British accent and the mangled intonations of an Australian one. She sounds like a kangaroo that is trying to seduce me, and it's honestly pretty confusing. Of course I turn out looking more like a badger than a cat—good thing it's only 5:00 p.m., which gives me plenty of time to reapply.

There's a knock on my door. It's Mom and Dad. I say yeah, fine, they can come in.

"Are you excited for your party?" Mom asks, as if I'm six years old and Barney is on his way.

"I guess."

"We just want to make sure we're all on the same page with the rules for tonight," says Mom.

I just stare, blinking.

"All we ask is that you keep the music at a reasonable volume," says Dad.

"You know, for the neighbors," says Mom.

"And make sure no one drinks alcohol," says Dad.

"But if they do, make sure you have their keys," says Mom.

"We'd much rather have kids sleeping here than driving home drunk," says Dad.

"But if people do sleep here, make sure they know they're not allowed to have s-e-x."

"Ugh. Gross, Mom."

"Okay, so do you agree to the rules?" Dad asks, crossing his arms.

"Sure, whatever, sounds fine. But you guys need to act cool, okay? The point of this party is to help my social life, not irreparably destroy it."

"Oh, we can be cool," Mom says, almost ominously.

"The coolest of the cool," Dad adds. I grimace and tell them very politely to please GET OUT OF MY ROOM.

After my second attempt at cat eyes, I have one eye angled up and one eye angled down, and a bunch of black smudges leftover from the first attempt. I may not be party ready, but I'm all set to rob a bank. Perfect!

I go down into the kitchen to get a soda and that's where I see the horror of all horrors: it's Mom and Dad dressed in full hip-hop attire, wigs and gold chains included, dancing to eighties disco.

"Cool, right?!" Dad calls out to me over the music.

Taxi!

Taxi driver: Where to, miss?
Me: Anywhere but here.

Hey, a girl can dream.

Darcy and Alexei come over around eight and help me corral the wild animals (parents) into the safety of their bedroom. We put on Iggy Azalea and throw confetti all around the living room to make it sparkle. Darcy says we need a beer pong table, so I reluctantly help her set one up.

"What even is beer pong?" I ask. "You just throw balls into beer cups and then drink them? Seems like a good way to catch germs. If you want to get drunk, why not just drink the beer? Why does it have to be a game?"

"It's more fun this way. The idea is you're trying to get the other team drunk faster than you're getting drunk," Alexei tries to explain to me.

"Why? So you can take advantage of them for the rest of the night? Seems creepy. How about everyone is just responsible for deciding how much alcohol they personally consume?"

"Chill, Lele, it's not as serious as all that. It's just a silly game that people have fun playing at parties. You don't have to make it dramatic," Darcy says. "Try to be a little more easygoing."

Story of my life. If I had a penny for every time someone told me to stop being so dramatic I could buy all of Miami and then everyone would be obligated to like me.

"Fine, everyone can play beer pong till the cows come home, see if I care."

"That's the spirit," says Alexei, who, being from Belgium, has probably never played beer pong. I consider throwing a Ping-Pong ball at his head.

• • •

It's nine thirty and none of the twenty-three Miami High students with Lisa Frank invitations have shown up. Darcy, Alexei, and I sit on the couch blowing into party horns and staring dejectedly out the window.

"It's only nine thirty," Alexei says. "People will be here."

"They were supposed to be here thirty minutes ago!" I am not hopeful.

"People are always fashionably late. That's just party etiquette."

"Who did we invite?"

"Everyone," Darcy says. "I invited everyone I know, like you told me to."

"Yikes. In retrospect that seems like a lot of people."

"Then it's a good thing none of them seem to be showing up." Darcy blows into her horn. It unravels, filled with air, and then coils back up, deflated.

Ten thirty and still no guests.

"Fine," I say. "So nobody wants to come to my party. So I'm a loser. Big deal. I have you guys. And my parents." I hang my head and pretend to cry. Being dramatic isn't all bad: it can be a great way to entertain yourself during hard times.

"Are you sure you invited people?" Alexei asks me and Darcy.

"Yep," we say in unison.

"Well, it's hard to have a party last-minute on a Saturday, a lot of people already have plans they've made in advance." Oh, sweet Alexei, trying to spare my feelings.

"That's okay, Alexei, you don't have to try to cheer me up. Worse things have happened in the history of the world than throwing a sad and lonely party that no one shows up to."

"You say it but you don't believe it," says Darcy.

"It's true, you know me so well!" I wrap my arms around Darcy's neck. "What is worse than this? Tell me one thing that is worse than this!"

"The Holocaust," Darcy deadpans.

"Yep, good answer, Darcy," I say, snapping out of my hissy fit and laughing. "Gooood answer."

At ten forty-five Lucy and Arianna and Mara arrive.

"Oh thank God," I moan in relief: at least my true friends still like me.

"Are we . . . early?" Arianna asks, almost nervously. The three of them look so cute in their bright, unpretentious party dresses, I just want to jump up and kiss them. So I do.

"No! You're not early!"

"Are we late? We really wanted to be fashionably late so your new friends wouldn't think we're losers, but we didn't mean to miss the party entirely."

"You're not early and you're not late, it's just that no one showed up!"

"Oh, Lele, I'm sorry." Mara strokes my hair.

"No, it's totally okay, because now look! My old BFFs can meet my new BFFs and everyone I love is here under one roof!" I introduce everyone to each other and am feeling a bit manic, bursting with love for my loyal friends while also actively battling off the disappointment of no one else showing up.

"I'm sorry it's kind of a lame night, but I'd love it if you guys hung around," I say. "Anyone can sleep over."

"Yeah!" says Lucy. "We can get fake drunk on root beer floats!"

"Umm, that sounds amazing." Darcy is thrilled at the idea. So we go to town on soda and ice cream until we're dizzy with sugar, making a game of throwing darts at the balloons, watching them pop one by one. It's a wonderfully good time and an epic bonding session, until I throw a dart and it goes point-first into Arianna's forehead. Oops. No real damage, but blood trickling down the front of someone's face does tend to put a damper on the festivities.

• • •

I can't get anything right, I am a walking disaster. It's been that way for my whole life, or as long as I can remember. When I was three years old I put one of my grandma's Valium up my nose. I mean, not on purpose or anything, I wasn't trying to get it up there. I honestly don't know how it happened, but next thing I knew it was lodged in deep and wouldn't come out—my mom had to rush me to the hospital before the Valium could get to my little baby brain. But maybe it did anyway and maybe that's why it takes a miracle for me to do anything right.

Another nightmare: The bell rings and school is out for summer. I rush out into the hallway where my friends—old school and new school—are gathered around my locker. They're ecstatic to see me, as they should be.

"Where have you been, Lele?" they cry. "We've missed you so much!"

"I was just in class," I say. "I'm here now!" I have to keep them at arm's length like fangirls while I open my locker. But that's when things take an ugly turn: my locker pops open and an endless pile of books topples out, flooding into the hallway. Dammit, I have to clean these up fast before I get in trouble, or worse, people start to drown.

"Could you guys just wait one second?" I ask. "I'll clean this up really fast, I swear." I frantically gather the books but whenever I put a stack back in my locker another dozen ooze out, now in liquid form, thick and black like molasses, spilling all over my shoes, which in this dream, are Louboutins and therefore very expensive.

When I look up from my tragically ruined shoes, I see my so-called friends strolling away, already on the far side of the hallway, laughing with their backs to me, everything in slow motion because, hello, this is a nightmare after all.

And, because this is not real life, I am able to steal a bus just in time to meet them at the school entrance. Of course they want a ride, they beg for a ride, but I just stick my tongue out at them and drive away. I can be very mature when I want to be. Serves them right. As it turns out, stealing the bus wasn't such a good idea, because soon after I get my revenge on those losers I go soaring off a bridge (an old-timey bridge that looks like it might have a troll living under it) and start to sink in the ink-black ice-cold water. Down, down, down, down.

That's when I wake up, only this time I'm not screaming. This time, a hellish nightmare is nothing to freak out over, now it's just the norm.

"Yep," I say, blinking my eyes open, "seems about right." These are dark times, my friends, dark times.

I want to pour myself a stiff drink, but because I don't have alcohol (and am still waaayyyy underage), I pour myself into my art instead.

Yes, that's right, I just referred to my Vines as my art. And I'll do it again! Art is self-expression in the form of something presentable as a way to cope with being a miserable outcast—I'm prrrreeetttyyy sure that's how it's been since the beginning of time. So, if I have to be an outcast I might as well document my misadventures and heartbreaks—maybe that way all the other outcasts out there won't feel so alone. A life without purpose is a life not worth living . . . is that a thing people say?

I get out my notepad and start brainstorming. If Alexei wants to be in a Vine with me, I'm going to have to make sure it's something good. Something impressive. In the light of the moon I scribble: *A girl abandoned by friends seeks revenge by stealing a school bus . . . How I act when my friends don't wait for me . . .*

Uh oh, it's 2:45 a.m., I have to get to sleep before three, otherwise . . . otherwise what? Otherwise I'll feel spooked, that's what. Taking over the world one Vine at a time is hard work, and a girl's gotta get some sleep.

11

Sometimes You Have to Prepare Yourself for the Hard Things in Life

(4,661 FOLLOWERS)

*T*oday is Sunday, but it's not just any Sunday, it is a very important Sunday. You might even say it's the most important Sunday of all time. Well, you probably wouldn't say that, but I would, because today is the Sunday I will call Alexei and make a plan to Vine with him.

I know, I know, what do I have to be nervous about? He likes me, I know that, and what's more, it was his idea to collaborate together. But you have to understand, this is my first real crush—I've never felt so unbearably butterfly-y about someone before. Sure there was that one kid Harry, who I dreamed would ask me to the fifth-grade dance (and then never did), but this is different! This time I have hormones and stuff or whatever.

So now I am programmed to second-guess myself, to experience an attack of insecurity and self-doubt every time his name enters my mind. Is it okay for a girl to call a guy—am I supposed to be waiting for him to call me? No, it was his idea to make a Vine together, right? So the ball is in my court, just where it belongs. Or, would I prefer the ball be in his court? When we talk about balls being in courts do we want them in our court or our opponent's court? I don't know—I'm not much of a sports person. Where was I? Oh right, should I be waiting for Alexei to call me?

I practically work myself into a panic attack trying to figure this out. Luckily, there are plenty of ways to procrastinate, and that is one thing I am flawlessly awesome at. I decide to kill two birds with one stone: I'll use the procrastination time to build up the courage I need to call. Now, if only I knew how to do that. . . .

There's one way to successfully distract yourself from discomfort, and that is to inflict a different kind of discomfort upon yourself. So, I decide to go on a run! I put on my Lululemon gear and set off for a jog around the block. I'm actually a surprisingly good runner. I say surprisingly because I'm basically the laziest person alive, but the truth is I have long legs and a lot of nervous energy to burn off.

After one lap, the endorphins and adrenaline really start to kick in. I'm alive and ready for more. Push-ups! Pull-ups! Sit-ups! Jumping jacks! I even sneak into my dad's downstairs gym to lift some fivers (I'm not frickin' Arnold Schwarzenegger after all). All right, all right, I think to myself, I am a strong and independent lady, and if I wanna call Alexei I should just call him. But no, I'm not ready.

Sweaty and panting, I rip out a piece of yellow lined paper from a legal pad that's been wedged under the treadmill and write out a sort of script for myself:

Hey Alexei, it's Lele. Just calling to see what you're up to today and if you maybe wanted to come over and film a Vine, like we talked about?

Simple enough. Okay, so it's not exactly Shakespeare, but I'm trying to make this as quick and painless as possible, and Lord knows Shakespeare more or less had the exact opposite goal. What if he doesn't answer? Do I leave a message? If I leave a message, should I basically say the same thing? What if I leave a message but he doesn't get it because he never checks his voice mail or something like that, do I call again? Or, what if he does get the message but chooses not to call me back. I do have a tendency to overthink things from time to time. I chew on the end of the pen until my lip turns blue. Cute, Lele, really cute.

Uh-oh, it's almost noon. If I don't call now, I might miss my chance completely. It's now or never. With great effort and will-power I pick up the phone and find his contact information. Remember when we used to have to actually dial someone's number? I don't, I think that went out of style entirely when I was about five. Shhh, it's ringing.

"Hello?" he answers, his voice husky and dreary.

"Hey, um, it's Lele, did I wake you? I hope not, I'm sorry if I did, but it's almost noon, so I figured you'd probably be awake. Not to say you're lazy for sleeping in, I mean it's Saturday, I actually wish I had slept in a little more. I just keep having these nightmares, so I wake up pretty early and can't go back to sleep. I mean . . ." Way to stick to the script. Jesus.

"It's okay." He laughs. "You didn't wake me up. I've been up for a while. Do I sound tired?"

"A little. I mean, in a cute way, I mean—no, forget that. Never mind. Listen." I shake it off, literally. "I'm calling to see if you want to come over and work on a Vine again, I think I have some ideas."

"Oh yeah? That would be super cool. I told my little sister I'd take her to the mall, so how about after, around three?"

"Three is perfect!" Okay, "perfect" might be a little overboard. Reel it in, Lele.

"You should come over to my place, my parents are out so we'll have the whole space to ourselves." Um, whaaaatttt? Did he just make this a date? Did he? Seriously, tell me, I don't know how to speak Boy.

"Cool, okay. Just text me your address and I'll come by around three."

"Awesome, talk soon." He hangs up. I hang up, feeling my finger-tips go numb. Well, this should be interesting.

12

When You Get Caught Bae Watching

(4,997 FOLLOWERS)

*W*ell, it's noon now, which means I have almost three hours to get ready. I start with outfits. I want to look hot and adorable/irresistible but also practical and like I'm not trying too hard. I try on five to ten outfits and land on jean shorts and a white tank top (low-cut, obvs), trusty white Converse to match and add a sporty, approachable vibe. If this outfit could talk it would say, "Hey, I'm easygoing but also classy and elegant, I'm everything you could want in a girlfriend!" At least I hope it would say that, but you honestly never know when your clothes are going to betray you.

As much as I would love to just head on over without fussing with my hair, I know this monster needs to be tamed if today is going to even have a chance at going smoothly. My inner artist/creator takes over and makes the executive decision to put it back in French braids so that it doesn't get in the way of my filming process. I've been giving myself French braids since I was in the womb, so this process is impressively quick (if I do say so myself) and goes off without a hitch. Sigh, if only the world was as easy to master as the French braid, my life would be so majorly under control it wouldn't even be funny.

In my tight jean shorts and hair braided back I think I look like Lara Croft from *Tomb Raider*. Or rather, the negative of Lara Croft, the Lara Croft of a parallel universe where brown is blond and black is white. But that's not the point, the point is that I look powerful. I even feel a little bit powerful after all that exercise. Note to self: maybe work out a little more often. Or, like, work out once in a while. Yeah, that's better.

By the time I've done my makeup (you know, where you put on pounds of foundation and lip gloss just to achieve the "natural" look), it's almost showtime. It takes me twenty minutes to walk to Alexei's house, and by the time I get there I am covered in a fine layer of sweat. *What would Lara Croft do?* I ask myself. She wouldn't care about some sweat, she would go right in there and be a total boss. I mean, I think that's what she would do. To be quite honest I have never seen the *Tomb Raider* movies, I've just seen Angelina Jolie on the posters in all her badass big-breasted glory. But from the looks of it, she wouldn't let a little bit of sweat get her down.

Alexei's house is one story but definitely, *definitely* not small. It stretches out across an emerald lawn like a cruise ship on a glowing green ocean. It's actually more like a museum of modern art, all geometrical and spacious. I know, I know, you don't care what his house looks like, but sometimes it's just nice to paint the scene a little, sheesh.

When I ring the doorbell I half expect him to answer without his shirt on, but sadly he is fully clothed. And he's not alone! There's a tiny girl in pigtails by his side. She's dragging a stuffed bear back and forth across the floor.

"Hey Lele! This is my little sister, Aya. Aya, this is Lele, I go to school with her."

"I'm four!" Aya holds up four fingers.

"I didn't know you had a baby sister! She's so cute!" I go into full-on gush mode.

"Lele is pretty and has pretty hair," Aya speaks into Alexei's leg. "She looks like Elsa from *Frozen*."

"Cute, and a genius, wow," I say. "Aya, I think you and I will be great friends." Aya laughs shyly, hiding her face behind the bear.

"She gets shy sometimes," he says. "Come in, I'll pour you some lemonade."

"Can't say no to lemonade," I say, and then immediately start replaying it in my mind. *Can't say no to lemonade? Can't say no to lemonade. Can't say no.* Did I just make myself sound like a floozy with no self-control? Agh, again with the overthinking! I'd take a chill pill if only I had one.

Inside, the house is perfectly air-conditioned. There's an easel where Aya has been finger painting and an array of photos of Alexei with Aya and their parents, who are, surprise surprise, very attractive. I swear this could be a family of Barbie dolls. What is his mom, like twenty? I squint at the photos, trying to figure out this sorcery. Alexei pours me lemonade and I thank him, but try to act cool about it like I'm not some kind of lemonade fiend in a helpless lemonade trance.

"Okay," he says, leaning on the kitchen counter, "where do we start?"

"Well, we start with a scenario or situation, and then stage it, basically. It's just you and me today, so we should do something simple that just involves two people. One I've been meaning to do for a while is basically about how much easier life is for guys than it is for girls."

"Ha! That's so not true," he says, smirking.

"It is true! Life is so much harder for girls!"

"Oh yeah, tell me one way. No, tell me two ways."

"Umm, okay, easy. First of all, guys can pee standing up practically wherever they want. A couple of weeks ago when we were walking home from school I had to pee so badly but I couldn't do anything about it. Meanwhile, you just went over to a tree and that was that!" Did I just say that? Suddenly, I don't care, I'll say anything. His smile and sparklingly warm blue eyes tell me that I can be myself, they tell me he's happy I'm here. Pray to Jesus that I'm reading them right.

"Okay, okay, that's fair. One more," he allows.

"Easy. That same day it was really hot out and you got to just take your shirt off, but again, there was nothing I could do. I was hot as hell, but could I take my shirt off? Noooo, 'cause I'm a girl."

"Hey, if you wanted to take your shirt off I would not have stopped you."

"Pervert!"

"Just sayin'."

"What's a pervert?" Aya asks. She's sliding around the floor on top of her bear.

"Remember we talked about grown-up words? This is one of them," he says.

"Pervert! Pervert! Pervert!" she chants while stomping her feet.

"Great, my parents are going to love this. You're a troublemaker, Lele Pons, you know that?" And there it is, that wink of his, as rare and beautiful as a comet.

I manage to snap myself out of this reverie and get down to business.

These are the scenes we film: Me struggling with my hair in front of the mirror, me struggling to find the right outfit, me having to pee *so* badly. Alexei easily combing his hair with one hand, Alexei easily picking out a T-shirt, Alexei easily peeing in the bushes like it's no big deal. Then, Alexei playfully nudges my shoulder and then, because I can't take the injustice, I punch him in the balls, just like I imagined doing when he tried to give me a high five. This is getting to be a habit.

All spliced together it looks really cool, like Alexei and I are old buddies, partners in crime, collaborators. And you can only tell a little bit how much I just want to climb on top of him and tear his clothes off with my teeth. I mean, what? Who said that? *Looks around suspiciously*

Aya, who has been watching us film very patiently, wants to go swimming.

"I could go swimming," Alexei says. "Are we all done with the video?"

"Yep." I click UPLOAD and smile.

"Awesome, do you wanna go swimming with us? There's a pool out back."

"Me?"

"Yeah, you do know how to swim, right?"

"Oh, yeah, of course, I just didn't bring my bathing suit, so, you know."

"You can wear one of Mommy's!" Aya shouts. "Swim-ming, swim-ming, swim-ming!"

"Good thinking, Aya," Alexei says. "My mom has tons of bathing suits. I'll grab you one."

"Ummmm . . ." Am I ready for Alexei to see me more than half naked? Yikes.

"Come on, it will be great. I don't want you to leave yet. I like having you around."

"Well, okay then! Sign me up." I blush like a ripe tomato, wait until he's in the hallway closet to gleefully bury my face in my hands.

There they are, those washboard abs etched from pure bronze glistening in the sun. Alexei is coating himself in sunblock—abs, arms, neck, chest—while I watch from the bathroom window, trying to squeeze myself into the microscopic spandex bikini that belongs to Alexei's mother, a.k.a Miami Barbie. The top zips down the front so you can adjust how much cleavage you wish to reveal, but I have to keep it almost all the way down if I want to fit into it at all. I'm

overflowing! I can't go out there like this! I look obscene! Porno-
graphic!

Alexei, on the other hand, looks like a cutout from an Abercrombie
& Fitch catalog—wholesome, classic. I prop my chin up on the bathroom window to watch him adorably blowing up a pair of water wings
for Aya. I slip into a pleasant daydream: Alexei is my husband and this
is our home, Aya is our precious daughter learning to swim, splash-
ing happily, everything has worked out, life has fallen into place,
I've found my Prince Charming and—HOLY MOTHER OF GOD!
Alexei's father pops up in front of the window, catching me in the act
of staring at his son. I jump back, holler like a baboon, fall on my ass.
The daydream vanishes; the spell is broken. Once again, I am a joke.
There's nothing I can do but laugh.

13

3 Signs That Show a Person Is Latin

(5,000 FOLLOWERS)

Quick question: Who on earth decided that Frisbee golf is a sport? Golf itself is barely a sport to begin with, but when you mix it with a plastic, Day-Glo, semi-aerodymanic disc, any semblance of legitimacy or prestige is zapped right out. It is an activity for the old and senile, the recently lobotomized, and, apparently, high school juniors. Coach Washington has us chasing these wayward flying saucers all over the soccer field for the entire ungodly forty-five minutes of gym—the sight is laughably tragic.

In case you're in the mood to be bored to death, this is how you play: You toss the Frisbee in the direction of a flag, which is supposed to represent a hole. You try to get it to the flag in the least amount of throws possible, then write down your number with a tiny orange pencil, then go on to the next flag, then the next. At the end of the game whomever has the lowest total of throws written down wins the game. I think.

I don't *really* know and I'm definitely not following the rules because I couldn't possibly care less and because as soon as I start paying attention then the whole thing will become real, and once you're someone who has played Frisbee golf you can never be someone who has not played Frisbee golf.

Coach Washington keeps shouting at me, "Lele, you're doing it all wrong. Come on, it's just like regular golf except with a Frisbee!" which literally means *nothing* to me. I'm sorry, do I *look* like Tiger Woods? Maybe I could pass for one of his foreign supermodel blonds, and after almost an hour of Frisbee golf I'm definitely in the mood to bash into someone's luxury vehicle. . . .

Okay, believe it or not, this story is not about Frisbee golf. It's about what happens after Frisbee golf in the locker rooms while we're changing out of these neon mesh uniforms and into our regular, non-night-vision-alien clothes. I've just opened my locker when my phone starts to ring. I forgot to put it on vibrate for school. And, because I am who I am, I can't just have a regular ringtone that comes with the iPhone (Sencha, Ripples, By the Seaside, Default, you know), I have to have it set to "Gasolina" by Daddy Yankee. For those of you who don't know it, this song is a fast-paced, rhythm-based, drum-machine treat that more or less just repeats *"A ella la gusta la gasolina (dame mas gasolina), como le encanta la gasolina (dame mas gasolina)"* over and over. In other words (English words): she likes gasoline (give me more gasoline), how she loves gasoline (give me more gasoline). In the world of Daddy Yankee (also known as Puerto Rico), "gasolina" can refer to either the street life or to a cocktail made from rum and fruit juice . . . it is unclear which "gasolina" this song is actually about.

Yes, this is my ringtone. Apparently I can't be normal, not even once. So, the ringtone goes off and it is *loud,* and everyone is looking at me like "ummmmm." Everyone, that is, except one person: *Yvette Amparo.* That's right, Yvette Amparo, sworn nemesis, is not staring at me, because she is too busy dancing to my reggaeton ringtone. She's *into* it; she *gets* it. Gasp! Maybe we're not so different, she and I.

Then, everyone's staring at her instead of me. The girls don't know what to make of it, it's like a giraffe at the zoo doing . . . I don't know, what would be weird to see a giraffe do? It would be like a giraffe at the zoo dancing to reggaeton. There you go.

When she notices everyone staring, she stops.

"What?" she asks with breezy, popular-girl confidence. "A Latina can't get down to a little reggaeton?"

"Whoa, you're Latina?" I say. I never knew, but Miami, duh. I mean there are a lot of us here.

"Puerto Rican, obviously." She frames her own face, imitation-diva style. "What did you think Amparo was, Japanese?"

"No, I thought it was just pure evil." (I can't believe I said that!)

"You're a riot." She laughs, like actually laughs.

"I'm Venezuelan, actually." It blurts out of my mouth. "I can't believe we're both Latina."

"Shut up," she says. "Your skinny butt looks like it's from Sweden."

"Hey," I say. "First of all, thank you for calling me skinny. But second of all, my butt is fat!" I turn around and demonstrate, jiggling clumsily back and forth. Always a jiggler, never a twerker.

"Wow, you're really serious."

"I'm ALWAYS serious," I say, and we both laugh.

"Hey," she says. "Are you gonna make a Vine about this?"

"You've seen my Vines?" I ask, surprised.

"Girl, really? Everyone has seen your Vines. You're hilarious, and now that I know you're not a bitch, I can like you just like everyone else does. Oh, and I like your new look, by the way. Very sophisticated."

OKAY, DO YOU KNOW WHAT THIS MEANS? It means pigs can fly, hell has frozen over, the moon is blue, cows can dance on ice, fish can swim—wait. You get the point: the unthinkable has become a reality: Yvette Amparo and I had a conversation that wasn't aimed at destroying each other's lives. For the first time in my life I truly believe that nothing is impossible.

Imagine how different these first months of school would have been had I known Yvette and I had this one deep-seated thing in common? Would it really be so politically incorrect for us all to wear signs with our race printed on them? Well, probably yes.

Luckily, I have found in my experience that if you want to know if someone is Latino, all you have to do is look for three telltale signs.

REGGAETON

Reggaeton wasn't always first on this list, but it's getting promoted ever since it identified Yvette as Latina and thus became an olive branch of sorts. From what I've observed, if you're not Latino, you don't get reggaeton. I mean, I barely even get it, probably because it's not something to "get," it's something to just feel, an excuse to just let it all go, leave the world behind. When a white person catches you wigging out to reggaeton, they try to pretend they don't see you, like you're breaking some major law by having a little fun and they want to make sure no one thinks they're part of this debauchery. Get yourself invited to one of our weddings, on the other hand, and you will be drowning in a sea of Latina ladies letting loose, no shame anywhere to be seen. As it should be.

THE TELENOVELA SLAP

The telenovela is a distinguished art form in which Latinos act out over-the-top dramatic situations and exaggerate every syllable for the sake of our entertainment. They kill each other for money, they sleep with each other's husbands/brothers/fathers/sons, and wear enough makeup to paint an entire town—in other words, it is a soap opera for the Latina lady (or gentleman, if that's the kind of thing he's into. No judgment). As you can imagine, with all of the elaborate backstabbing that goes on, there is also a fair amount of slapping. You can spot a Latina girl by her courage and audacity to slap a bitch. It doesn't matter who you are—male, female, ugly, attractive, hero, villain—if you cross a Latina, you *will* get the telenovela slap.

LOUD CURSING

Latino guys and girls are more, let's say, self-expressive than your average person. We feel our feelings deeply and aren't ashamed to demonstrate them to the world. For example, if your mom calls you to tell you to come home when you're having a perfectly good time with your friends, you might start cursing loudly (in Spanish) into the phone, not having a care in the world about who is around to hear you. And, yes, we Latino folk do have a great deal of respect for our parents, but that doesn't mean we can't curse at them. In our culture, at the appropriate time, a round of loud cursing is just the way we relate to each other. Other times, I'll throw a curse word or two at my mom and end up getting telenovela-slapped.

So, there you have it, the Lele Pons official guide to spotting a human being of Latino origin. Of course, just because you can spot their Latino-ness doesn't mean you will automatically know what type of Latino they are. Mexico, Spain, Venezuela, Guatemala, Puerto Rico, Costa Rica, Argentina . . . the list goes on and on. A Latino or Latina can be from any of these places and you don't want to assume which, because when you assume you make an ass of you and me, and also you will be risking the dreaded telenovela slap.

Don't say I didn't, say I didn't warn you. (Quote by Taylor Swift, least Latino person on the planet.)

"You'll never believe what happened today in gym," I say to Alexei when he calls me later that night. "Yvette and I realized we're both

Latino and I think now we don't hate each other anymore." He's taken to calling me fairly frequently, just to say hi or tell me about something funny he thinks we could film. Sometimes he says he just wanted to hear my voice, which is pretty intimate if you ask me.

"So she likes you now because you're not just a white girl? That's sort of racist."

"Well, sort of. More like racial elitism."

"Sure."

"Anyway, that's not really the point. The point is now we gotta film '3 Signs That Show a Person Is Latin.' Can you come over in like an hour?"

"Yeah!"

"Great, love the enthusiasm. Oh, and Alexei?"

"Yeah?"

"You'll have to be okay with getting slapped."

CUT TO: Fourteen takes of the telenovela slap later and Alexei is icing his face, trying not to cry. Way to take one for the team!

14

And Thus . . . a Friendship Was Born

*A*h, December, month of jolliness and togetherness and possibility, month of Styrofoam snow and spray-painted frost and waiting in
line at the mall to get photographed with a fat old man who is most
likely a disgruntled pervert with a shaky financial history. And no,
I'm not talking about Uncle Freddie, who is in Miami with his wife
and three children for the entire month. Let's be real, December is
really Santa's month, whether he deserves it or not.

You'd think that being sixteen I would no longer have to go
through the whole ordeal of dressing up and waiting in a forty-five-
minute line to get an annual Santa pic, but alas, you are mistaken.
Uncle Freddie and Aunt Sylvia and their darling Kyle, Suzie, and
Johnny are in town and spirits are preternaturally high. *Preternatural* is a word I learned in English last week that basically means
"supernatural" or "beyond natural." So why not just say supernatural, you might ask? Well, earthling, because preternatural sounds
oh so much cooler. Plus, it never hurts for people to think of you as
the smart one in a group. Hey, do *not* call me a nerd, okay? I'm just
slowly working on my new brand of mystique and sophistication.
Lele 2.0, to be revealed in 2016.

Anyway, so we're waiting in line with Uncle Freddie and Co., the kids high on gummy bears and the grown-ups buzzed on white wine spritzers. I'm surrounded by bumbling imbeciles. Lovable imbeciles, *my* lovable imbeciles, but imbeciles nonetheless. Johnny says, "Where do monkeys like to hang out? The monkey bars!" Squishing the so-called punch line right up against the joke so no one has time to guess the answer or even understand that a question was being asked. Uncle Freddie follows this up with "What's the difference between your mom and a bowling ball? You can only fit—"

"Okay Freddie, not in front of the kids," says Aunt Sylvia.

"Come on, they're too young to even know what I'm saying."

"Let's keep it light."

I put my face in my hands, imagine I'm somewhere else. I'm on a beach with Alexei, and waiters in Speedos are serving me piña coladas. They fan me, feed me grapes; they've all written "Lele is queen" on their chests in blue paint. I open my eyes and, to my dismay, I am still in the Palm Beach mall with the entire Pons clan, each of us wearing some combination of red and green. My outfit is a red polyester dress with big green buttons on the shoulder straps and a white puffy-sleeved shirt billowing out the top. I do my best to keep my eyes on the ground in a valiant attempt to go unseen, but my efforts are in vain.

"Ew." I look up to see a girl, about my age, in a leopard-print dress, immaculately flat-ironed hair, and bubblegum-colored lip gloss. She's staring me down like I'm a leper.

"Excuse me, are you talking to me?"

"Yeah," she says, "I said ew, because your outfit is completely gross."

"Bitch!"

"Slut!" This voice comes from a third party. I turn around to see (gasp!) Yvette Amparo with (gasp!) her family, staring down Leopard Girl with more tenacity than I've ever seen.

"Whoa. Hey, Yvette, I didn't see you there," I say, wondering how long she and her family have been standing behind us.

"Are you going to let her talk to you like that? Hey, Leopard, who do you think you are? You think you can just go around commenting on people's outfits like you know what the hell you're talking about? You're wearing leopard print, girlie, which puts you at the very bottom of the fashion totem pole. As far as I'm concerned you're the least qualified human to criticize anyone's fashion sense, and I'm fairly certain nobody asked for your useless opinion, so buh-bye, walk along, sweetheart." Yvette waves her acrylic nails at Leopard Girl, who is now a deer in the headlights, scampering away with wide eyes and trembling legs.

I'm just as stunned. "Thank you, I uh . . . I don't know what to say, that was really sweet of you."

"Yeah, well, no one's allowed to talk to you like that but me, right?"

"That's right. *Puta.*"

"*Pendeja!*" We laugh, our parents eye each other suspiciously.

In a daydream, Yvette and I get our revenge on Leopard Girl. Mercilessly, we tie her to a tree, we roll her up into a rug, all the while "Do You Believe in Magic?" by The Lovin' Spoonful plays on repeat. Ahhh, I think I've found my happy place.

"Lele? Lele?" Mom snaps me back into reality. "Who was that girl? Is she a friend of yours?"

"Yeah," I say, thinking about Yvette. "I guess she is."

15

Nobody Ever Believes Little Kids in Scary Movies / How Little Kids Wake You Up on Christmas

(5,892 FOLLOWERS)

So, turns out Yvette isn't so bad after all. Sometimes your greatest enemy is actually the most like you. Yvette saw herself in me and freaked out, figuring this town wasn't big enough for the both of us—it's all very cinematic. We hate the same things and the same people, she's actually the smartest and funniest person I know, besides myself of course. So what if she has a chip on her shoulder? I can relate to that sometimes, to be quite honest. I think if we join forces we'll be unstoppable. We'll throw parties that people rave about for months and invent a secret language so no one can decode our texts—all the guys at school will want to date us and all the girls will want to be us. Hell, even the girls will want to date us and even the guys will want to be us. We will be rulers: first we take Miami, then we date the world.

But for now it's winter break and I am beyond thrilled to be away from school. Although, it's not much of a vacation with Uncle Freddie and the gang scampering around our house all day like rabid mice. I try to spend as much time in my room as possible. I've fashioned a makeshift lock out of pushpins and a chain-link brace-let so that my room can be a secluded sanctuary for sleeping, eating, and Vine making. It may not be *all* that professional-looking, but this is my office, my studio, the setting where the magic happens.

In years from now, my house will be a museum, my room blocked off with red velvet rope, and a tour guide will say, "This, THIS is where Lele thought up the material to put in her Vines. Some say she's the greatest genius of the millennial era . . ." Really, you guys, they will say this.

Until that point, however, my four-year-old cousin Johnny is sharing my room at night, sleeping on a cute little trundle mattress that pulls out from under my bed.

Johnny is really sweet, but he sort of creeps me out. He reminds me of one of those kids from horror movies who somehow is the chosen one in the family to be constantly contacted by the super-natural, I mean, preternatural element. He's constantly spooked and on guard, staring at the walls like he sees something no one else can see. I believe in ghosts, so all this kid has to do is stare into nothing with that fixed, dreamy gaze and I jump right on board with the notion that the house I live in is, in fact, haunted.

I have a lot of empathy for the kids in horror movies: nobody *ever* takes them seriously. I can relate. So, when I come home from my morning jog to find Johnny sitting up in bed, hands over his eyes, I want to believe him that there's something in the closet.

"What is it, Johnny? What's in the closet?"

"It's a monster. It has black hair and a black face." He whimpers into a pillow, brown eyes wide and glossed with fear.

"Okay, let's check this out." I grab a baseball bat to show him that I am taking him very seriously, then open the closet and peer in. Nothing. Nothing but a disorganized pile of my shoes and some articles of clothing piled on top of that. I'm not great with neatness.

"Look, no one's in there. You're safe." I turn back to face him. "I was on your team, I wanted to believe you, I really wanted there to be a monster and for you to have your little-kid victory of finally being right for once, I'm sorry that it didn't turn out that way."

He starts screaming, bloody murder, and pointing aggressively.

"Behind you!" he shrieks. "He's behind you!"

"What? Where?" I swing back around, only to see my lopsided ball of clothes and shoes.

"Johnny, is this what you're seeing? These clothes sort of look like a monster. I guess."

"No! He has a black face and black hair! And whenever you look at me he comes back out!"

"Johnny"—I turn back to face him—"are you messing with me? There's no—" And that's when I feel it: two slimy hands wrapping around my ankles. I try to run but it's too late. The hands pull me down into the closet, I try to grip the carpet, hold on to anything I can, but I'm dragged deep into the bowels of the house and then deeper, into the fiery pits of *Hades*.

LOL, yeah right, I'm just messing with you. Did I mention I have an active imagination?

Having kids around is scary enough as it is without adding monsters to the mix. Seriously, what is with them? They need to eat around the clock, they are loud and insist on climbing everything, they're amused by the stupidest things ever, and they *never* get tired. I don't know how they do it, but if you didn't make them go to bed they honestly never would.

And nothing gives them more energy than Christmas. NOTH-ING. Last night, Johnny and Kyle and Suzie stayed up until two in the morning waiting for Santa Claus, and are now banging on my door screaming "PRESENTS! PRESENTS! PRESENTS!" It is six in the morning, I don't give a f**k about presents. It's six in the morning, I wouldn't get out of bed if Alexei was downstairs standing under the mistletoe, covered in whipped cream and strawberries, wearing nothing but an elf's hat. Okay, maybe I would get up for that.

The Pons family has two main Christmas traditions. The first, I've told you about already—you know, the one with the mall and the waiting around for a chance at a photo op with Santa while dressed in embarrassing clothes. The second is exponentially more lovely, something I actually look forward to. I don't know where you come from, reader, or if you're blessed with snowy Christmas mornings, but there's a better chance of seeing snow in hell than in Miami. Well, maybe that's a slight exaggeration, considering hell is most likely a fictional place, and it did snow once in Miami thirty-six years ago. But anyway, the night before Christmas, the Pons family gathers around the dining room table and makes chains of paper snowflakes to hang around the house. I'm not talking like eight or nine snowflakes here and there, I'm talking about hundreds upon hundreds, all painted with glitter-glue for a magical sunlit-morning-snow look. We stay up late drinking warm apple cider and make bets on who will fall asleep first. Whoever falls asleep first gets their face drawn on (PG stuff only, e.g., no penises), and whoever wins the bet gets to do the drawing. Whoever stays awake the longest gets to hide the presents all around the house and laugh while everyone struggles to find them. It's an odd tradition, yes.

This year around midnight, Mom says, "I'm just going to rest my eyes for a second."

"Sure, sure. Go ahead, take a break," I say encouragingly, because I'm betting on her to be the first one out. She closes her eyes and in seconds is talking in her sleep. Mom is an impressively intelligible sleeptalker:

"Don't forget to turn off the electric cars," she mumbles, and then, "Is this the one with the roller coasters?" The rest of us laugh so hard it hurts.

By 2:00 a.m. I reach the end of my snowflake-making capabilities, so I pull a blanket over Mom and (lovingly) draw a small snowman on her left cheek—it's super adorable if I do say so myself—then drag myself to bed where I fall instantly into a deep and peaceful sleep.

"Lele! Lele! Lele! Get up! Presents!"

"Go away!" I put a pillow over my head, trying to block the sound. *CRASH!* They break through my makeshift lock and bound into the room like jungle animals. Johnny and Kyle jump up on my bed while Suzie walks right up to my face and screams, "IT'S CHRISTMASTIME!!!!!!!"

I'm sorry, but what are we feeding these kids, cocaine? I never thought I'd say it, but I think I'm ready to go back to school. I love my family but I've learned a very important lesson this winter vacation: they are extremely frightening.

16

Puberty Hit Her Like . . .

(600,000 FOLLOWERS) (WHAT??!!)

*Y*ou guys, I went on a jog EVERY SINGLE DAY OF CHRIST-MAS VACATION. Christmas vacation was like a sweet little cocoon; I curled up in my den of hibernation as a caterpillar and came out, if I do say so myself, as a FRICKING BUTTERFLY. I exercised, I got a tan, I put highlights in my hair, went shopping two or three times, and best of all, I GOT MY BRACES OFF! Finally! I had almost forgotten what it's like to not look like a crew of robots has colonized my mouth. Would you believe me if I told you my abs are almost as flat as Darcy's now? I can rock a crop top like a super-star and nobody can stop me. Hallelujah.

Oh, and after Cameron Diaz shared "3 Ways to Tell If a Person is Latin," I jumped from six thousand followers to six hundred thousand! I literally don't know how to process this information. I keep getting phone calls about unfamiliar words like *deals* and *sponsorships* and *representation* and *brand image* . . . am I going to need a man-ager? Who knew having a following could be so complicated? Ooh, I like the sound of that: "a following" . . . it's like I'm a cult leader.

On our first day back at school, I show up wearing a hot little dress from Brandy Melville, and beige suede Korkys wedges. I have cranked it up to the next level and everyone is noticing. During first-period English I keep catching people staring at me, but in a different way than they used to. Now they see something they like and can't get enough of. That's right, bitches, my smile says to them, Nerdy girl is all grown up.

"Hey, Lele." Alexei stops me after class. "You look . . . hot." My mouth hangs open as he walks away.

When gym rolls around, I worry that changing into that hideous uniform might kill the magic of my new look (how will I *ever* take off this little black dress with holes so casually and conveniently cut into the sides to reveal where my waist curves in?!), so I tell Coach Washington that I have terrible cramps and opt to sit on the side-lines. What a beautiful hour: me in the bleachers without a care in the world while the other girls run laps around and around the track field. Everyone is sweaty and gross, while I remain a goddess of hot-ness, hair blowing in the wind high above the common folk. I feel like I'm on top of Mount Olympus; I feel like I'm in a movie.

Yvette and her gaggle pass me on the track and Yvette stops to catch her breath.

"Wish that dumb mall bitch could see you in that dope outfit, Lele. She'd shoot herself in the face."

"That's a tad extreme, but thank you. I accept your kind words." *I accept your kind words?* Will I never learn how to speak to people?

"You're seriously so weird," she says. "Wanna have lunch with us today?"

"Whoa, me? Really?"

"Yeah, why not?"

"Can I bring Darcy?"

"Sure. Yeah, she's cool."

"Okay then."

"We meet at the front gate and then walk to Tommy's Pizza."

"See you there."

"Awesome, see you there," she says. "On Wednesdays, we wear pink." She winks at me in this chillingly cool, self-aware way that leaves me in awe. First day back at school is shaping up to be a memorable one.

"Shut up," Darcy says, eyes wide. We're walking toward the front gate and she cannot keep her cool. "You have to be kidding me."

"I am not kidding you, Darcy. She just ran right up to me and invited us to eat lunch with them."

"Off campus."

"Correct."

"We're eating lunch off campus with Yvette Amparo."

"That is correct."

"Do you know how rare this is? Nobody gets invited to eat off campus with Yvette and her posse."

"Yeah, speaking of that, do they have a name or something? I mean I feel like any real popular clique needs to have a group name, like the Plastics or the Pink Ladies or the Heathers or the Pretty Little Liars or . . . the Jawbreaker Murderers?"

"Hm. I don't think they do. Maybe you should suggest one and then they'd invite us to be permanently part of the group."

"Maybe."

"It's so weird that she invited you, of all people. I mean, I thought she hated you."

"Yeah, that's the thing, she did hate me. And I hated her. Then we realized we just hated each other because of how similar we are. I think that's what happened anyway. At the end of the day I'm not really one to hold a grudge."

"I guess stranger things have happened," Darcy says, fixing the barrettes in her newly braided hair.

Yvette and the Fleek Four (obvi the clique name is a work in progress) look like an army waiting for us at the gate. They're all wearing black and the same impeccably applied cat-eye makeup, clear lip gloss. Yvette's eyes could cut through ice; man am I glad I have her on my side now.

"Hey, Lele. Hey, Darcy. Thanks for joining us! Come on, let's get the hell out of here." She leads the crew off campus and we follow her down Fourth Street to the corner of Ocean Avenue, where Tommy's Pizza awaits us, a 24-7 oasis in the desert of high school hell. Emily, Cynthia, Maddie, and Becca huddle together, pretending that Darcy and I aren't here. They order Diet Cokes and nothing else. Oh, so it's that kind of lunch. Sigh.

"How happy are you that Frisbee golf is over?" Yvette asks once we're outside with our Cokes. Cynthia lights a cigarette.

"Oh, super glad," I say. "Although now we're probably going to just have to participate in some other humiliating sport. Once swimming season comes around I'm going to be longing for the Frisbee golf days."

"Oh my God." Yvette laughs. "That is so real. I am with you one hundred percent."

A truck full of guys drives by and all five of them whistle at us, calling out obscenities too obscene for even an X-rated film. If only their mothers could see them.

"Men are pigs," Becca says. "They don't deserve to share the planet with us." The other girls giggle.

"Amen, sistah." Cynthia exhales smoke.

"Please don't blow that in my face, Cynthia," Yvette says. "I just got a facial."

"Sorry," Cynthia mutters, turning away.

"Speaking of men"—Yvette laces her fingers together and rests her chin on them—"what's going on with you and Alexei? I saw the Vine you guys made together, it was so cute. Are you dating?"

"Oh, uh . . ." I freeze, I've never had to talk to anyone about Alexei before. "No, we're not dating. Just friends."

"Really? You guys seem really close," Yvette says.

"We've hung out a bunch and it doesn't seem like it's going any-where . . . I mean, he did tell me he liked me but—"

"He told you he liked you?!" Yvette's eyes are bulging out of her face. Is it THAT SHOCKING that he likes me? I mean, I'm not ugly.

"Mmm-hmmm."

"Oh my God, Lele, he's in love!" Yvette is practically squealing.

"You think?"

"I know boys, Lele, trust me. You should totally date him."

"Well, he hasn't asked me to be his girlfriend or anything, so I don't know."

"Men are so confused," Cynthia says. "They have no idea what they want."

"Does Alexei Kuyper really count as a man?" Maddie asks. "I mean, isn't he such a boy?"

"Oh, he's a man," Becca says in a way that makes me a little nauseous. The rest giggle. Blech.

"He'll come around." Yvette smiles, almost wickedly. "Especially now that you're so goddamn sexy, if you don't mind me saying so."

"Oh, I don't mind." I swat at her playfully. "Tell me again."

"Especially now that you're so goddamn sexy!" she says again and I fake-swoon; we laugh like long-lost sisters. The other girls sulk, Darcy included.

In fifth-period marine biology I wouldn't be able to pay attention to what Mr. White is saying if you paid me a million dollars. Some-thing about a hundred different species of fish and their scientific names. For example, the shortnose sturgeon is actually called *Acipenser brevirostrum*. It sounds more like a spell you learn at Hogwarts than a fish, which I guess is pretty fascinating if you think about it . . . but I can't think about it! All I can think about is how crazy this day was and the six hundred thousand followers I have on

Vine. Life is changing fast and I have visions upon visions swirling around my mind, so many ideas to turn into Vines! I jot them all down while Mr. White chatters on in the background:

- Boys whistle at girls, girls throw Diet Coke in their faces.
- Girl-on-girl jealousy.
- Boys vs. men (alternative title: boys are so confused).
- During marine biology, girl uses Potter-esque spell to turn teacher into a shortnose sturgeon.
- Instant makeover.

Instant makeover. I write it out over and over. Is that what happened to me? No, I put effort into my new look, I worked hard, I suffered for this body! But wouldn't it be great? A makeover as instant as instant coffee. Just add water. Extremely nerdy girl waves at friends—braces, glasses, bad skin. Suddenly, she's hit by a book called *Puberty* and is automatically a beauty queen. CUT TO: her friends all hit themselves with the *Puberty* book trying for the same effect. Sadly, the magic doesn't work on them.

Marine biology flies by like this, and by the time the bell rings I have three pages of new Vine material. Damn it feels good to be a gangsta.

17

How to Recover from a Bad High Five

(600,102 FOLLOWERS)

"So, today was . . . different." Darcy catches me at my locker after class, still chewing the straw from her Diet Coke.

"I know! What a trip. Can I be honest with you though? I am so hungry I could eat your face."

"Me too! What's up with the no-lunch thing? No wonder they're so skinny."

"Right? Yvette wants us to go off campus with them again tomorrow, so I guess we'll have to bring our own snacks to fill up on beforehand."

"Are you serious? We're hanging with them again? Oh man, Lele, do you know what this means?"

"Ermmm . . ."

"You're popular now. We're popular. This is insane."

"Hollerrrrr!" I put up my hand for a high five. Darcy goes in for the kill but misses my hand and we both topple from the momentum of failure.

"That was embarrassing." She grimaces.

"Yeah, we're gonna have to work on that."

In my room we binge on curly fries and spend the next three hours coordinating the dopest secret handshake you've ever seen. By the time we have it perfected we look like Lindsay Lohan and her butler in *The Parent Trap*. They were cool, right?

18

You Belong with ... Her?

(600,552 FOLLOWERS)

*A*mazing news. Yvette is throwing a party with the sole purpose of getting me and Alexei together!

"What, why?" I ask. She's pulled me under a staircase in the language building and is stroking my hair like I'm a sad cat as she speaks. How is she this comfortable with being so touchy? Isn't she worried I'll think she's a big lesbian? No, she isn't, because Yvette doesn't worry about anything, she is too cool for worry. Maybe she's a cyborg? One of those *Austin Powers* Fembots? I wouldn't be surprised.

"Because, silly, I know he likes you and you're obviously head over heels for him! You don't strike me as the shy type, but something is keeping you two from making it happen and I, for one, am getting impatient. You're my friend now, and I like Alexei just fine . . . this is what I do for people I like."

"Okay, Cupid. If you say so."

"Eeeeeeeeeeeeee! Yay. So excited. Friday at my house, spread the word. Kisses!" She saunters off, bouncing up the stairs. This girl is a roller coaster, whenever she's around I feel like I have to hold on to something.

• • •

So now here we are, Yvette and the Roller Coasters and me, blasting Beyoncé in the Amparo mansion, drinking virgin piña coladas. Well, mine is virgin, they're really going for it with the rum. Don't get me wrong, I get it, but I don't feel the need mostly because I find that I act plenty drunk without adding alcohol to the mix. People drink to keep up with me! Plus, since I turned sixteen and got my driver's license I've been the designated driver—and that gives me *all* the power, muahahaha!

"I'm not kidding, it was like THIS big." Becca holds her hands apart to demonstrate the size of what looks like a Subway sandwich. "I was shocked. I mean, shocked." The others squeal and flap their hands in disbelief. They look and sound like a flock of gulls.

"So what did you do?!" Yvette gulps her colada.

"At first I was like, 'Oh my God, Jackson, no way. There's no way that's going to fit.' But he was like, 'Trust me, I can make it work.' But I said, 'No! It's going to hurt!' And he said he would make sure it didn't hurt, so then I let him go down on me for basically a million years."

"And . . . ?"

"And he was right. It fit. And it didn't hurt. Only a little bit in the beginning."

More squealing, more hand flapping.

"I cannot believe you lost your virginity to Jackson Clark!" Yvette approves. "Becca, he is so hot."

"So much better than my first," Cynthia says. "Remember Eric McCullough?"

"Wasn't he only at Miami High for like one semester in ninth grade?"

"Mmm-hmm!"

"Ewww, Cynthia."

"I know. He was so creepy. But I was really bored at Jessie Jacobs's party, so I figured why not? And it wasn't the worst thing in the world, the kid was good with his hands."

"Oh my God, stop talking, you're going to make me throw up."

Yvette puts a hand up to Cynthia and then turns to me. "What about you, Lele? Who'd you lose it to?"

"Oh, um . . . well, funny story, I uh . . ."

"Have you never done it?!" Yvette asks me this as if she's never heard of a tragedy so great.

"Yeah. I mean no, I haven't."

"Shut up!" She drops her jaw for dramatic effect. The way she's staring at me you'd think I just told her I'm a martian spy. "What the hell are you waiting for?"

"I don't know . . . I'm not necessarily waiting, it's just never happened. I've never had a real boyfriend and—"

"Boyfriend shmoyfriend," Maddie says. "Just pick a guy, someone with experience, and get it over with."

"Nonsense!" Yvette interjects. "She's obviously going to lose it to Alexei. Maybe even tonight. Oooh, this is so meant to be!"

"I don't know about that."

"Don't you like him?"

"I do, definitely. But I want it to be . . . I don't think I want it to happen at a party."

"Uhh . . ." She looks at me like I've just descended from a UFO. "Why not?"

"A party is a public place! I'll only get to lose my virginity once, it should be . . . special." I feel my cheeks get hot and wish we could change the subject.

"Lele, losing your virginity is not something you 'get to do,' it's something you get out of the way so you can start enjoying sex. And it's not going to be special . . . it takes like five or six times before it's special."

"I know it's not going to be like fireworks bursting in the air the first time or whatever, I'm just saying I want it to be . . . thoughtful. I want to look back on it and not wanna puke. You know? I at least want . . . somewhat fond memories. And unless it's on Brangelina's yacht after the Oscars, a party isn't the best environment for that."

"Ugh, fine," Yvette says. "Be a romantic. But we'll see how you feel once he shows up wearing a hoodie zipped open with no shirt underneath!"

And we do see how I feel once he shows up: absolutely miserable. Rock-bottom miserable. No good, very bad miserable. Why? He's shown up with ANOTHER GIRL.

Oh, and they're KISSING.

I'm walking down Yvette's notorious carpeted spiral staircase in a skintight pink-floral dress, hot as hell (but in a classy way) when I see him by the Amparo bar, pouring a drink for a little pixie girl with dyed pink hair and a lip ring. My heart stops and thoughts race in triple speed: *What the . . . okay, stay calm, deep breath. Wow, she's pretty, and very unique-looking; does he think she's cooler than I am? It's probably nothing to worry about, she's probably like his cousin or sister or just some girl he doesn't even know . . .*

Just as I'm thinking this they clink their glasses together and he leans in for a kiss. Not just any old kiss, but a passionate one. A slow, passionate, unnecessarily long kiss. With tongues. Disgusting. Alexei looks up and sees me standing there, frozen on the staircase, no doubt with a look of sheer horror plastered onto my face.

"Oh hey, Lele!" He waves enthusiastically, as if he hasn't just ruined my life. I try to wave back but I can't—my arms feel heavy as lead, I couldn't lift them if my life depended on it. I can't feel my face and the whole room seems to have entered a slow-motion time warp; all I can do is turn and run back up the stairs.

So there goes Yvette's great plan, there go my future hopes and dreams of being Mrs. Alexei Kuyper. That's it, game over. Imagine a pixilated video-game Lele appearing on the screen, X's over her eyes.

"Okay, so there's a tiny glitch in my plan." Yvette tries to calm me down while I try to not hyperventilate in the bathroom. "We just have to rework it a little, that's all. Do you know how easy it is to break people up these days? I bet they're not even that serious. Lele, please take a deep breath, you're scaring me."

"Me? Oh, I'm fine." I sigh, realize I've been holding my breath so long my face is turning slightly blue in the mirror.

"Yes, you're more than fine. You're a knockout in this dress, seriously. Just go downstairs and enjoy the party like the goddess rock star you are and let him eat his heart out. You just be you and by the end of the night he'll forget all about what's-her-face. Okay?"

"Yvette, I don't want to be rude, I know this is going to be a great party, but I don't think I can do it. I think I need to be alone. I'm just not in a party mood." I brace myself, certain she's going to either launch into a vengeful tirade or give me the cold shoulder. I fear the return of evil Yvette.

"Oh, babe, I totally get it. This sucks, I've been there before, trust me. Will you do one thing for me?"

"Sure, I think."

"Go home and be super good to yourself, because you deserve it. Take a bubble bath, pour yourself a glass of champagne, do some frivolous internet shopping. Like honestly, watch some *Real Housewives* if you have to."

Whoa. Not what I was expecting. I guess this party has been filled with surprises, the good, the bad, and the ugly.

Back at home I try to summon the energy to get into the bath, but I can't, so I lie in bed staring up at my ceiling imagining big red letters that read "REJECTED" stamped across my forehead. Alexei has a girlfriend. I honestly didn't see this coming. I could see him not being interested in me, but I couldn't see him choosing someone else instead. And maybe Yvette's right, maybe I could win him over, but I don't want to be that girl who steals someone's boyfriend. Also known as a boyfriend stealer. It's not right.

I'm not much of a writer, but I feel the need to channel my pain in some way that doesn't involve getting out of bed. I grab a pen and paper and get to work, boosting my self-esteem by telling myself I'm a regular F. Scott Fitzgerald. Anyone worth their salt has been rejected, after all. Although, I think that's just something people say to make you feel better, because, really, anyone who is alive has been rejected at one point or another, it has nothing to do with greatness. Anyway, here's the short story I end up writing when I should be losing my virginity to Alexei in Yvette's parents' hot tub. Okay, fine, maybe I would lose it at a party after all. Hot tubs are romantic, right? I've seen *The Bachelor*. (Note: All characters appearing in this work are fictitious. Any resemblance to real persons, living or dead, is purely coincidental.)

You know when you have a really hot next-door neighbor boy whose second-story bedroom window is aligned perfectly with your second-story bedroom window? Oh, you don't? Sucks for you. You've never seen the "You Belong With Me" video by T-Swift? I, like Tay-Tay, have perfect visual access to the often-shirtless hottie next door, and in a mere two days of his moving in, I found myself completely in LOVE. That's right, bitches, it wasn't just a crush and it wasn't just hormones, it was TRUE LOVE. I loved his blue eyes bright as the Miami sky; loved his swishy blond hair, so impeccably groomed it would put prepubescent-era Bieber to shame; loved his tan, hairless chest; loved those muscle lines by his hip bones that trailed diagonally down leading to his— Wait, what were we talking about!?! Oh, right, it was true love. True, silent love, expressed solely through words written in Sharpie on notebook paper, held up to windows. Swoon.

There was just one problem: our love was star-crossed. Not so much because our families were long-time arch enemies who spilled each other's blood for sport, but more because he had this hot girlfriend who, YOU GUESSED IT, was a cheerleader at our school: the high heels to my sneakers, short skirts to my T-shirts. Do I really have to spell it out for you? She was a freakin' beauty queen, okay? Then there's me: tall, long blond hair, big boobs. Ugh. It was so unfair. But I wasn't going to let my ugly-duckling looks get in the way of winning the man of my dreams. And you know what? He wasn't exactly *un*interested in me. Sometimes he would just sit on his bed holding up signs with clever little messages on them like "Hey" or "What's up?" and I would hold up a sign in response with something like "NM, U?" and we'd laugh and bat our eyelashes at each other like two . . . like two . . . I don't know, what bats its eyelashes? Humans? That's it: we'd laugh and bat our eyelashes at each other like two humans. So I devised a plan to win him over: I'd wear my cutest T-shirt with the least amount of holes in it, sit cross-legged on my bed, and use my red Sharpie to write out the words I've always wanted to write to a man and show him from a safe distance: I Love U.

As fate would have it, the moment I held up my sign was the exact moment that Hot Cheerleader Girlfriend decided to show up—appearing from nowhere as if teleported from the Parallel Universe of Preppy Perfection—to stand right next to him with her arms crossed, looking like she was going to straight-up murder me. And that is what happened: she murdered me. She took out her slingshot and before I knew what was happening, my life was cut short by a rock the size of my fist. The worst part? She wasn't even mad at him. She blamed the whole thing on me and THEY lived happily ever after. Now they're married with two children and live on a cul-de-sac and he's always like, "Honey, I'm home!" and there are picket fences EVERYWHERE. The best part: now that I'm dead I just haunt them all the time. So I guess in a way even I lived (or, died, actually) happily ever after.

The end.

See? Not much of a writer. But I get about a million points for imagination, if I do say so myself, and quite frankly, in this situation, my opinion is the only one that matters.

#GIRLONVINE

January to April

19

When People Honk at Me for No Reason

(1,650,000 FOLLOWERS)

*I*t's hard to stay sad about Alexei and No Name Girl when I'm blowing up on Vine! I don't know what I'm doing right (besides just being myself), but I have another million followers now and ten million loops! Boy, if I had a dollar for every loop I'd . . . well, I'd clone Alexei and make five of him and never be lonely again. Anyway, I guess people think I'm funny, or pretty, or funny and pretty . . . that or they just really like watching me get punched in the face.

Either way, all these followers are translating into endorsement deals and party invitations—it's not quite true love but it will do for now! I even got invited to Coachella (plus all the super-dope parties) to hang out in the celebrity tent, which is um, a *very* big deal. That's not until April, but I am counting the days.

In a way, I've always wanted to be famous. When I was seven I figured out how to record myself singing and burned it onto a CD. Then I burned that CD until I had about ten of them that I tried to sell to kids at school for twenty dollars each. Sadly, no one at school bought it. The album was called *Lucky Penny* and sold a total of one copy, which went to my dad. This is how a seven-year-old works the music industry. I cried all night in my room until my mom came in and gave me a very classic motivational speech about practice and determination and how fame doesn't happen overnight and blah blah blah. It didn't cheer me up, but I pretended that it did so she'd leave me alone and I could go to sleep.

I've always wanted to be famous but I never knew I would be. I guess in the back of my mind I always knew. The funny thing is, my mom was wrong about fame not happening overnight. Yesterday nobody knew who I was, today I'm walking down Lincoln Road and nobody will leave me alone. I gotta be honest: I'm not sure I like it.

The more I walk the more tense I get, worrying that I'm going to do something stupid and everyone will see. This is undeniably an insane concern, as any fame I have right now I got specifically from making a fool out of myself and broadcasting it to the world. So what if I mess up in real life? Somehow it feels different, like my space is being invaded, like the right to go about my day has been taken away from me. Out in the real world I haven't invited anyone to stare at me, but they are.

Two young girls, maybe ten or eleven, approach me for my autograph, which I totally don't mind because they're so young and cute. If anyone, these are the people I've been making Vines for, young girls who need someone to relate to, to tell them everything's going to be okay because life is actually really funny and not as scary as it seems.

"You are like seriously the best Viner," one says. "We totally love you." She's wearing a shirt that reads ANGEL in pink plasticky letters that look like they'd be partially sticky to touch.

"Girls! That is so sweet. Do you guys Vine?" I'm signing napkins for them, as if this will be worth anything *ever*. Do I have to start carrying around pictures of myself? Or is that their job? Like, if you want an autograph you gotta supply the photo. Are there hard rules for this? Is there a famous person's guidebook I can refer to?

"No, we're not allowed to have our own social media accounts until we're fourteen," the other one says. She has streaks of glitter in her hair and green gel barrettes.

"That's probably smart. Be kids for now, you have your whole lives to be slaves to the internet."

"Do you think the internet is a bad thing?" Plastic Letters Girl seems confused.

"No, no, it's just a complicated thing. You can end up spending too much time on it and not spending enough time doing real things . . . or, like, also for example, there are some dangerous people on the Web who you have to be careful of."

"Like killers?" Green Barrettes seems concerned. No, agh, I didn't mean to scare them. I have to backtrack.

"Well, sure, but you don't have to be worried about them. You just have to be smart. I didn't start using social media until I was fifteen actually." The girls nod their heads, wanting to hear more. What the hell is going on? Am I a mentor now? I can barely get my own life together, how am I supposed to be a voice of wisdom for young girls? I'm too weird to be a role model! What if I can't handle the responsibility?

"What about that hot guy, Alexei, is he your boyfriend?"

Ah, finally a question I know the answer to. "No."

"Why not? He's cute."

"Yes, he is cute. But listen, there is a lot in life that is more important than boys. Find something you love doing and focus on that instead. The right boy will come to you." I don't know where that came from, but it sounded great! And the girls look like I just fed them a big dose of wisdom! Maybe I can be a role model after all.

On the drive home I'm feeling a little tense, so I stop at a Starbucks drive-through for a caramel Frappuccino. There's not a lot in this world that can't be fixed with a Frappuccino, I always say. Driving away with my deliciously blended beverage, I pump up the jams ("Pursuit of Happiness" by Kid Cudi), and come to a stop sign, where I make a complete stop, LIKE YOU'RE SUPPOSED TO

DO. However, the bozo behind me feels that my coming to a complete stop at a stop sign is an inconvenience to him, so he lays on his horn for an inappropriately long amount of time. And, as you know, horns in real life don't sound like *beep beep* (have they ever?). No, it's much more like *bwwaaaahhhhgghhhhhh*. So obnoxious.

Now, my nerves are on edge already, what with the perverts and the impressionable admirers and all, so when Mr. BMW honks at me, I just can't take it anymore. I put my car in park, remove the air horn from my glove compartment (a present from Dad for if I'm ever being attacked), walk calmly up to his car, and tap on the window. When he rolls it down, agitated and huffy, I lean over, smile, and blow the horn directly in his entitled face. That's right, the world can't mess with Lele Pons.

Lele: 1, World: 0.

20

Girls Will Be Girls

(1,655,236 FOLLOWERS)

*A*fter a week of ignoring texts from Alexei, he shows up at my house with a bag of marshmallows and a Hershey's bar.

"What is this for?"

"I thought we could make s'mores, isn't that what you call them?" he says. "But I forgot the graham crackers at checkout."

Awwww.

"You also forgot the campfire."

"We can use the stove. I do it all the time." Suddenly Mr. Belgium does s'mores all the time? Well then!

"Hm."

"Can I come in?" he asks.

"Now isn't really a good time. I'm uh . . . I'm . . ." I look back into the house for a clue. "I'm organizing the pantry."

"You're organizing the pantry?"

"Yep."

"Well, can you organize it later?"

"No, it needs to be organized immediately."

"That doesn't make sense."

"You don't make sense!" Oops.

"Lele. Why are you mad at me? I thought I was imagining it but you've ignored my texts for like ten days and now you're being . . . extremely weird. So what's up?"

"You brought a girl to Yvette's party. Ugh, I don't know, it's totally stupid, but you told me you liked me a million years ago and I thought something could happen between us but it never did and Yvette said it's just because you're shy but obviously you're not that shy if you can make out with some random girl in front of everyone so I guess this whole thing has been in my head—but no, it wasn't all in my head because you did say you liked me didn't you? I'm not mad at you, I'm mad at myself for thinking it was more than it was—no, actually, I am mad at you because you never bothered to tell me you have a girlfriend. This whole time! You never thought to mention it?"

"We should talk." He sighs. "Can I please come in?"

"Fine. I guess the pantry can wait."

"Okay, look," he says, sitting on the corner of my bed. I sit on the other end of the room so that he doesn't get too comfortable and think everything's fine. "When I first met you I thought you were amazing, and I knew I liked you right away. As more than a friend. But the truth is, I had a girlfriend back in Belgium, and she moved out here with her family. I knew when I moved that they were considering moving too. Our parents have always been friends, so we sort of grew up being close. Her name is Nina . . . she goes to Cour D'Elaine, that private school in Lake Buena Vista . . . I guess what I'm trying to say is I thought you and I could be something, but when Nina showed up I knew I couldn't break things off with her. I just didn't know how to tell you." His cheeks are flushed and his words come out flustered and breathy. He seems genuinely distressed about all of this, and a little frantic. I find myself feeling sympathetic.

"Whoa. That is a lot of information."

"I know, and I'm sorry. I really am. But I've told Nina all about you and she's fine with us being friends. I want to be your friend, Lele, even if we can't be together right now. I hope you want to be my friend too."

"You know what? Yeah, I do. I think we're good as friends. And that's obviously what was meant to be, so yeah, I'm in."

"Really? That's so great. I would hate to lose you."

"Same!"

"Awesome." He comes over to hug me. He's a good hugger . . . so warm and snug and— No, Lele, don't even think about it. "Friends forever?"

"Friends forever? Yikes, Alexei, that's a pretty girly look for you and I don't know if it works."

"No? BFFs? Homies? Bros?"

"Are you having a stroke?"

"Maybe!" We laugh and he punches me lightly in the arm. I punch him back, full force, and he topples like a skinny flamingo.

Alexei asks if I want to play video games at his place, or would I rather organize my pantry?

"Fine," I say. "You called my bluff. I don't have to organize my pantry; I never had to organize my pantry. Who am I, my mom?"

"Knew it."

We head over to his place and he tries to explain to me how to play this ludicrously elaborate game called *Destiny,* but I can't figure out the controls. How are you supposed to remember which button to press at what time? Every time I want to make my character jump I accidentally make him walk backward, and all the motion on the screen is making me dizzy, so I keep dying over and over again and eventually Alexei gets bored of playing such an amateur. Why can't I do this? I mean, the general demographic of video game players are mostly boys who are not all that bright, and yet they seem to figure this out just fine. Ugh.

"I'm over it," I announce after watching myself get blown up for the fifteenth time. "Let's make those s'mores." We picked up some graham crackers on the way over.

"Finally! I thought you'd never ask."

Watching a marshmallow melt might be one of my favorite things of all time. The shift from white to gold to brown, the way it starts to bubble before going black and turning to goo on the inside, it's basically magical. I like mine burned to a crisp on the outside, molten on the inside. Alexei likes his to have just a touch of golden color to it, nothing more. He says it's because marshmallows are so pretty and he hates to see them get destroyed. I tell him he's a wimp.

He laughs and then gets serious. "You know," he says, "it really means so much to me that . . ."

Okay, I have to be totally honest, this is where I lose my will-power and let myself drift into a fantasy daydream. In my mind, Alexei is slowly taking off his clothes—he unbuttons his shirt, unbuckles his belt, and soon he's down to his black boxer briefs and—

"Lele, are you even listening to me?" Snap back to reality, a sad, sad, sad reality where Alexei is fully clothed.

"What? Oh, uh, yeah, what's up?" I say, trying not to blush.

"You weren't listening to me! Look, your marshmallow is ruined." He turns off the flame.

"No I like it like this. Mmmm, nice and uh, charcoal-y. I dih dis om purpose," I mumble, mouth full. "I wah listenin', I pwomis."

"You're such a liar!" Alexei laughs. "I was telling you how much you mean to me and you were totally checked out!"

"Aw man, I'm sorry I missed that."

"You should be, jerk."

"You're a jerk!" I pluck a marshmallow from the bag and throw it at him.

"No you didn't!" He throws one back at me and next thing you know we're engaged in a full-on marshmallow fight.

CUT TO: Alexei and I exhausted on the couch, the living room filled with a flurry of wayward marshmallows. His parents are sure to love me.

21

So This Is What Popular Is Like

(1,900,552 FOLLOWERS)

*A*lmost two million followers on Vine. They just keep coming. And the more followers I get the more obligated I feel to provide them with entertainment. Filming Vines has become almost like a full-time job, and I hardly have time for schoolwork anymore. Even when I do have time it's the last thing I would want to do—thirty-seven calculus equations, who needs that? Who needs anything when you have the wonderful world of Vine?

Sigh, if only that were true.

All of Miami High is following me on Instagram but still no one really knows me. I mean, no one really knows anyone in this life, but the difference is everyone at school thinks they know me. They think I've given them some highly intimate peek into my life; they think they can become my friend just by watching a few of my Vines. But that's not the truth. The truth is I keep a lot of my life private just like anyone else and I wish people would take the time to get to know me, just like anyone else. Long story short, blowing up on Vine hasn't helped me to discover my truest self or feel any less alone.

But don't get me wrong, my life is dope and I do dope things. People think I'm cool and want to be around me; I attract crowds like moths to a flame, I am in demand. I can't begin to explain how strange all of this is: I had no idea Lele 2.0 could possibly turn into Lele 8.0, which is essentially what has happened.

Steve Tao, one of my favorite DJs of all time (Okay, fine, so he's the only DJ I've ever heard of. So I'm not Miss In-the-Know, what are you gonna do, sue me?), is hosting a gigantic event downtown and has asked me to do a set! Meaning, he wants me to choose some songs and hang out onstage looking cute. I've never done anything even remotely like this, and I'm super nervous—I just know I'm going to fall on my face or my boobs are going to accidentally pop out. I take Alexei, Darcy, and Yvette along for moral support, and none of them are complaining. This is the coolest thing that's happened to any of us, and I made it happen. As far as anyone is concerned, I am a straight-up queen.

"The girls are seriously so jealous," Yvette gushes as we walk around to the back VIP entrance, following the directions Steve texted me. "I thought Cynthia was going to die. She has such a crush on Steve, I'm pretty sure she'd have his babies on the spot."

"That's disgusting," I say, and Yvette laughs. That's the other thing: no matter what I say, people laugh at it, whether or not I'm trying to be funny. Everyone assumes what I'm saying is funny and laugh just so they're not the only ones missing the joke. Cynthia and Maddie and Becca and Emily follow me around, hanging on my every word like I'm some sort of prophet, meanwhile just last month they scoffed at me, treated me like a freak. They're a bunch of shallow bitches and no way am I taking them with me on my rise to stardom, if that's even what this is (I mean, two million is a lot of followers). You might think Yvette is just as shallow as they are, and in a way you're totally right. The difference is, Cynthia, Maddie, Becca, and Emily are followers, parasites, while Yvette and I are natural-born leaders, which is mostly where we relate. And besides, there's something oddly comforting about her—when she's at my side I know she's got my back. I suspect she's not your average fair-weather friend popular girl, and that she's actually fiercely loyal. She's ride-or-die, and I admire that.

I give the bodyguard my name and he checks me off on a fairly short guest list: Lele Pons + 3. He wraps purple paper bands around our wrists, so delicately and ceremoniously that I almost feel the four of us are marrying him. He points and says, "Down the hall and up those stairs right there. Steve is just at the top, you'll see him." I put my palms together and give him a sort of Japanese-style thank-you bow, then head down the hall with my crew trailing behind me like baby ducklings. I remember not so long ago when Yvette led the march, now it's me in my high-waisted jean shorts and a crushed-velvet bare-backed halter top. Holler.

"Lele! Thanks for coming!" Steve is sitting on a blue velvet arm-chair surrounded by carafes of vodka and cranberry juice. Either I'm hallucinating or he's wearing a hot pink polo and a matching head-band. Is this real life? Guys and girls in distractingly neon outfits flutter around the gutted-out side-stage area, smoking cigarettes, taking selfies.

"Yeah, of course, wouldn't miss it. Thanks for the invite!" I say, grinning.

"It's great to finally meet you. I feel like I've known you forever just from watching your wacky little videos. I love them, by the way, very spot-on. Super topical."

"Ha, yeah. Well, thanks so much. Thanks for watching. This is Alexei and Darcy and Yvette. Guys, this is Steve."

"We know who Steve is." Darcy smiles, shaking his hand. "Great to meet you."

"Pleasure," Yvette says with a quick twinkle in her eye, before turning away like she has somewhere better to be, someone better to text. Steve watches her ass as she swivels. Clever girl.

"Dude, this is so dope." Alexei has taken on a strange hipster-bro hybrid voice that is neither attractive nor endearing. "Great venue. Really sweet." He holds one hand above his eyes like a visor to look out past the stage and onto the industrial-chic room where an audience will soon gather—exposed pipe, smooth concrete floors.

"Thanks, man. Here, everyone, grab a drink." He pushes the tray of liquor toward us and gestures to a stack of plastic cups. My three musketeers flock around the alcohol, pouring and mixing like they have no shame. I pour myself a glass of cranberry juice and pretend to go for the vodka but set it down as soon as Steve looks away. What the hell was that, Lele? Afraid he won't think you're cool because you don't like to drink? Afraid to be yourself all of a sudden? Get it together.

By the time Steve's set starts, Yvette and Darcy are legitimately drunk, giggling and bouncing around, bumping into things, flirting with anything they come across. So far, this is the first time in my life I'm not feeling like the foolish baboon of the group. I'm standing to Steve's right while he mixes his tracks with one hand, easy and relaxed like he doesn't have a care in the world. The crowd is overwhelming, they roar and holler, they break glow sticks and pour the chemicals over their bodies, girls climb up onto guys' shoulders and take their shirts off, guys down their beers and throw the cups onstage. A network of laser lights crisscrosses over the crowd, shifting and spiraling—I get a touch of vertigo.

"Thank you, Miami!" Steve calls out, switching records. "This is my new friend Lele Pons, she's gonna take over for a hot second. And if you like what she does you can check her out on Vine. She's a big star. Here's Lele!"

I step out to midstage and wave awkwardly at the crowd.

"You're hot!" someone calls out.

"Take off your shirt!" says another. Animals.

I tune them out and focus on the computer screen Steve has

laid out for me. He showed me how to choose tracks and blend them into each other, how to adjust the rhythm and the beat, but in the heat of the moment all of that goes out the window. Luckily, as it turns out, clicking around aimlessly and *acting* like I know what I'm doing does the trick! So, crisis averted on that front. Note to self: *always* open with "Paper Planes" by M.I.A. Instant crowd-pleaser.

The roaring and hollering continue and escalate, so I know I must be at least doing a little bit okay. Steve comes back out and brings my crew along with him, who at this point are so wasted they can't stand straight and somehow Yvette's tongue has been dyed blue.

"Lele is a rock star!" Yvette shouts into the microphone. Steve pops a bottle of champagne and shakes it over the front row. Alexei and Darcy drink from the champagne geyser; everyone has lost their goddamn minds.

Backstage, I get lost among a frenzy of Steve Tao's friends, fans, and a fair amount of guys and girls who don't totally seem to understand where they are. A few people I've never seen before approach to tell me they loved seeing me up there and they think my Vines are hilarious. Everyone says this as if they're reading a script, as if they're in a daze, only half present.

Is this what being popular is like? Being surrounded by people without having anyone to really talk to? Everyone knows your name but no one cares to know any more than that? And why? Just because I got in shape, lost my braces, and posted some wacky videos on the internet?

I've always been this person, so it feels strange that all of a sudden people approve of who I am. It's all very Emperor's New Clothes; someone said they thought I was cool and it started a domino effect until suddenly everyone felt they had to like me or else it meant something was wrong with them. But I'm just the same person I've always been. It's so disingenuous! It's so fake! I want real connections; I want to believe that people can like even the nerdy, loner version of me. I wish people could appreciate me as Lele 1.0.

So far, all being "famous" has done is teach me just how shallow most people really are.

But I could get used to the glow sticks. Definitely not complaining about the glow sticks.

22

How to Stop a Party from Getting Shut Down

(2,700,200 FOLLOWERS)

$\mathcal{R}$emember when I used to go to parties and get mercilessly ignored? Well, now I get invited to parties hosted by celebrities like Kendall Jenner, and sometimes I even get invited to parties being thrown in my honor. Either way, whatever party I attend, I'm never ignored. Mom and Dad keep reminding me that fame can be a double-edged sword—which I think means it can be awesome but can also hurt you if you're not careful?—and to always stay grounded.

"You're still a normal high school girl, Lele, don't let your head get too big."

"Please," I say. "When have I ever been a normal high school girl? And besides, I got this."

Although I have to admit, sometimes the attention is a bit too much to handle and I want to scream out: "Hey! Shine the spotlight over there! Nothing to see over here, folks!" and then run home into the comforting, humbling arms of my mom and dad. You know, like when I'm about to sneeze and know I'm going to make the most ridiculous face, or when I lose my hand-eye coordination and spill my drink everywhere, or when the police show up—I miss the days when I was invisible.

"Say what?" you might say. "The police showed up? Man, Lele is hard core." And you'd be right to say this, because it's true, I am hard core, but that's not the point of this story. Let me tell you how it went down.

Have you ever been to a warehouse party? Well, now I have, and I'm here to tell you that they are *insane*. People pay money to dance for hours on end pressed up against sweaty strangers while getting their eardrums blown out by blasting techno music. It sounds horrible, and it kind of *is* horrible, but also pretty fun in a YOLO sort of way.

Yvette's cousin Danny is a club promoter who hosts this event (a.k.a warehouse party) downtown called Cacophony (which is a fancy word for an unpleasant mixture of sounds), and Yvette says he'd love to have me there as a celebrity guest. Me? A celebrity guest? Obviously I can't say no. So we put on the shiniest, most neon clothes we can find and take an Uber to a dark corner of downtown where everybody mulls around stealthily like vampires and meet up with Danny, who takes us to the front of the line and stamps our hands with a red smiley face.

Yvette starts to let loose right away, bouncing and jerking her body around to the *ntz ntz ntz* of the music. I'm taking a good look around at the spacious room cast in dark red light when a flock of girls in pseudo-hippie festival attire descends upon me with wide eyes and big smiles.

"You're Lele Pons," one screams over the music, stroking my hair, clearly high out of her mind.

"I am! Hi!" I consider moving her hand off my hair but she seems like she's on a roll, and I might as well just let her do her thing. Plus, it never hurts to make a new friend.

"Come dance with us!" another says. "We think you're amazing."

"Oh, ha." I'm glad it's dark enough that no one can see me blush. "Thank you. That's sweet."

"You have to dance with us. Oh my God, this night is incredible. Lele, you're a goddess. You guys, isn't she a goddess?"

The rest agree in unison and pull me by my arms into the center of the room, where bodies writhe around like a snake pit. Despite the intensity of the scene it actually feels amazing to move with the music and let my troubles melt away. Yvette finds us and pours a water bottle over my head to cool me down and we just keep moving for what feels like hours, probably burning thousands of calories. I've just lost track of all concept of time and space when a concerned murmur starts moving through the crowd and quickly becomes an eruption of frantically scattering bodies shouting some variation of "The cops are here! Come on, let's go!"

"The cops?" I turn to one of the girls. "Why would they be here? This isn't illegal is it?" My stomach turns—I'm too pretty for prison!

"Not if you're twenty-one," she says, dipping away into the crowd.

"Oh, shit! Yvette, I can't go to jail."

"Oh my God, Lele, calm down. Follow me." She grabs my hand and pushes through the dispersing crowd as the sirens approach and the music comes to an abrupt stop. I follow her up to the bar, where we duck under a curtain and are suddenly in a very narrow hallway.

"Police!" I hear a booming voice just on the other side of the curtain. "Nobody move!"

"Come on!" Yvette tugs my hand and we run down the hall to a clanky metal staircase that leads us to a door that opens up into an alleyway. The secretive back exit, nice. I can see the red-and-white swirl of siren light at one end of the alley, so we know to keep running in the opposite direction. When we make it to the cross street, we're panting and laughing, finally in the clear.

"Jesus Christ, Yvette! What the hell just happened?"

"The cops show up to this sort of thing all the time. We're going to need to get you a fake ID."

"Hate to be such a wet blanket, but maybe in the future we could just go to legal parties."

What an adventure! I witnessed my first warehouse party and almost had my first run-in with the cops! At home I collapse onto my bed and scribble a newly inspired thought onto a notepad:

How to stop a party from being shut down: If you go to a party, always keep a police uniform in your purse. That way, if the police show up, you can pretend that you're one of them and say, "Hey, I got this one under control, you guys can just move along." Then sit back and watch the magic continue.

23

Partied Out

(3,145,000 FOLLOWERS)

*O*ne party, two party, red party, blue party. I've been going to so many parties and no two are alike! Some parties are big and some parties are small, some parties are fun and some just aren't at all. Some parties have alcohol and some have balloons, some parties have piñatas shaped like Looney Toons. Some parties are—okay, you know what, you get the point: I'm a very talented poet. Who has been going to parties and letting schoolwork slide like a kid at a water park (oops!). But, as it turns out, not all parties are worth the effort. Some parties you'd be better off not going to. These parties are called thirteen-year-old birthday parties.

I've never understood kids' birthday parties. The kids are happy just to roll around in the mud, while the parents use the opportunity to socialize. Apparently this phenomenon lasts all the way into the early teenage years. It's Saturday night and I'm dressed in pastels with my hair in a side braid hovering awkwardly in the far corner of the room where Josie King's son is celebrating his thirteenth birthday. Along with two hundred of his closest friends. I don't know anyone here and I've been alone with the chocolate fondue fountain for basically an eternity while stampedes of newly hormonal thirteen-year-olds swarm the dance floor—I'm bored and scared and seconds away from drinking chocolate straight out of the fountain.

Maybe I should back up for a second. Last week I got a call from Josie King herself (who is an A-list movie star, obviously. What, do you live under a rock?) saying that her son, Ryan, just loves my Vines and would like to invite me to his thirteenth birthday party. At first I was like ummmmmm, but then she hurried it along and I realized that this was not an invitation, but a proposal: I would show up to her son's bar mitzvah, sign some autographs for the kids, and go home with ten thousand dollars. Yes, please! How did it feel to be hired by Hollywood royalty? Amazing. Unreal. Preternatural. But once I got there the magic faded. A celebrity's child's thirteenth-birthday party is still a birthday party, which means the majority of the guests are going through puberty literally as the party is happening.

Which means they have no chill. Which means CALM THE F DOWN, YOU MONSTERS!

"You're not Miley Cyrus," the birthday boy observes rather astutely when I meet him.

"No, honey," his mom says somewhat nervously, like she's trying to placate a wild animal. "Miley Cyrus would have cost Mommy a couple million dollars. And that's just ridiculous. You said you love Lele—you watch her videos all the time."

"I do! I just wanted Miley. But this is okay—hi, Lele! Thanks for coming to my party." His cheeks are chubby and freckled. A couple million dollars? Maybe I shouldn't have gotten so excited about ten thousand. I sigh deeply; this is going to be a long night.

So, I drink cranberry juice at table eleven with Ryan and his best friends while the guests mingle with their toothpick-impaled crudité and "I Gotta Feeling" by the Black Eyed Peas rages on high.

Things could be worse.

There are worse ways to make ten thousand dollars. Right? That is, until Ryan's BFF Carl starts asking me what kind of "sex stuff" I've done and then I know I have to get outta there.

I excuse myself from the table of child perverts and head to the chocolate fountain, which is now where I've been for the past twenty minutes, just eyeing the clock and avoiding conversations with grandparents and family friends who want to know how I know Ryan. Oh boy.

I'm chewing one fingernail and basking in the joy of knowing I get to leave in three minutes when a boy in a turquoise blazer throws a football to his buddy and it knocks into the chocolate fondue fountain, spraying liquid chocolate all over me like I'm in the splash zone at one of those sad Sea World shows. At first I gasp, horrified, then I just shrug; who am I kidding? Being covered in chocolate is the highlight of my night.

I think from now on I'll stick to parties for free hosted by my own age group.

24

Old Friends Are Best Friends

(3,200,000 FOLLOWERS)

"*R*emember when if you wanted to watch a TV show you had to know what time it was going to be on and then make sure you were there to watch it?" Lucy asks us, plucking out the red M&M's from a pack and setting them aside. We're in Arianna's room—Lucy, Mara, Arianna, and me (the old school gang back together again)— lounging casually after a long Wednesday as if nothing has changed. As if I wasn't ripped from the comforts and safety of my lovely circle of friends, as if I'm not becoming an accidental internet sensation. (I know it sounds exciting, but just the thought of it makes me feel like there's an elephant sitting on my chest or like I'm falling through thin air. It's like I'm falling through thin air *while* an elephant sits on my chest.)

"Sure, I remember," I say, my head resting in Mara's lap. "I used to rush through dinner so I could be sitting in front of the television as soon as *One Tree Hill* came on."

"TBT *One Tree Hill!*" Arianna says from her bed, where she's completely horizontal, draped across it from left to right instead of head to foot.

"And then after that it was like, if you wanted to watch something you had to make sure you remembered to DVR it," Lucy continues, "but now all you have to do is look it up on Hulu or, like . . . buy it the next day on iTunes."

"Great story, bb," says Mara. "Can we talk about something interesting now?" The love we all have for each other is epic and undying, so it's okay to talk like this from time to time.

"I got paid to go to a thirteen-year-old's birthday party this weekend," I say.

"What? Like as a babysitter?" Mara asks.

"Um, no, like as an internet celebrity, right, Lele?" Lucy is impressed.

"Yeah, I guess so," I say. "You guys, life is getting weird. The weekend before that I went to a warehouse party and we ended up running from the cops. I don't want to ever run from the cops again—it was exhausting. Actually, all of life feels exhausting these days."

"Whoa," says Arianna. "And you're literally never tired. This must be serious. We need to do something to relax Lele ASAP."

"Actually just hanging around here watching Lucy with her weird aversion to red M&M's is quite soothing."

"It's not a weird aversion." Lucy pouts. "I'm allergic to them." Then she throws one at my head. I eat it.

"Well, we're glad you still want to hang with your boring non-famous friends," Mara says.

"Oh my God, Mara, you are not my boring friends. I'm the boring one. Did you not hear me? I went to a kid's birthday."

"And ran from the cops at a rave."

"Oh, hush. Enough about me. What have you guys been up to?"

"Like, studying for the SATs and stuff. I'm trying to get my score up to the two thousands," Mara laments. "Ms. Smarty-Pants over here already has a 2250. Bitch."

"Arianna?! You do? I mean, I'm not surprised, but wow, congratulations."

"If ya wanna go to an Ivy League that's how it's gotta be. Actually, it should be higher. I'll take it one more time."

"Jeez, how many times are you supposed to take this dumb thing!?" I ask, getting nervous. Am I falling behind? Do I even want to go to college? No, I don't. School makes me anxious and the performing arts make me feel at ease—so why not just follow my passion? Why not just skip college and go straight to performing for the world? Have I ever really stopped to ask myself what will make me the happiest? Well, I'm asking myself that now, and the answer is not college.

"However many you want," Arianna says. "One is totally fine though."

"Yeah, I only took it once," says Lucy. "No way I'm doing that again. Don't worry, you're good with one. What did you get?"

"Errmmmm. I uhhhhh . . ."

"Have you not taken it?!"

"Umm, well, not myself, no. But I uh . . . know people who have?"

"Lele, please don't freak out." Arianna puts her hand on my knee; she always senses when I'm going into panic mode. "You don't need to take the SATs, just keep being yourself and it's going to be great. College isn't for everyone."

Gulp. I know Arianna meant that to be helpful, but do I really not want to go to college? I haven't had time to really think about it—am I running out of time? Is my college hourglass draining sand as we speak? I've successfully blocked the SATs from my mind, probably due to my test-taking anxiety and denial issues, but that doesn't mean I've made any major decisions about my future yet! Did the elephant on my chest just gain fifty pounds? What a jerk.

IT'S TIME FOR A SHOPPING SPREE

Every now and then the world is too much pressure and you need to let loose. And, now that I have some of my own cash to spare for the first time in my life, I'm letting loose at the mall, in the first-ever Lele Pons shopping spree! Now, I gotta be honest, this spree lasted hours and would take forever to recap, so I've condensed it into a mega-convenient, ultra-cinematic montage for your reading pleasure:

12:30 p.m.: Arianna, Lucy, Mara, and I storm into the Westfield mall with hungry eyes and fierce determination to tear the place apart.

12:35 p.m.: Straight to Bebe! We try on leather jackets and over-the-top stilettos and (ironically, duh) a bunch of those tight-fitting shirts that actually have Bebe spelled out in rhinestones. Selfies off the hook!

1:20 p.m.: Tiffany's! Sure, we're not getting married anytime soon, but what's the harm in trying on a couple dozen diamond rings? Answer: no harm! Thank you, lovely salespeople at Tiffany's!

3:00 p.m.: Time for practical purchases (feather boas are practical, right?) We head to Top Shop for purses and dresses, scooping things off the shelves left and right like big spenders, throwing hats and scarves in the air for that special montage essence. We leave the store with at least three bags each, stuffed full with jeans and sequined tops and Fendi knockoffs, all of it paid for by yours truly. A girl's gotta show gratitude for her ride-or-dies!

5:00 p.m.: Here's where things get crazy. As you know, I only own two pairs of shoes. As we pass through the first floor of Nordstrom, slow-mo, my eyes rove over clusters of red-soled Louboutins and Jeffrey Campbells and Jimmy Choos, boots and flats and sandals and heels—I have to have them all. This is what a life of severely depriving oneself of shoes will do. In the span of an hour I go from owning two pairs of shoes to owning thirteen. Oops. Needless to say, my girl squad is very impressed.

6:15 p.m.: After six hours of shopping we literally cannot keep going, and collapse outside Wetzel's Pretzels. We have shopped until we dropped, and it feels good. I almost don't remember why I was so stressed in the first place—oh right, college. *No, Lele, refocus:* your shoe life has begun and that is something to celebrate! Something to celebrate with cinnamon Wetzel's! Nom nom nom nom. Sigh, life is good.

25

Yeah, Yeah, Happy Valentine's Day

(3,780,888 FOLLOWERS)

$\mathcal{L}$et me tell you the story of my first Valentine's Day as a pseudo celebrity. Hint: it was equally dismal as all the other Valentine's Days before it and probably all the ones after it as well.

I wake up at seven in the morning because *dear God* Valentine's Day is on a *school day* this year. The universe truly shows me no mercy. In my white pj's speckled with pink hearts (intended to attract Cupid, or whoever the hell is supposed to take care of your needs on this stupid day), I sleepily stroll out into the kitchen and, to my surprise, find a wicker basket the size of a small boat resting on the counter.

OhmyGod ohmyGod, candy and presents for *me*? I'm sorry for all the mean things I've said about you, Mr. Valentine, you are truly a saint. After unwrapping the yards of cellophane around the basket, I pluck out a box of Godiva chocolates and get to work devouring them.

The way I (and anyone who isn't a total psycho) eat a box of chocolates is like this:

1. First, I throw away the cheat sheet. I don't like a piece of paper ruining the mystery for me.

2. Then I bite into them one by one to see what's inside. That's right, I honestly don't care how many chocolates are in the box, I will taste-test each of them before making my pick. If I bite into one and it turns out to have coconut or almonds inside, I leave them be (these flavors are for psychos). If I bite into one and it turns out to be caramel, toffee, truffle, vanilla ganache, raspberry ganache, coffee, praline, peanut, cinnamon, white chocolate, hazelnut, mint, raspberry cordial, or solid milk chocolate, then I eat that one right away. As you can imagine, this means I eat many in a row.

3. When I'm finished with those, I go back to the almond and coconut ones and eat the chocolate shell around it, leaving just bits and shreds behind.

4. However, if the outside chocolate shell is *dark* chocolate, then, yeah right, I would never eat that, I'm not a psycho.

5. By the end, what used to be a box of twenty-two artisan chocolates looks like a brutal massacre. As far as I'm concerned this is the correct and proper way to eat chocolate.

So, I'm in full-on chocolaty heaven, singing to myself as I lick my fingers. I'm singing, "Somebody loves me, somebody loves me, la di da di da . . ." when I stop to wonder who the basket is actually from. There's an envelope. I go to open it, telling myself to be realistic. Lele, I know how much you want this to be from Alexei, but it is *not* going to be from Alexei.

DO NOT EXPECT IT TO BE FROM ALEXEI, YOU HOPELESSLY ROMANTIC LUNATIC.

And I'm right, it's not from Alexei.

To my utter, total, horrified dismay the card reads: Happy Valentine's Day, Lele! Love, Dad. UGGHHHHHHH! Just then, my dad *pops up* from under the center island, where he has been apparently snacking in secret this *whole time.*

"Happy Valentine's Day, pumpkin!" He wraps his arms around

me and squeezes me until I think I can feel my intestines. I swat at him but he just squeezes tighter. Jesus H. Christ, is there no mercy? I mean, I love my parents, and I am *so* grateful to have a dad who cares about me (I've seen what happens to girls who don't have that), but does being a minor internet celebrity mean *nothing* these days?

What is the point of having fans if they don't send me Valentine's Day presents?! And what about all those creepy guys who comment telling me to get naked and wear lower-cut shirts etc., did none of those ever translate into stalkers? Not even the nice kind of stalker who sends flowers once a year? Jerks.

"Yeah, yeah," I say to my dad. "Happy Valentine's Day to you too."

"What did you get me?!" Dad asks, mock-horrified.

"Ugghhh," I say, shuddering.

The day drags on. I'm surrounded by a disgusting jungle of pink Mylar balloons and teddy bears holding satin hearts. They're everywhere; it is a total nightmare, a parade designed to remind me that I'm going to die alone.

Over three million followers on Vine but not one suitor.

No one to love. I'm basically just like Marilyn Monroe. Or Lucky from that one song "Lucky" by Britney Spears.

During sixth-period Spanish I'm too deep in a sugar coma to even pretend to understand what Señora Castillo is talking about. The room is a blur of heat and disappointment. How much candy did I actually eat today? Let's say I had ten pieces per class, that's ten times six plus the strawberry milkshake I had at lunch with Yvette. Whoa. I probably gained a billion pounds today, which is totally fine seeing as I am going to die alone, so no big deal. I put my head down on the table and try to fall asleep, block out the cruel world for a while. Just then, my phone buzzes. It's Alexei:

ALEXEI: Hey, wanna make a Vine later tonight?

ME: Sure. Don't you have plans?

ALEXEI: Yeah, I'm taking Nina to dinner. But I mean after that I can come over.

ME: I'm fine with that if Nina's fine with it.

ALEXEI: Oh yeah, she's totally fine with it. She's super chill.

ME: The chilliest.

ALEXEI: Was that sarcasm?

ME: Hm? 😈

ALEXEI: Oh, Lele.

ME: Oh, Alexei. Do you have anything in mind to film?

ALEXEI: Not sure, but was thinking it could be titled "Valen-vine."

ME: Alexei, I'm not going to lie, that was the lamest thing I've ever heard.

ALEXEI: You love it.

Okay, so I don't have a Valentine this year, but I have a friend and a collaborator, a partner in crime, dare I say a valen-vine? And that counts for something, right?

26

What You Feel Like Doing Versus What You Do When Your Crush Just Ended a Relationship

(3,789,900 FOLLOWERS)

*T*o be *quite* honest, it's not so terrible being single on Valentine's Day. Mom and Dad are out at a nauseatingly romantic dinner, so I have the entire house to myself—in other words, I am the queen of the Pons residence. I put on a pink wig to get in the spirit and some of my parents' old disco clothes from back in the seventies, when they thought they were cool. I *cannot* believe they used to wear this clown attire—and not just them, it was everyone! In thirty years are we going to look back at our clothes and think they were ridiculous? Are our children going to taunt us mercilessly? And if so, what will the clothes be like then? I remember in 2001 I thought by 2011 we'd be wearing plastic blow-up clothes, but obviously I was wrong about that, so who knows? Then, of course, in 1968 they thought by 2001 we would be deep into space travel, so there's really no way to predict what will be going on in the future.

Anyway, so I'm wearing a hot pink wig (sort of like Natalie Portman's in *Closer* except even more stripper-y), black sparkly bell-bottoms, and a turquoise halter top. I crank up Gloria Gaynor on the sound system and put on a highly elaborate show for myself using a spoon for a microphone.

"'At first I was afraid, I was petrified . . .'" I sing into the mirror, hand to the mirror, hand to my face. I hop up onto a kitchen chair, bump one shoulder up and down, power-step up onto the table, head bounce, head bounce, arms and face up to the heavens, singing "I Will Survive."

"Uh, Lele?" Record scratch, the party's over.

It's Alexei, standing in the open doorway, looking like someone just punched him in the stomach, but also sort of like I just made his day.

"Oh my God, you didn't see this."

"I kept ringing the doorbell. I called your name a few times . . ." He starts to laugh. "I have honestly never seen anything like that in my life."

"You didn't see anything!" I shriek à la "you can't sit with us!" and jump off the table, hoping I make it look sleek and graceful like Catwoman.

"It's not embarrassing, it was adorable."

"Fine. I mean, thanks. So, what's up? I thought you were on a date."

"Nina and I broke up."

WHAT? I want so badly to jump back up on the table and get down to Soulja Boy. I want to dance on the roof of a car driving around town so everyone can see me. I want to run across the beach, arms flailing, singing, "I believe I can fly." R. Kelly was a perv, but that song, come on. I beeelieve I can fly!

"Lele, did you hear me?"

"Huh? Oh, yes, of course I heard you." I shake myself out of it. "I'm so sorry, Alexei. What happened?"

"We're both just becoming different people since we came to Florida. We're moving in different directions. And she got pretty upset when I told her how much you and I have been hanging out.

She asked me to not be your friend anymore, and I just couldn't do that."

"Awww!! I mean, oh, Alexei, I'm so sorry." I give him my best sad look and wrap my arms around his neck. When he can't see my face I grin like a maniac fresh out of the asylum.

27

When People Tell You to Calm Down

(4,000,000 FOLLOWERS)

I spend a few days wondering if Alexei is going to ask me out now that he's single, but then I get distracted by the topic of my burgeoning career. See, when you're a social media figure, there isn't a lot of time for boys. JUST KIDDING. Can you imagine if I were really that obnoxious? Celebrities are always going on about how they don't have enough time for love because they're so busy working all the time, and when they're not working, they're partying and it's all just so time-consuming!

If I'm going to be very real with you, a good chunk of my waking hours are spent sitting on the couch on my phone scrolling through Instagram and Twitter feeling utterly inadequate. On Instagram, there are four types of people who feel the need to constantly show you how superior their lives are compared to yours. They are:

THE FITNESS MODEL

Okay, I get it, you do yoga and you eat super "clean" foods (whatever the hell that means). It's *awesome* for you that you have a dope body and are proud of it, really, but dear God I don't want to see it in a bikini on a regular basis paired with captions like "I've never felt better in my whole life #YogaBabes #GirlsWhoWorkOut #Fitness." #EffYou #GetOutOfMyInstagram #WhyAmIFollowingYouAnyway

THE PARTY ANIMAL

This person goes out *a lot* and wants you to know all about it. He or she has tons of friends, and it's very important you know all about their #SquadGoals. Here's a group selfie of us on the roof at the W, here's a group selfie of us drinking fancy drinks by a pool . . . it's endless. This person also often is guilty of the "fancy lifestyle" posts: a limo, a private jet, a newly popped bottle of Moët & Chandon. Please get over yourself before I have to go to your house to tell you how deluded you are. You're seventeen, you don't have a private jet!

THE HAPPILY EVER AFTER

Newly engaged or just basic, bottom line in love, this person (let's be real, it's *normally* a girl) posts pictures of Bae playing beach volleyball or Bae holding a puppy or Bae grilling up some burgers, and the caption is always something like "I love this man more than anything in the whole world #Blessed #LuckyInLove." These people are the cruelest brand of human. I wonder if they realize they are basically just telling you how unlovable you are and will always be. EVIL.

WORKING GIRL (OR GUY):

Welp, you've got your dream job and you have never been happier or more proud of yourself. It wouldn't be good enough to just enjoy your success day to day, you have to post pictures of yourself in the fleekest work clothes or beaming with your "dream" coworkers. Captions are normally along the lines of: "Can't believe I get paid to do this! #LivingTheDream #Blessed." #GetOffMyInstagram #WhyAmIFollowingYouAnyway

In reality, there are actually more like one hundred different types of Instagram show-offs, especially if you consider all the subcategories within the four categories I just outlined. (Should we call it Instagram InstaShowOff? Note to self.) And maybe it's all a lie, maybe they have really lame lives and are just trying to make everyone think otherwise, but I fall for it every time!

I sit on the couch with my sweatpants and my pint of Ben & Jerry's wondering how everyone could be doing something cool with their lives except for me. So why don't I just unfollow these people if they make me feel so bad about myself? If you even have to ask, then you obviously don't have Instagram. The thing is addictive, and when you unfollow people with fabulous lives, the FOMO just gets worse.

Darcy comes over so at least I'm not sitting on the couch alone. We're in it together, watching *SpongeBob* because neither of us can muster the energy to change the channel. OKAY FINE YOU GOT ME! I LIKE SPONGEBOB! HE IS EASILY, HANDS DOWN, THE BEST SPONGE THERE EVER WAS AND EVER WILL BE. Am I right or am I right? It's Sunday and we're both feeling pretty lazy—there's a canister of Pringles open between us and every now and then Darcy will start to doze off. Then SpongeBob does something to make me laugh and it wakes her right up.

It's a regular day, a day like any other day, until out of nowhere it takes a dark and regretful turn. Here's what goes down:

A very tiny sliver of Pringle gets stuck in my throat, so I cough, trying to get it to move, bitch, get out tha way.

"Whoa, calm down," Darcy says.

"What? I am calm. I just had a Pringle in my throat."

"You were coughing like a lunatic, I thought you were gonna die."

"You thought I was gonna die so you told me to CALM DOWN?"

"Lele, it's gonna be okay, just breathe."

"What are you talking about? I am totally fine."

"Try to calm down. Let's breathe together."

"Are you frickin' joking me right now? I AM calm! I HAD A PRINGLE IN MY THROAT AND NOW IT'S GONE AND I'M FINE."

"You don't sound fine. Here, let me help." She puts her hands on my shoulders and starts massaging them. I push her off.

"DARCY, WHAT THE HELL ARE YOU DOING? I AM TO-TALLY FINE AND CALM AND GOOD."

"You're obviously not!"

"I. AM. CALM!" I roar like King Kong and just lose it completely. I tear up the couch, throwing pillows and kicking at the wall. I pull my hair until wispy blond strands start floating around the room.

"Hey, Alexei, it's Darcy." Darcy has grabbed my phone and is speaking into it. "Lele is sort of freaking out, I need backup." Uh-oh, the stress of existing in the public eye may be starting to get to me.

Alexei shows up like he's frickin' Hercules here to save the day. I'm half mad and half dreamy-eyed that he felt I needed rescuing. They lie me down on the couch and Alexei gets an ice pack for my head. My very own personal nurses!

"You're overwhelmed, Lele," Alexei says. "You're cranking out Vines every day, I think maybe you've been under a lot of pressure. You should try taking it easy, maybe take some days off." He's not always the brightest crayon in the box but he's sooooo sweet. And hot, have I mentioned that he's hot?

"That's nice of you to worry but—wait a second, are you wearing a headband?" I don't know why I didn't notice before, but Alexei is wearing a red terry-cloth band around his head. Not pushing his hair back, the way girls wear them, but actually around the circumference of his head like he's a tennis player. But he isn't a tennis player, which can only mean one thing: he's doing this in the name of style.

"Yeah, so what?"

"It looks weird."

"Steve Tao was wearing one, you didn't think he looked weird."

"Um, yes I did. He always looks weird, that's part of his thing."

"Well, I like it."

"It's kind of bro-y," Darcy says.

"It is," I agree. "Like, you're wearing a plaid button-down shirt, it doesn't go with a headband at all. A headband is something you wear with like a jersey or something like that. Something really bro-y."

"So, what you're saying is the headband is a bro item of clothing and the shirt is not?"

"Correct. The shirt is more hipster," Darcy says.

"OH MY GOD!" It hits me. "Are you transforming into a bripster?"

"What's a bripster?"

"It's a combination of a bro and a hipster. You were kind of being one at the Steve Tao show but I didn't think anything of it. Now you've got this headband and—"

"Hold on, hold on, I am neither a bro nor a hipster." He's from Belgium. He's a Belge-bripster? Heh.

"Maybe not today, but you're on your way to being both. A hybrid. It's a dangerous breed of human. And by dangerous I simply mean despicable."

"What's so bad about it? I don't get what's going on right now." He's cute when he's confused.

"Look, Alexei. Respectable girls don't like bros, and they don't like hipsters. Now, if you're like a little bit into sports that doesn't mean you're a bro and if you're a little bit into J. D. Salinger that doesn't make you a full-blown hipster, it's when you've really embraced a certain lifestyle that you become one or the other. Then, there's this new trend, where a bro type will start taking on certain hipster qualities, and the two start blending into each other. Like, a true bro would never read a book, but once he's crossing over he'll probably start reading some Hemingway or Chuck Palahniuk—"

"Oh, totally," Darcy adds. "Bripsters love *Fight Club*."

"Exactly. That's a crossover point. There are hipster things and there are bro things, and then there are the crossover points that point to the hipster bro. Or, the bripster, as I said before."

"And you're saying a headband is one of these crossover points?"

"Yes. And that plaid shirt."

"Jesus. Seems complicated."

"Not really. If you love beer pong, you're a bro. If you love shopping at Amoeba Music, then you're a hipster. If you play your records on a Crosley turntable specifically as a seduction tactic, then you're a bripster."

"So . . . bripsters are kind of just bros who picked up a few lifestyle tricks based on wanting to hook up with more girls?"

"Maybe. It's hard to pinpoint the evolution of the bripster."

"Indeed. He is an elusive creature." Darcy puts on a phony professorial voice. "Anthropologists don't have a strong understanding of him yet. All we know is that he is unpleasant."

"It sounds fine to me. You like sports but you're creative too, so what?"

"Ugh, no. Alexei, don't you get anything? A bripster is not CREATIVE, he just picks up little qualities here and there designed to trick girls into thinking he's creative so that they're more likely to sleep with him. He owns props. Everything he does is intentional and—you know what, never mind. Be a bripster, see if I care."

"Okay, Lele, let's calm down."

"What the!? I swear to God I'm gonna—" I sit up to throw a swing at Alexei but Darcy holds me back. My poor little friends, they're going to need a straitjacket and some horse tranquilizers if they want to restrain me.

28

When Everyone's Out Partying Except You and Your Friends

(4,200,250 FOLLOWERS)

*A*s I just outlined in the previous chapter, I would be lying if I said my life was always fun. I would even be lying if I said my life was fun half of the time. However, this reality is unacceptable when you're a social media star—actually, it's unacceptable no matter who you are. No matter who you are, your social media followers expect you to be having fun ALL THE TIME. ESPECIALLY when you're a high school girl.

"I can't believe it's already Friday," Darcy says. She's flipping through a magazine on my bed while I examine my pores in the mirror up close. "Should we go do something fun? Are there any parties?"

"Ugh, Darcy, I can't even. I mean, we could . . . maybe we even should, but it seems like so much effort. How do people do it? After a week of school I just wanna eat cookie dough and watch VH1."

"Fine by me. Oh, look!" She has her phone out now, scrolling through Instagram. "Yvette and the Sausages are out at Lure." We started calling Yvette's crew the Sausages based on the way they squeeze into skintight dresses, and Lure is a nightclub in downtown

Miami where high schoolers go to pretend they're much older than they actually are.

"What?! Why didn't they invite us?!" I'm so annoyed I almost choke on my cookie dough.

"Probably because we don't have fake IDs."

"Ugh. I could have a fake ID if I wanted. That's not fair, I wanna go to Lure! Man, Darcy, I can't catch a break."

"Oh, who cares, we're having a fun night in."

"No, we're having a fun night out."

"We are?"

"Well, people will THINK we are." I have an evil glint in my eye, I can feel it. Glinting.

"What the hell are you talking about, Lele?"

"You'll see. Just trust me."

It's time for Operation InstaParty.

Here are all the tools you need to make it look like you're out having fun when really you're just home doing basically nothing:

One large black sheet

You'll use this to hang up as a backdrop for your photos for the illusion that you're in a dark nightclub, maybe even one of those extra-hip bars with the photo booths that are half ironic but half not.

One selfie stick

You'll use this to make it look like you've asked strangers to take photos of you.

Martini glasses

You'll pose with these to make it look like you've ordered fancy drinks. Really, you can use any type of cup depending on what sort of outing you want to make it look like you've been to (e.g., red plastic cups if it's a college party), just as long as you don't use the Little Mermaid sippy cup you have from when you were a kid that you still drink out of sometimes when you REALLY need cheering up.

Hot outfits

If you want people to think you're out being fabulous, you gotta dress the part.

It takes us twenty minutes to hang up the black sheet because the pushpins keep falling out and Darcy doesn't have great balance, but we finally get it in position and are ready to go. The rest of the shoot is fast and easy—it only takes us ten minutes to shoot an experience that *would* take hours of our time if we were to go out and actually do it. Our time-saving skills are impressive, in my humble opinion. We wear matching white turtleneck halter tops and colorful skirts from American Apparel, then drink a number of different juices out of a number of different glasses while we pose for the selfie stick. The result is about thirty-five pictures of us having the most adorable and classy kind of fun. Then, we put on "Get Low" by Lil Jon and film some selfie-stick dancing to send out on Snapchat. When you're a sixteen-year-old girl, if it happened on Instagram but not Snapchat, then it didn't happen.

InstaParty accomplished!!

"Seemed like you had fun on Friday," Yvette remarks in the locker room on Monday. I detect a sort of sly snarky sarcasm in her voice. A hint of jealousy, perhaps?

"Oh yeah, it was a lot of fun."

"What club were you at?"

"Just a new club." I shrug. "Downtown."

"Awesome, what's it called?"

"Umm . . ." I look around, trying to be discreet. My eyes land on a padlock on a locker behind Yvette. "Kwikset," I say. Dammit.

"Kwikset? That's the name of a club?"

"Mm-hm," I say, hoping she doesn't Google it.

"Weird, I haven't heard of it."

"Yeah, well, it's really new."

"Right. Whatever you say. Hope your time at Kwikset was awesome."

"It was dope, thanks. How was Lure?" I ask, but she's already walking away.

29

How to Get a Boy's Attention / That Friend Who Always Cheats

(4,318,722 FOLLOWERS)

*A*lexei invites me over after school on Tuesday. At first I want to say no for the sake of playing hard to get, but then I say yes for the sake of not wanting to seem like I'm playing hard to get. As it turns out, he didn't just invite me over, but he also invited a bunch of guys from school. At first I was disappointed that he didn't want to spend time alone with me, but then I was excited when I realized he thinks I'm cool enough to hang out around his friends. Then I was disappointed again when I realized that all they wanted to do was play video games, which, in case I haven't made clear, I think are total and complete bullshit. Can you believe that a bunch of high school boys would rather play video games than hang out with a real-life girl? A blond girl with big boobs? A blond girl with big boobs who is also an emerging internet celebrity? I know, it's sad, but it's true.

"You guys wanna play 'never have I ever'?" I ask.

"Isn't that kind of for middle schoolers?" says Jake.

"Um . . ." I say, "isn't *Mario Kart* kind of for elementary schoolers?"

"NO!" they all shout in unison. Jesus.

"*Mario Kart* is an awesome game that will be awesome for the rest of time," Alexei says, brow furrowed, thumbs flailing. Nothing kills a crush like seeing a guy gripping a video game controller, in my humble opinion.

"Okay, fine," I say. "I think I'll go swimming then. Oh no, I didn't bring my bathing suit! I guess I'll have to go in naked . . ." Nothing. No response. The guys stare into the screen with more tenacity and robotic lust than ever before. "Are you guys kidding me? Okay, this is ridiculous, I'm putting an end to this RIGHT NOW." I walk up to the TV and pull the plug.

"Noooo! Lele!!!!" You'd think I just murdered their mothers.

"Oh my God, you did NOT just do that. Now all our scores will be erased!" This comes from Brian, some random sophomore who is 99 percent bro and 1 percent hipster.

"Yes, I did just do that, Brian. I am a girl, and I am here to hang out with you. And no, I do not like video games. And yes, I am a little bit needy. So this is what we're going to do. We're going to get our asses up off the couch and do something that is fun for all of us, okay?"

As it turns out, these boys respond surprisingly well to a dominant woman.

"Yeah, no problem." Alexei hurries to get the words out. "What do you want to do?"

"Literally anything other than video games."

"Cool," says Brian. "How about basketball?"

"Yeah!" Jake and Alexei high-five each other.

Ugh, why did I have to say "anything other than video games"? I forget how narrow-minded boys can be. Note to self: when dealing with boys, be specific.

Well, fine, I'll play basketball, but I'm not going to play by the rules. Why? Because I'm a renegade, I'm a rebel . . . and also I don't know the rules.

I'm on a team with Alexei against Brian and Jake, and I would hate to lose and for Alexei to think we lost because I'm a girl, so I decide to do whatever I have to do to win. I clutch the ball tight against my chest whenever anyone gets too close and I'm not afraid to ram a shoulder bone into the opponent when I have to. When Jake or Brian try to call me out on it I just play innocent and make my eyes extra doe-like. *Who, me? I'm just a girl, I don't know what I'm doing.* At one point I'm about to do a layover (or is it a layup? Or a layout? Yikes.), but I could use some extra height, so I jump up onto a lawn chair and *SWISH!* Victory.

"Lele, you can't do that," Brian protests.

"Aw, come on, guys, don't be sore losers. I'm sorry I'm just really talented at basketball."

"You're out of your mind," Jake says, but he's laughing and giving Alexei a smile that says, "Hey, she's great, you should put a ring on it." I don't know why this fantasy involves me being objectified so majorly by Alexei's friend, but hey, that's for my therapist to figure out.

(No, I'm not in therapy, but the way things are going I'm sure I'll be on that couch in no time.)

30

Frenemies / That One Person You're Friends with Only at School

(4,850,544 FOLLOWERS)

uys aren't the most fun to hang out with, but at least you always know where you stand with them. With girls like Yvette, you never know. First she hated me, then she love, love, *loved* me, and now she oscillates daily between affectionate and coolly distant, as if she's vaguely suspicious of me. I constantly feel as though I'm under her microscope, and it is exhausting.

"I literally have no idea if that girl likes me; it's like she has split personalities," I say to Darcy at lunch. We've decided to take a day off from Yvette and the Sausages to regain our energy and get back in touch with our truest selves. We're sitting on a grassy hill behind the English building and Darcy is braiding my hair.

"I think she likes you. She admires you, I can tell."

"Then how come she gets so . . . bitter out of nowhere? And she never invites us to cool places, even after I went out of my way to include her at the Steve Tao show!"

"Lele, is it really not obvious? Do I really have to explain it to you?" Darcy rolls her eyes.

"Um, yes. I'm not very bright, Darcy, you know that." I like saying this every now and then, because I actually am very bright and everyone knows it, so it doesn't come off as self-deprecating and annoying. It also doesn't come off as bragging, because technically I'm putting myself down, but since everyone knows I am an undeniably smart girl, saying I'm not draws attention to the fact that I *am*—it actually is bragging. It's a very sneaky way to brag and I'm proud of myself for inventing it. Oh wait, someone already did. #HumbleBrag. Sigh.

"She's jealous. You're getting a lot of attention and she's not. She doesn't invite you places outside of school because whenever you're around you get the attention, which means she gets less. When it's just her and the crew, she's the star, and that's how she likes it."

"Interesting. But she always wants to talk to me at school. Most days she treats me like I'm her best friend. But I don't think she's texted me even once to hang out."

"At school she's still the star. People here know her and remember when she was the queen bee. Outside of school literally no one knows her. But you, you're a real star!"

"I'm just an internet personality, I don't know if that really qualifies me as a star."

"Um, hello, you have almost five million followers. You have a legit following. That's a lot of fans, girl."

"Yeah, I guess you're right." I smile, feeling lucky to have what I have.

"Don't give it much thought. You're school friends, nothing wrong with that."

"Is that like a thing?" I ask. School friends? What even is that?

"Duh. It's when you hang out at school but then don't really know each other after sixth period."

"That's severe!"

"Yeah, well, life is severe," Darcy laments with a heavy sigh.

"Whoa, way to make it dark, bb."

"You're welcome."

Hmm, is Darcy going through something right now? It's always a shock to remember you're not the center of the universe: other people have problems too.

The next day I decide to test out Darcy's theory. When I see Yvette at the front gate I run up to her and cover her eyes with my hands.

"Guess whoooo?" I say.

"Oh my God, you crazy bitch!" she squeals gleefully, turning around to laugh with me.

"That's my name, don't wear it out."

"Missed you, where were you last night?"

"What do you mean?"

"Maddie had some people over, I thought you'd be there."

"No one told me about it!" I do a cute fake-angry routine that is actually real anger covered up masterfully.

"I just assumed you knew about it. You're so in the know. I mean, you're so in the loop that the loop literally forms around you."

"Is that what you think?" We're walking up the main building steps and I'm overcome by a sudden desire to be honest. "It couldn't be farther from the truth. I'm actually still a loner outsider slash outcast slash loser. Having Vine followers hasn't changed any of that."

"Really? Wow, I never would have known. Sorry, bb, next time something's going on I'll make sure to let you know." She puts a hand on my arm, genuinely apologetic. I feel like a puppy that has rolled over to get its belly scratched. The main goal is for Yvette to not see me as a threat. Hey, that rhymes. Anyway, apparently she didn't mean for us to be school-only friends, glad I handled that before it got out of hand. Man, the world keeps throwing me curve balls and I keep knocking them out of the park.

In fourth-period gym Coach Washington tells us we're entering the tennis quarter.

"Find a partner, make sure it's someone you can tolerate, as you will be playing tennis with her for six weeks. If you can't find a partner I will find one for you, and once I've picked a partner for you, there's no arguing with me, so I suggest you figure it out on your own."

Good God, what is it with this lady? She's so disgruntled and resentful—what did we ever do to her? Yvette jumps to be my partner and we choose the court farthest from the gym, pressing up against the senior parking lot. In other words, we're far enough from Coach Washington that we can goof around and gossip, making up our own rules as we go along, only falling in line when she comes over to check on us. We clumsily whack the ball back and forth for a bit, then get right up against the net so Yvette can tell me about how Becca is probably moving to Spain to be with a guy she met there last summer.

"WHAT?!"

"Shh, Washington will come over! Be cool."

"Be cool?! After you just told me that one of our friends is leaving the country for some random guy? She's only sixteen; it's nuts."

"It's not as crazy as all that. She comes from a pretty international family. Her parents are originally from London."

"London? I'm pretty sure that doesn't affect the insanity of the situation. They're just going to let her go?"

"They're not in love with the idea."

"Do they know the guy or something? Is this even legal? A sixteen-year-old needs to be living with a guardian, right?"

"Eh"—Yvette shrugs—"I dunno. I think it's all very romantic."

"I guess . . . but . . . how does she know he's not some psycho? They spent a summer together and she thinks she knows everything about this weirdo?"

"Lele, you are so adorable. You genuinely care about the people in your life and their well-being. But look, Gavin is not a psycho, I've looked through his Instagram."

"First of all, of course his name is Gavin, it sounds like he was born to be a European womanizer."

"LOL, Lele, why are you assuming he's a womanizer?"

"He sounds like one!"

"Well, I'm going to go visit if she does decide to move. I've always wanted to see Spain, you should come too."

"How old is this guy even?"

"I dunno, does it matter?"

"Um, yeah, what if he's like seventy?"

"Wow, Lele." She jokingly smirks. "Didn't realize you were so closed-minded." She throws a tennis ball at my head. I catch it.

"I didn't realize you were such a pervert!" I throw it back.

"It takes one to know one!"

"Ohhhhh man, now you're asking for it." I hop the net and attempt to tackle her to the ground. Coach Washington starts blowing her whistle at us, running over with arms flapping, and we almost die of laughter.

When sixth period ends I find Yvette by the lockers and we walk together to the front gate.

"What are you doing for the rest of the day?" I ask, thinking we could hang out, chillax, etc.

"Homework and then dinner with my family," she says. "See you tomorrow." Then she heads off abruptly without another word.

Wait, so we are school-only friends then. Darcy was right. Darcy is always right.

The weirdness gets weirder about five hours later, around eight at night, when I go out with myself to Ben & Jerry's, a tradition I've had for as long as I can remember. It's actually not so much a tradition as much as it is me going to Ben & Jerry's as often as I possibly can. Anyway, so I'm walking up the street toward the mothership when I see none other than Yvette Amparo strolling toward me. She's wearing the cutest dress I have ever seen: pale pink jersey-fabric bell skirt attached to a black spandex top with a scooped neck and off-the-shoulder sleeves. I'm wearing sweatpants.

"Lele?"

"Yvette?! Hey, what are you doing here?"

"Oh, this is kind of weird, but I always go out for ice cream when my family is driving me crazy," says Yvette.

"Whoa, me too. Which is always," I tell her.

"Same. I have a gigantic family and they're all nuts."

"I'm an only child, but my parents are pretty intense." Yvette smiles knowingly, follows me inside.

On our way out of Ben & Jerry's we hug good-bye and voilà! Our outfits are magically switched. I'm in her adorable outfit, she's in my sweatpants, and by the time she's realized what's hit her I'm running down the street.

Fast.

Okay, fine, so that last part didn't happen, but with Coachella approaching I really have a one-track mind, and that track is outfits.

31

When My Friend and I Ask to Go to the Bathroom During Class

(5,000,001 FOLLOWERS)

*C*oachella Coachella Coachella!!!! What a magical name for a music festival. Legend has it if you say it six times in a row your skin will turn glow-in-the-dark and you'll never be heard from again. Fine, so I made that up, but someone's gotta make up the legends and it might as well be me. Ohhhh my God, I can hardly contain my excitement as I write this, but here we go:

Steve Tao has invited me to fly out to California to hang out with him in the VIP tent and backstage. *Me?!* In California?! What if I explode from excitement on the plane and then the flight attendants have to clean my brains off the windows? And the chairs . . . you can't get anything off those.

Darcy has ever so kindly volunteered to come with me, and at the very last minute Alexei announced that he's had plans to go to Coachella since before he even moved to America, which I think sounds suspicious. He probably made that up just so he could spend time around me without seeming desperate. You know, since he's in love with me and I'm going to have his babies or whatever.

We're missing school for this, which would count as unexcused absences, which means we'd have to make up the time we missed in detention, which is why we plan to keep this excursion under wraps. And as much as it pains me, that means *no Vines*. I mean, yeah, we'll tape some there, but we can't post them until we leave. That's right, we're going off the grid, into the wild . . . we're just like Lewis and Clark navigating the wilderness of the West with nothing to sustain them but each other's company and faith that everything is going to be okay. Okay, so it's not *quite* like that, but you get the picture. When we get home we'll forge doctors' notes and be welcomed back with open arms. After literally seven straight hours of debating and convincing, my parents decided that "you're only young once" and that I should go, as long as I promise not to do drugs or get myself killed—which are both very fair rules. Alexei's parents don't seem to care what he does with his time, and Darcy's happen to be on vacation, which is completely and totally fate, in my humble opinion.

It's like the *universe* wants us to go to Coachella.

The flight is uneventful: Alexei and Darcy take sleeping pills and, out of sheer, torturous boredom, I draw things on their faces. Nothing vulgar, just mustaches and glasses and a Harry Potter scar on Alexei's forehead. I spend hours staring at the bathroom door wondering how people manage to have sex in there and why they would even want to. First of all, it can barely fit one person, let alone two people bumping up against each other. Second of all, it smells like a combination of sewer water and chemical lemon Pine-Sol and I can barely spend two seconds in there without throwing up. But hey, whatever floats your boat, who am I to judge?

Our hotel in Palm Springs is called Ace Hotel and it is the coolest hotel in the world. It has this very desert-y Native American feel to it with shabby chic beds and antique maps on the walls and a pool where you can lounge and order food and drinks from hot waiters. But that's not what we're here for.

For those of you who don't know, Coachella is a three-day music and art festival where anyone who is anyone goes to hear their favorite bands and take ecstasy and get naked and take pictures and we are here, in the middle of it all, in the eye of the storm! In reality, it's not as savage as all that, but it's an overall let-loose good time.

The three days are a whirlwind I won't soon forget:

Outkast, Arcade Fire, Lana Del Rey, Lorde, Dum Dum Girls, Ellie Goulding, Muse, Haim, Sleigh Bells, Kid Cudi, Krewella, STRFKR, the Naked and Famous, Cage the Elephant, Little Dragon, Toy Dolls, Skrillex, Girl Talk, Chvrches, AFI, and the 1975. Kendall and Kylie Jenner and Selena Gomez and Justin Bieber and Emma Roberts and Paris Hilton and Katy Perry and Leonardo DiCaprio and Jaden Smith and . . . David Hasselhoff, who I had to surreptitiously Google as to not give away how young I really am.

A gigantic spaceman towering a hundred feet above us and an animatronic robot and jacaranda trees the size of buildings made of lights that blended from orange to pink to yellow to blue to green and miniature architectural designs set up for you to go inside—a gingerbread house and a lifeguard stand and a house made of Popsicle sticks (which is cool to look at if you're hallucinating, I heard, but I didn't take any Molly, are you kidding?)—and green and purple palm trees and an illuminated kaleidoscopic rotating portal that you could walk through and a room-size caterpillar growing an entire garden on its skin and a forty-five-foot tall knot of twisted metal tracks covered in canvas containing multicolored lights that interact with shadow to create a dramatic spectacle and a field of cardboard sunflowers and a roadrunner made of metal scraps that holds a swing in its mouth and a completely mirrored tower that turned everything into a cube like a chunk of space had been cut geometrically into facets and we discovered that the whole universe is really a diamond.

We danced and we sang our hearts out and we never slept. We'd never done anything so beautiful.

The fantasy life comes to an abrupt end on Sunday night when we're boarding the plane back to Miami.

"Oh man, I got so many dope pictures for Instagram," Alexei says.

"No, you can't post anything, remember? We said no photos so we don't get in trouble."

"Oops. I, uh, sorta already posted some."

"Alexei, you beautiful creature, I am going to murder you."

32

Lele's One True Love: iPhone

(5,199,900 FOLLOWERS)

"*W*elcome back, you three," Mr. Contreras says the next day, all snarky and snide. "How was Coachella?"

"Ermmmm . . ."

"Uhhhhh . . ." The whole class is glancing between us and their Instagram feeds, practically green with envy. You know how jealous people are, they want to ruin everybody's fun.

"You know what, screw it," I say. "It was the most incredible thing I've ever done in my life. We hung out with celebrities and saw all our favorite bands and just went totally wild and I don't regret it for one second. So sound the alarms! Bring out the guillotine! You can take away my life but you can't take away Coachella!"

"Okay, I think you took it a little too far," Alexei says.

"Fine," Mr. Contreras says. "As a punishment for skipping school I'm taking away all your phones. For a week."

"Nooooooooooo!!!!!!" I holler—this is much worse than the guillotine—then, "Wait a second, you can't do that, you're just our English teacher." Good thinking, Lele.

"So I can't keep it all week. But I can take it away right now, for this hour."

"Nooooooooooooo!!!!!" It hurts, it really does. We hand them over and he puts them on his desk, WHERE I CAN STILL SEE MY PRECIOUS BABY. It's like he's taunting me on purpose.

As Mr. Contreras, a.k.a Hitler, a.k.a the Devil, lectures about literary devices (hyperbole, alliteration, foreshadowing, etc.), I catch myself drifting into a lovely daydream, and I don't stop it from happening:

I'm brave, I'm an adventurer, I climb up on my desk and take big, teetering steps from desk to desk while Mr. Contreras is scribbling on the board, all the way to the other side of the room, where I snatch up my phone and hold it over my head like I'm an Olympic champion!

Snap back to reality, oh there goes gravity: I am alone, without my one true love, without my sunshine. Mr. Contreras took my sunshine away, and I'll probably never forgive him for that. Doesn't he understand my phone is my life? Without it I would literally be nothing—or, I at least wouldn't have achieved internet stardom, that's for sure.

Once I have my phone back I cling to it like a mother reunited with her long-lost child. I make a vow to never let it out of my sight again.

The next morning a highly sleep-deprived Lele is sleeping through her alarms. I apologize for speaking about myself in the third person, but that's the sort of thing that starts to happen when I'm so deliriously out of it.

"LELE! Get up!" It's my mom, shaking my feet poking out from under the blankets. I kick her away. "Get up, get up, get up! You're going to be late for school and you already missed so many days of school from your crazy shenanigans!" Zzzzzz. Also, Mom and Dad let me go to Coachella, so it's sort of her fault too, right? "Lele, if you don't get up right this minute you're grounded!" I can hear her voice in this distance but I just don't care.

"Five more minutes," I mumble.

"No more minutes! If you miss any more school you might get suspended, is that what you want?"

"Sure. More time to sleep."

"Agh, Lele, I've had enough of you." She leaves the room; for a second I think I'm in the clear, but when she comes back she has a small cupful of water that she THROWS ON ME.

"Mom, you're crazy," I slur, eyes still closed. "I'm gonna get you back for this."

"Oh, okay, I know what will get you up."

"Nothing."

"I'll think of something," she says, super proud of herself. "I'll just take this." Oh no, it can't be, anything but that. I hear her scoop my phone off the nightstand and start to walk away.

"No!" I jump out of bed and beat her to the door. "Hand it over and no one gets hurt."

"Yep"—she practically pats herself on the back—"works every time."

That was the beginning of a very weird phone day. By that I mean my phone went through some weird stuff. I guess God is also punishing me for skipping school by antagonizing my most treasured possession. I never would have thought that God and Mr. Contreras were in cahoots.

First, during gym, I have my phone secured into my underwear elastic so I can keep tabs on it at all times. While I'm playing tennis against Yvette, my phone goes flying into a nearby tree and falls to the ground. I run to it, cradle it, and am ecstatically relieved to see that it is still fully intact, unscratched and unharmed.

Then, as I'm walking through the field where the guys are playing golf, I accidentally drop my phone and some bozo whacks it with his golf club! Again, it goes flying, and again it is magically uninjured.

On my way home from school, walking with Darcy, I say some-thing funny (like I often do, no big deal) and it makes Darcy laugh so hard that she bumps into me and knocks my phone out of my hand. It spirals into the street just as a car is coming. I consider jumping in front of it but reluctantly opt to let the car run over my phone. This is the naïve part of my day when I start to feel like maybe I'm being protected by angels: my phone has survived its third attack of the day. Not a scratch! Miracles do happen, and they happen to me!

But it looks like my luck just ran out. When I get home after my long, trying day and set my phone lightly on the dining room table, INSTANT SHATTER.

The poor thing finally caves under the weight of the world and erupts into a million slivers.

I worry I may never love again.

33

Better Grades / White Girls at the Movies

(5,850,551 FOLLOWERS)

*B*ut I do love again. As it turns out I am due for an upgrade, and the iPhone 6 is super dope. I get it in white and gold because I'm feeling like a straight-up rock star these days. I don't even get a case, 'cause I'm a badass bitch and I don't learn from experience.

In third-period calculus, we get back the results from a recent pop quiz and to my dismay, but not surprise, I have received a D minus. Yikes. I'm a smart kid even if I don't pull straight A's, but a D is D-pressing. Still, pop quiz?! Come on, people, how am I supposed to do well on a math test if I don't know about it enough in advance to write all the answers out on my hand? Seems unreasonable, TBQH. Of course Darcy, who is sitting next to me, gets an A. Why's this girl gotta be so smart all the time? I bet she barely even studied. School just comes naturally to her. I want to be proud of her but I'm just jealous.

"What did you get?" she asks.

"D minus."

"Oh, I got an A."

"Yes, Darcy, I can see that. You're literally holding it up in my face."

She laughs, I laugh, she laughs, I laugh, all the while I'm holding a lighter up to her test. She doesn't notice until it catches fire and the smell of burning paper fills the room.

Oops. I'm immediately sent to the principal's office and, as it turns out, lighting fires in class is a very serious offense.

"Lele, what were you thinking?" The principal, Mrs. Lombardo, is sitting behind her desk littered with Doctor Who bobbleheads and pictures of what I presume are her children. She has short grayish brown grandma hair and is wearing a beige pantsuit. There are posters of cats in human outfits on the walls and one of Garfield hating Mondays.

"Do you have any idea how dangerous lighting paper on fire in a classroom is? What if it had gotten out of hand? What if you set the whole class on fire? The whole school? Did you even consider that for one second? I could have you expelled, permanently. I could even call the cops, Lele, do you understand that? Do you think you can just do whatever you want because you're a little bit famous? I mean, I honestly want to know what you were thinking."

My first instinct is to tell her that I'm not a little bit famous, I'm almost a lot famous at this point (closing in on a billion loops viewed!!!), but I bite my tongue. Note to self: "Almost A Lot Famous" is a great idea for a Vine.

"Well"—I sigh deeply—"to be really honest, I let jealousy get the better of me. Darcy Smith, the girl whose test I lit on fire, is a good friend of mine, and she's a lot smarter than I am. Maybe not in every way, but definitely when it comes to school. And that makes me feel bad about myself." I let my eyes get a little watery; the last thing I need is getting arrested for setting a small fire, and you can't send a girl to jail who is being open and vulnerable with you about her emotions, right?

"So when Darcy started bragging about the A she got on this pop quiz even after she knew I got a D minus, I went a little crazy. I put my lighter under the paper as a joke at first but then I realized how easy it would be to actually set the thing on fire. But then I felt terrible. I'm so ashamed of myself, Mrs. Lombardo. I just want to be happy for my friend. I didn't think I was being cruel, I thought of it as a practical joke, but now I see how wrong I was to do what I did. I don't know who I've become. I feel so pathetic!" At this I burst into tears, half of which are dramatized and half of which are real.

The dramatized tears come from me wanting Mrs. Lombardo to feel extremely sympathetic and take pity on me. The real tears come from my realization that I really don't feel confident in who I am or comfortable in my own skin. I'm achieving internet success at such a young age, and that is super cool, but it doesn't mean I'm any closer to knowing what I want from life or feeling loved. As I cry I realize it's mostly because until that moment I hadn't realized how insecure I'd been feeling for so long.

"Oh, honey." She hands me a box of flamingo-pink tissues and leans in like she wants to pat me on the head. "I remember when I was your age, I was so insecure. We all were so insecure, that's part of what it means to be a teenager. Most people don't start feeling good about themselves until they're in college. Or right after college when they get their first job. For some people it's not until they're in their thirties. Or forties. For some it's not until retirement. I think most people never feel good about themselves, to be honest. Or, TBQH, as you kids say these days." Wince. "But hey, in a way that should make you feel a little bit better, you're not alone! Feeling bad about yourself is something almost everyone struggles with at one point or the other, and the people who don't are probably psychopaths. Like my ex-husband, for example." Grimace. "I think a great way to start feeling better about yourself is to celebrate your peers for who they are and realize that you're different than they are, but that doesn't mean you're any less special. You're special for being you, and they're special for being them. No two people are the same, and that's what makes us all beautiful! I know this is all very Dr. Seuss, but trust me! I've been around long enough to know these things." Oh my God, could she be any more oblivious? "I guess what I'm trying to say is, don't compare yourself to other people, focus on your strengths, and love yourself unconditionally, even when you're feeling weak. Well, that speech went on longer than I thought it would. Did I get through to you at all, Lele?" At least her intentions were good. And I do want to avoid being expelled.

"Yes, Mrs. Lombardo. That was very helpful. You definitely made me feel less alone."

"Fantastic. Now, I'm going to send you back to class with a warning. I don't want to hear about any more of this acting out, all right? I know you mean well and I know you can DO well, okay? Try applying yourself every once in a while." She scribbles on a red slip and hands it to me, "Give this to Coach when you get back to class so she knows you've come to see me."

"I will. Thank you so much, Mrs. Lombardo." I curtsy awkwardly as if she's some sort of duchess or prime minister or . . . I don't know, someone fancy.

Phew, that was a close one. If I got expelled or arrested my parents would most likely disown me. Then I'd probably have to live on the streets as a beggar. Or I could ask each of my Vine followers to send me a dollar and then I'd be rich as f**k. Note to self: hmmm, interesting.

But the hard part of the day isn't over. I wait for Darcy at her locker after school and she is PISSED.

"Lele, are you out of your goddamn mind? You could have hurt someone. And now I can't even show my parents how well I did on that quiz."

"Eeesh, yes, that is uh, really hard, and I'm sorry." I try to genuinely care that her parents will never see the results of this one particular pop quiz. "Look, I figured you'd be mad, and I would be too if I were you. What I did was really selfish. When you got an A I took it as a sign of my own incompetence . . . but your success isn't about me, it's about you, and I realize that now, and I'm happy for you! I know I can work harder and maybe one day we can both get A's. But honestly, as I'm saying all this, I realize I don't even care about getting good grades. Academics aren't my passion in life, they're yours, and clearly you excel at them—"

"And you excel at what you do! You have over five million followers on Vine, do you know how rare that is? You're a performer and a comedian and you're doing astronomically well. You're reaching more people than I ever will with my good grades."

Darcy is so right. But to be nice I say, "Nah, that's not true. You're going to become a scientist and cure AIDS probably."

"Probably, yeah."

"See? Love your confidence. I admire it."

"I think you're more confident than you think you are."

"Oh, please. Wanna go see a movie?"

"Yeah! I'm in the mood for something scary."

"Me too! I heard *Oculus* is scary as hell."

"Let's do it."

In the cool dark of the movie theater, Darcy and I sit with our feet up on the chairs in front of us. It's 4:00 p.m. and the theater is practically empty. Darcy's nibbling on popcorn and I've got a box of Red Vines, a bag of M&M's, a bag of Sour Patch Kids, a giant soft pretzel, and a large Coke. See, I deal with fear by eating as much sugar as possible. One of the many differences between Darcy and me (which I am here to celebrate, not use as an excuse to feel bad about myself) is the way we deal with scary things.

Darcy is fearless, while I am a scaredy-cat through and through. I spend the entire two hours shrieking and hiding my eyes and thrashing around in my chair while Darcy remains cool, calm, and collected. She even laughs a few times, which is absurd, because this movie is *chilling*. A mirror has been haunting these siblings for decades and it may have been the reason their father killed their mother and himself and stuff is always appearing in it and it's always warping reality and I never know what kind of horrors are going to pop out at me and I wonder if I'll ever feel safe again. But Darcy isn't fazed. Note to self: Darcy is a true badass bitch.

This afternoon's Vine, entitled "White Girls at the Movies / Darcy Is a Badass Bitch":

White girl Lele sees the grim reaper appear in her home and faints out of fear. Black girl Darcy walks into the room, sees the grim reaper, and beats the sh*t out of him without thinking twice. Terrified, the poor guy runs away down the street, never to return again.

34

When Two Boys Like the Same Girl Versus When Two Girls Like the Same Guy

(6,266,200 FOLLOWERS)

*H*ere we are again, tennis with Yvette. She always wins, because apparently she went to sports camp growing up or some preppy crap like that. Camp never worked out for me, personally. You all know about the time I gained twenty-five pounds at camp, and one year I went to sleep-away camp in Massachusetts and on the first day I broke my arm during ropes course and made my parents come pick me up. I've been a natural-born klutz since day one.

Anyway, Yvette has just kicked my ass in tennis and we're walking to the vending machines for some water.

"So, any developments with Alexei?" she asks.

"Not really. I mean, we had fun at Coachella."

"But he's single now, right?"

"Yeah, so?"

"So, why hasn't anything happened? He's single, you're single, shouldn't you be dating by now? Or at least hooking up?"

"I dunno . . . I haven't wanted to rush things. He just got out of a long relationship."

"But you still like him, don't you?"

"Duh."

"And he likes you?"

"He said he did. I don't know. What are you getting at?"

"I'm not getting at anything. I'm just trying to get a better understanding of the situation." She presses A1 for her bottle of water, retrieves it, and casually walks away.

"'Trying to get a better understanding of the situation' my ass," I mutter to myself, then press D7 for a Coke because f**k it.

What was that all about? Does Yvette like Alexei? Is she trying to swoop in on him? I swear to God I will cut a bitch. I know I'm supposed to be enlightened now and celebrate all my female friends instead of competing with them, but if one of my friends OR ANYONE tries to take Alexei from me there is no telling what I will do. Sure, Alexei isn't my boyfriend, but he's the one that I want. And he better shape up, 'cause I need a man, and my heart is set on him, woohoo. Sing it, Olivia Newton-John as badass bitch Sandy in black latex.

Oh wait, I forgot that it's the twenty-first century and I don't actually need a man. At least that's what my head tells me . . . other parts of my body don't seem to be in agreement.

Here is another instance where guys have it much easier than girls. When two guy friends like the same girl, they actually bond over it. They're all like, "Hey, check out that ass, yeah, high five, we both agree that ass is cute!" Such simpletons. Sometimes they'll go as far as to say things to each other like, "You deserve her, man, I'll step down this time," or "Let's just say this one's off-limits. Wouldn't want to let a girl get in the way of our friendship. Bros over hoes, man, bros over hoes."

Do you like my impersonation of a guy? I think I've nailed it.

But when two girl friends like the same guy, however, it's total bedlam. All vows of loyalty and friendship forever are thrown aggressively out the window and the fierce competition begins. Okay, yeah, there's girl code, but that's only if one of you has already dated him. With new guys, all is fair, because this is war. It's hard to believe, but we will actually end friendships over liking the same guy. Granted, we normally will refriend each other after a short amount of time once we realize that said guy was completely and 100 percent not worth it, but still.

The concept of avoiding a guy because our friend likes him is quite foreign to us and difficult to comprehend. It's weird, you would think guys would be the more competitive ones, what with all that testosterone and all, but no, it's girls who fight each other to the death in the name of lust.

What's that even about? Evolutionarily speaking, I mean. Because, if there's anything I've learned in biology it's that everything about us is the way it is because of evolution (quite different from what I learned at my previous, Catholic school). Maybe it has something to do with how men don't need a particular woman to reproduce, but for women to reproduce they need the right man to help feed them and provide shelter so they whack the bad guys over the head like a carnival game. Sounds like some antiquated gender norm bullshit to me.

See? I know some things.

Take that, Darcy, I can be smart too.☺

35

Flirting Gone Wrong or Right?

(6,388,991 FOLLOWERS)

*A*lexei comes over after school in his bro tank top and hipster Converse. I'm waiting for the day he shows up with ironic glasses and a leather satchel. We watch some Jon Stewart off my DVR and all I want is to ask him if he likes Yvette. *No big deal, but do you have a thing for Yvette? 'Cause I think she has a thing for you.* I try it out over and over in my head but it sounds clunky and obvious. *So Yvette was asking me some weird questions today . . . What do you think of Yvette? Is she your type? . . . Soooo who would you rather date, me or Yvette?* Ugh, is there no winning this?

"I'm gonna grab a soda," Alexei says. "Want something?"

"Yvette loves you!" I blurt.

"What?"

"I mean she likes you. I mean I think she likes you."

"What?" He laughs. "Where is this coming from?"

"She kept asking me questions about you during gym today. It sounded like she wants to make a move."

"Lele, Yvette is a big flirt. She likes everyone. She tried to kiss me at her party back in September but I pulled away. She's just not my type. I mean, she's a cute girl, for sure, but I don't feel anything for her."

"Oh." YVETTE TRIED TO KISS ALEXEI!!!! RAGE!!!

"Did you really think I would date Yvette Amparo?"

"I dunno. Maybe."

"Eww, why do you think so low of me?" He lightly punches my shoulder.

"Because you're gross and a weirdo." I lightly punch him back. Even though Yvette and I are frenemies now, I still don't trust her. Wait a minute. I don't trust her because she's a frenemy.

"Um wow, look who's talking." He punches again, this time a little harder, but still friendly, maybe even flirty? Then, out of left field, seized by my subconscious mind, I punch him back, but this time it's aggressive, and *in his face.*

I see the pain flash across his eyes.

"What the hell? What did you do that for?"

"You only hurt the ones you love!" Another terrible thing to blurt out. Dammit, I am out of control today. "I mean, I'm sorry! I mean, I didn't mean to hurt you!" Oh my God, oh my God, did I just tell him I love him? He's going to laugh at me now, isn't he? Or worse, he's going to leave. I just know it, he's going to turn around and leave. No, he'll laugh at me and then leave.

But I'm wrong. He doesn't laugh and he doesn't leave. He's quiet for a second, and then inches slightly closer to me. He puts his hands on my cheeks and pulls my face toward his and I swear I can hear music playing. Loud, victorious music, fireworks bursting all around while his soft lips are pressed against mine.

He's kissing me.

THIS IS WHAT I'VE WAITED FOR ALL MY LIFE!!!!

This kiss. Oh my God. He's an amazing kisser. It's like I can feel the entire world through my lips. Is that weird? That's how awesome it is.

Then it gets even better.

"So you love me?" he says, so close to my face that I can smell the Winterfresh on his breath.

"Maybe."

"Maybe I love you too."

And that, ladies and gentlemen, is the end of our story, because at this point Lele dies of happiness . . . she lived a good, good life indeed.

36

Crushes Always Call at the Worst Moments / When Your Crush Comes to Your House

(6,900,000 FOLLOWERS)

Sadly, I did not die in that moment that was quite possibly the high point of my life. I continued to live and rode out the excitement of being loved until Alexei had to go home for dinner and the excitement of being loved was replaced by a feeling of longing and anxiety. Does this mean he's my boyfriend now? He told me that maybe he loves me! When is he going to call me? How am I supposed to act when I see him at school tomorrow? These are the types of neurotic questions that raced through my mind.

But now it's the next day after school and I'm feeling nice and satisfied after a day of the two of us note-passing in English and hand-holding at lunch and tongue-kissing in the hallways.

Life would be perfect if it weren't for the fact that Mom has just called me into the kitchen and has a very angry face on. It's that face she gets whenever she's decided to read me the riot act.

"Uh-oh," I say. "This doesn't seem good."

"You bet it's not good, Eleonora Pons." I cringe at the harsh sound of my birth name. "I just got a phone call from your guidance counselor saying that you've been skipping school not just for Coachella, and failing tests left and right, and set a girl's math test on fire? Is this true?"

"Who the hell is my guidance counselor? I've never met such a person."

"Well, she exists, and her name is Mrs. Morgan, and she is very concerned about you. Do you know where D's and F's are going to get you? Community college, that's where. Or some state school— is that what you want? I thought you wanted to go to a rigorous university where you could be with people who challenge you and motivate you to learn. You think you can get that by failing eleventh grade?" She's practically red in the face and her voice is about a hundred notches louder than it needs to be.

"I don't know, Mom, I think that's always been what you want for me. I've never been particularly good at school, and I used to feel bad about it, but I'm trying to embrace who I am. I'm not academic smart, I'm Lele smart and I'm creative, and funny; the world thinks I'm funny. Did you know I have almost seven million followers on Vine now? I have a huge fan base and I'm only six- teen; to be entirely honest I don't think I need to go to college, at least not right away. I want to take some time off to focus on . . . myself. College isn't going to make me happy . . . you know how I am, Mom, listen to me, college will be oppressive and it will keep me from developing my career. As an actress. Maybe even as a singer."

"Your career? You can't make a career out of little internet videos! You need an education in this world. Good God, Lele, you're letting fame get to your head. You can't get by on temporary popularity, Lele, you can't—"

That's when my phone lights up and I see that Alexei is call- ing. Oh God, I want to answer it so badly—I can't even begin to explain how much I long to answer the phone and end this unex- pected bombardment of emotion and hysteria that is, quite frankly, detrimental to my delicate little psyche—but I know I can't. I bite my lip and nod along to the tirade.

Mom isn't done, not by a long shot. "You can't think you're special just because people like you on the internet right now. What about tomorrow? What about in a few years when this whole thing blows over and you're left with nothing to fall back on because you haven't been educated? What then?"

Call from . . . Alexei ❤, Call from . . . Alexei ❤.

"You think you'll be able to just come crawling back to your dad and me? Well, you're dead wrong, because that won't be an option. I suggest you take a good hard look in the mirror and start to turn this around; if you don't have the grades to start applying to colleges in November, then you won't be welcome in this home, do you understand?"

"Yes," I say hurriedly. "I definitely understand. I hear you loud and clear."

The call goes to voice mail. Dammit.

"Really? I thought you were going to háve a lot to say about this." Mom frowns.

"Not today, Mom. You're the parent and I respect your wishes. Talk later!" I run back into my room and hit CALL BACK.

"Hey, you've reached Alexei, a.k.a. A-list, a.k.a. Axxy. Just kidding, don't call me those things. But you can leave a message and I'll probably call you back." *Beeeeeeeeep.*

Nooooooooo! I'm too late! I've lost him forever!

My phone dings.

Ooh, a text from Alexei:

Hey, taking care of Aya now, can't talk. I was just calling to see if I could take you out tomorrow. Like on a date.

Whhhaaatt? Is he for real? Of course he can take me on a date, that's all I've ever wanted! I write back:

Yes!

I instantly regret the winky face, but it's too late.

Psh, it's all going to blow over, yeah right, what does my mom know anyway? It's so not fair: one second she's my champion cheerleader, swearing she'll have my back no matter what, and the next she's switching into her "overprotective mother" persona in overdrive to make up for time spent being easygoing. I have a Dr. Jekyll and Mr. Hyde situation on my hands and it can be very disorienting. I just need to remember that I'll never be able to make everyone happy: at the end of the day I need to make decisions based on what I know I need. And I know I need to act.

This is what I find myself thinking as I'm tearing through my closet looking for the perfect first-date dress, tripping over all the new shoes I've bought. I can build a career off this moment in my life if I want, I'm a highly capable young lady. If I go to college I'll just be wasting valuable time! Right? Do I want to go with a classic little black dress or is that too funereal? Electric-blue cocktail dress or is that too slutty? Pale pink bell-skirt dress with one off-the-shoulder sleeve or is that too childish? Do I own nothing appropriate for a first date? Where is he even taking me? What if it's not that fancy and I'm overdressed? What if after thinking this I decide to wear something casual and I end up being underdressed?! This is how my train of thought goes and soon I've forgotten all about my mom and her antiquated opinions.

I decide on a black corduroy skirt from American Apparel over a slate-gray leotard, kitten heels, and a white blazer. Do I look dope? Yes, I do.

The doorbell rings. Christ, he's early. Does he want to come in? Holy Christ, I hadn't thought of that. After a day of reorganizing, this place is no place for a love interest: childhood stuffed animals and baby dolls and princess dress-up gowns and board games litter the floor. I frantically shove them all in a closet as fast as is humanly possible (I probably look like I'm on crack), then hurry to the front door. On my way, I pass Mom, and can't help but shove her into the nearest closet as well.

Quick mirror check—hair, eyes, lips, boobs, fleek, fleek, fleek, and fleek—then open the door like the cool, calm, collected, easy, breezy, beautiful girl that I am.

"Hey, Alexei," I say. "Wanna come in?"

"Oh, thanks, but we gotta go. I made a reservation for eight."

"Lovely," I say, and step outside. I can vaguely make out the sound of my mom butting up against the closet door.

#ZEROTOHERO

May to June

37

Guys Change When in Front of Their Friends / When Bae Embarrasses You

(7,700,502 FOLLOWERS)

*A*lexei is proving to be quite a romantic. And a gentleman. He opens doors for me, he pulls out chairs—I honestly thought chivalry was long dead, but I guess I was wrong.

After sharing tiramisu on Friday at the Cheesecake Factory (he's seventeen after all, not Bill Gates), we rent a paddle boat and paddle around the marina like a couple of ducks in love.

On Saturday we pack a picnic and go to the beach. He rubs sunblock on my back and lets me win at beach volleyball and tries to teach me how to surf but I keep freaking out as the waves get close and I always topple over, my life flashing before my eyes each time.

On that note, let's talk about the ocean for a second. Can you believe people still go in there? I can't believe it. The whole thing is so unpredictable and aggressive. The riptide can just pull you under whenever it decides to get strong, and waves can get huge out of nowhere and sharks live in there and decomposing bodies from the Titanic probably. I know the ocean is supposed to be this beautiful, majestic, God-created masterpiece, but it really gives me the creeps.

"Okay, the sun is setting, I'm getting out of here before I get eaten by a night creature," I say, dragging myself out of the water and onto the sand like a dying whale.

"A night creature?"

"Yeah, you know, like a sea monster. You know, if they exist they gotta come out at night."

"Ummmm, I don't think those are real," he says.

"I'm not taking my chances."

"You're adorable."

"I know."

He tackles me and pins me onto my towel. He tries to tickle me but I'm strong and I ram my body into him and knock him over so that I'm the one pinning him down. He's caught off guard, for sure, probably really impressed that his girlfriend could potentially be a professional wrestler.

He starts kissing me passionately and then we're side by side and the sun is setting and everyone's gone home and we're the only people on the beach. He starts to peel the bathing suit off my shoulders and I almost want to let him but something doesn't feel entirely right. Have I known him long enough to let him see me naked? If I get closer with him now and then he breaks up with me, I'll be extra devastated. I want to be naked with him right here and now but I can't ignore the instinct to protect my-self.

"Not yet," I say, stopping his hand. "I'm sorry."

"Don't be sorry, babe." He props himself up on one elbow and kisses my ear. "We can wait as long as you want, I don't mind."

"Whoa, really?"

"Yes! Of course, what do you think I am, some kind of animal?"

"I don't know . . . you hear a lot about teenage boys being so . . . you know."

"Horny? Desperate for sex? Yeah, we get a bad rap."

"So really then, you can wait? Won't you get frustrated?"

He laughs. "Probably, but I can wait."

"Wait a second, are you just saying this because you'll secretly be sleeping around behind my back?"

"What?! No! Of course not. You're my girl."

Oh my God, he said I'm his girl! In a simpler time he would have given me a bracelet with his initials and we'd be going steady.

"Well that is all I needed to hear. And I mean, you know, it's not that I, uh, don't want to. I do want to. I just want it to be right. When it feels right."

"I totally get it. I don't want to rush things either."

"That's grea— Wait a second, you've, like, done it before though, right?"

"Nope."

"What?" I sit up. "But you seem so . . . confident. Plus, you were with Nina for so long."

"I seem confident? That's ridiculous. I mean, I'm not unconfident, but I'm definitely not experienced. Nina was a year younger; she wasn't ready either. I mean, we did other stuff, don't get me wrong, but I wasn't going to pressure her into something she wasn't comfortable with."

"Wow, so we're both . . ."

"Yeah. For now." He raises his eyebrows at me like a lecherous predator and we laugh. Then I tap his shoulder.

"Tag, you're it," I say, before running away across the sand.

Fun: check.

Funny: check.

Gets me: check.

Good kisser: check.

Hot: double check.

Chivalrous: check.

Respectful of me and of women in general: check.

Is a mature adult: zero checks. D minus, at best. Ugh.

What happened, you ask? I'll tell you what happened. After that lovely and romantic day at the beach, we got hamburgers from Jack in the Box and walked through Acadia Park, some sappy 1950s love song playing in my mind (probably "Earth Angel"). We sat down on a park bench, perched on top of the bench so that our legs dangled over the backboard, his arm around my shoulder.

Just then, Jake and Brian walk up, smoking a joint and looking all bro, no hipster.

"Oh, hey, guys," I say, seeing them before Alexei does.

When he looks up and sees his bro buddies approaching he suddenly gets panicky and twitchy like he's been possessed and abruptly pulls his arm off me so that I have no support and fall off the bench in a backward somersault. But not a cool backward somersault, I'm talking graceless and embarrassing backward somersault.

"Hey, guys, what's up?" Alexei stands to give them high fives like he's some tough, big man on campus who don't need no lady holding him back. Gasp! He's Danny Zuko! He wishes.

"Uh," Brian says, "is that Lele? Did she just fall?"

I stand up, brush leaves out of my hair.

"Yep, it's me. I'm fine though. Thanks for asking. I don't think I broke anything. I guess that's to be determined though." I glare at Alexei.

"Well, we were just thinking of going to see a movie, you guys interested?" Brian asks.

"Sounds great guys," I say, "but I have to be up early tomorrow for a . . . for a thing. An important thing. So, see ya later." I sling my purse over my shoulder and start to walk away.

"Lele, wait!" Alexei calls. "I have to give you a ride home! Where the hell are you going?" He catches up to me, grabs my hand. I pull it away.

"Are you embarrassed to be seen with me or something?" I snap.

"What? No, of course not."

"You practically pushed me off a bench when your friends walked over."

"I was just caught off guard. It didn't mean anything. I swear to God!"

I believe him and forgive him but don't tell him so. It's much more fun to watch him squirm all the way home.

I freeze him out all of Sunday, during which he leaves me five voice mails, each one a long apology speckled with corny jokes and even the occasional awkward song. It's delightful.

On Monday he shows up to English with a dozen roses and the whole class thinks it's so romantic. Okay, I think it's a little romantic too, but I don't make a huge deal about it because, let's be real, this is how I'm gonna expect him to treat me regularly, whether he has messed up or not.

"Please forgive me," he says.

"I do, I forgive you." The class goes awwwwwwwwww and I lean in closer so only he can hear me. "But if you ever drop me again you'll barely live to regret it." He gulps.

Coach Washington is absent today, so we have a substitute gym teacher who throws us a bunch of handballs and leaves us unattended. An hour to do whatever we want; I'm not complaining.

"So, I hear you and Alexei are finally a thing," Yvette says as we take a slow stroll around the track field.

"Yeah, it's hard to believe it's actually happening. But it is."

"Have you done it yet?!"

"Ugh, grow up, Yvette," I say. "But no, no we haven't."

"Why not?! Oh my God, you have to."

"Slow your roll, bb, I'm not in a rush. Oh hey, look, there he is!"

Alexei bounds toward us diagonally across the field, zigzagging through girls playing soccer, approaching the giant game of Connect Four (imagine it: the game Connect Four except it's three feet tall), and keeps on running, gaining speed so he can jump over it. He runs, he jumps, he lands straddling it like a bull and the whole thing goes down, Alexei and all. Frisbee-size chips go flying. I cringe, hide my face.

"Well"—Yvette smirks—"you might have missed your chance now. I do hope it's not broken."

"Bite me," I say. But secretly I'm pleased: now Alexei and I have both fallen over in front of each other's friends. The score has officially been evened.

38

Don't Believe What You See in Magazines ... Sometimes / When You Have the Worst Luck

(7,980,000 FOLLOWERS)

"*W*hy were you running across the track field in the first place?" It's after school and I'm brushing my hair in front of the mirror. Alexei is sitting on my bed with an ice pack on his crotch.

"Hm?"

"When you and that Connect Four set got intimate, you were running over to me; it seemed like you wanted to tell me something."

"Oh yeah! I completely forgot. You're the first Vine user to reach one billion loops." The brush drops from my hand.

"I'm sorry, what?"

"Yeah, look." He pulls up my Vine on his phone to show me. It's true: I've reached one billion loops. That means my videos have been viewed a total of one billion times. And I'm the first person on Vine to reach it. I stare at the numbers trying to digest them, make them feel real. But it won't sink in. This must be a dream.

"Alexei, is this real life? I've had dreams like this before."

"You're not dreaming, this is real life."

"Ugh, people say that in dreams all the time, it's lost all meaning."

"Lele, you're being ridiculous, look." He pinches me on the arm, hard.

"Good God, was that necessary?"

"Yes, it was. You're tripping. Just open your eyes and acknowledge that you're absolutely slaying on Vine. You broke a record, Lele, you're frickin' awesome."

I pause for a moment, stare into space. I can feel the information finally soaking through my muscles into my blood and straight to my brain.

"Eeeeeeeeeeeeeeeeeeeeeeeeeeeeeeee!" I shriek at the top of my lungs, jumping up onto the bed like I'm five years old again and have the capacity to get excited about Santa Claus and the Easter Bunny and ice-cream sundaes. I bounce around, dance with my arms flailing—I don't care who sees, even Alexei, who, in fact, can see me.

"Dance with me!" I pull him by his hands. "This is a cause for celebration! Pop the champagne! Hold the phones! Alert the press!" With my help he hoists himself up so that he's standing next to me, and for one happy moment I'm the belle of the ball holding hands with my prince.

"Aghhhhh," he groans, putting his hands to his crotch. "The pain!" And he collapses back onto the bed. Well, it was nice while it lasted.

While Alexei nurses his own wounded testicles (sorry for TMI, but it's not my fault he's a moron), Yvette, Darcy, and I head out to our second Steve Tao show. Yvette heard he was playing downtown, and asked if I could possibly get us into the VIP section again. I said, "Let me check. Your question has been submitted for review and the answer is DUH, because I'm mega famous now and can have whatever I want!"

Yvette just glares at me, utterly repulsed.

But now we're hanging backstage and her tune has changed to one of gratitude. We're sitting on a white leather couch drinking gin and tonics (mine is just tonic) as roadies set up for the show and randos mull about trying to look important.

"Congrats on the one billion views, by the way," she says, trying to make it sound casual. But she can't, there's no way to make it sound casual; I have gone where no girl has gone before. I'm expecting a phone call from the president any minute now. He's so cute.

"Oh, thanks, it's no big deal." I shrug, picking up a nearby issue of *Teen Vogue*.

"You're so weird," she says. "You swing from arrogant to modest every five minutes."

"Hey"—I take on a fake-pretentious theater-snob voice—"it's hard being famous, all right? I'm trying to find the perfect balance." She rolls her eyes and we laugh.

Flipping through the glossy pages of *Teen Vogue,* an endless array of airbrushed faces pop out at us. Enhanced lips and contoured cheekbones and extended eyelashes galore. It's practically like watching a cartoon. A cartoon where everyone is more attractive than you are. One male model with abs so chiseled they create shadows on themselves has sparkling green eyes that look too good to be true.

"Everyone in these magazines is so fake," I say, thinking of all the work they'll have to do on me if I'm ever in a magazine.

"I know, right?" Yvette says, then gasps. She grabs my arm. "Lele, look." She points straight ahead.

"What am I looking at?" I look up from the magazine at the growing crowd.

"Right there, next to the girl with the yellow dress. That's him!" She can't believe it; neither can I. And yet, it's true: the male model we were just objectifying is off the pages and standing before us. No, I'm not forcing you, reader, into some mystical magical fantasy world where images come to life, I'm saying that the guy who modeled for this Tommy Hilfiger shoot in *Teen Vogue* is now, today, hanging out backstage at the Steve Tao show.

And guess what? He's just as gorgeous in real life. Damn.

"Whoa, I guess that's one man who doesn't need airbrushing," she says.

"Ehhh, I don't see it." I grab the magazine and hold it close to my face in an attempt to conceal how unbelievably hot I think this guy is. What if Yvette sees me blushing and tells Alexei about it as a ploy to steal him for herself? Does she still secretly want him? I never did get to the bottom of that.

"Come on, let's go talk to him."

"Nah, I'm good. But you go. You should talk to him."

"Fine, I will," she says. "Catch ya later." And she's off to the races. Wow, look at her go, that girl knows how to flirt! Maybe she doesn't have a thing for Alexei after all. Or maybe that's what she *wants* me to think.

I don't really get how DJ-ing works exactly. Like, this is a music show but he's not really playing any songs, he's just mixing other people's songs together. What I'm trying to say is that there's no opportunity for that "Hey, I know this song!" feeling—or, there is, but when it hits it has nothing to do with the artist you are here to see. Basically, the purpose of a DJ is to play for people who really wanna get pumped up. Or, "turnt up," as the kids are saying these days.

So, I stand in the front row happy to be in my own company, bumping along to the multitude of rhythms and cheering whenever a song I love splices into another song I love in perfect harmony. Which, I admit, is pretty dope.

At one point, Steve brings out a birthday cake, and starts balancing it on his head. The crowd goes wild. I don't totally understand, but hey, that's rock 'n' roll. Oh, no, wait, it's not rock 'n' roll, it's . . . DJ-ing culture?

"Who wants cake?" he calls out, causing the crowd to cheer even louder. Then, without warning, he hurls the cake into the audience—Lord knows why. Lord knows why Steve does half the bizzarro things he does—and I can see it heading straight for me. Uh-oh, uh-oh, uh-oh, my mind races; I'm frozen in place and can't think to jump out of the way. Plus, I could go for some cake.

SMASH! It hits me right in the face. Mmm, vanilla icing. With cake in my ears I can hear the muffled sounds of laughter and applause. I could be embarrassed but suddenly I'm too hungry to care. Plus, this will make for a super-dope Vine. I'm so glad Darcy's there with the camera, just as long as Steve is willing to play himself and we're able to get it all in one take—actually, scratch that: we'll film as many takes as we need to get it right, even if it means I have to take seventeen cakes to the head. #DoItForTheVine!

I wipe cake from my eyelids and see Yvette making out with model boy. Luck is a weird thing, isn't it? Some people have it; other people get hit in the face with cake in front of hundreds of people.

39

School Is Fun / When You Hear an Old Song That Everyone Knows the Dance To / When You Forget It's Not Friday

(8,189,000 FOLLOWERS)

*O*kay, so I may not excel at academics, but I pretty much dominate the part of school that happens in between classes. The hallway high fives, the lunchtime shenanigans—I lead it all. Just being my weird self has finally translated into universal respect from my peers. They look to me for the fun; they look to me for validation. I didn't ask for this, but I have gradually become the queen bee of Miami High.

But I'm not your average queen bee. Sure I'm pretty and tall like typical queen bees, but I don't abuse my power, I don't rule through intimidation and exclusion and dictator-like regulations. I just want everyone to have fun and to like who they are, and I don't want anyone to ever feel the way I did when I started out at Miami High.

If I were to put out an official royal newsletter it would say something like: *Be not afraid to embrace your truest self, for Miami High welcomes and celebrates the nerds, weirdos, freaks, outcasts, and overall eccentrics.* Imagine trumpets blaring as these words are read off a scroll to an entire kingdom.

It's Friday and those of us in sixth-period Spanish are growing rest-less. Those last few minutes of school are the hardest to sit through, especially on Fridays. As Señora Castillo's green marker squeaks across the white board, we all glance at the clock, willing it to move faster. My God is it painfully slow. Tick . . . tick . . . tick . . . I have time to start a family and grow old and die in between each second; it's practically torture.

But then the glorious moment comes. The three o'clock bell rings and we burst out of our seats, throw our pens and papers in the air, cheer like we've collectively won the World Cup.

"Sit your asses down!" Señora Castillo snaps. "I mean . . . *sien-tense.*"

"But it's Friday!" I protest.

"Bitch, you trippin'," Señora Castillo says. Okay, so she doesn't say that, but that's the look she gives me. *"No es viernes,"* she says, super smug. *"Es jueves."*

It's Thursday, not Friday. How could this be?!

Bubble = burst. Parade = rained on.

When Señora Bossy-Pants finally does let us out of prison, I meet up with Darcy by the lockers. It may not be Friday but at least I get to go home, so things have been worse.

"Wanna get a family pack of Kisses and watch *Beverly Hills, 90210*? The old version, obviously," I ask.

"I have to study for the calc test tomorrow," she says, because *everyone* wants to burst *all* my bubbles today. "And you probably should too."

Just when I'm about to strangle her, the first "Yooooouuuu" from Soulja Boy starts to play. Everyone freezes. The music is coming from a radio inside one of the open classrooms. It may be 2014, but the Soulja Boy dance from 2007 is just like riding a bicycle: nobody ever forgets how to do it.

202

"Let's go, people!" I call out, and we all fall into line. This is our jam and we know it by heart. See, when this song came out we were only eleven—while you were out voting for Obama we had nothing else to do but practice this dance over and over and over again.

"Soulja Boy off in this hoe . . ." Okay, so we never figured out what we were singing back then, but we can crank out the choreography without a single misstep.

A bunch of white and Latino kids plus Darcy.

40

How Others See Your Little Siblings Versus How You Do / We've All Gone Through Them Lazy Days / How You Are Outside Versus at Home

(8,400,999 FOLLOWERS)

*M*y life is good, right? I have friends and fun and a boy, I even have some fame, which is more than most can say! So why do I feel so . . . overwhelmed? My mom is pressuring me to get better grades and I'm pressuring myself to be the perfect girlfriend and my followers are pressuring me to keep churning out Vines like I'm a machine but I AM NOT A MACHINE! I am just one girl! Am I ever going to get to relax again?

Alexei obviously likes me a lot, but I still don't feel like I can be myself around him. It's weird, because I am always myself, but as soon as he comes around I feel this overpowering need to be lady-like and cutesy. Like a doll. Is that what men want? A doll? I don't know, I just don't know.

On Saturday night Alexei picks me up and takes me to see *Godzilla 3D*. Not the most romantic movie of all time, but we make out through most of it anyway. The dress I'm wearing is too tight at the waist—it makes my waist look smaller but it also makes it so that I can barely breathe. I keep having to suck my ribs in so that my chest has room to expand within the dress so that I can get enough oxygen. But still I end up gasping for air. I try to make the gasps sound cute and nonfrightening. The things we do in the name of looking hot!

"Are you all right?" Alexei whispers in the dark.

"Oh yeah, I'm fine." I cross my legs and lace my fingers over them as if I'm Jackie O. at a gala or something.

When he drops me off I kiss him good-bye and hurry into the house. As soon as the door is closed behind me I literally rip the dress off my body. Just then, Mom walks in.

"Oh, Lele, what are you doing this time?"

"I was on a date wearing this stupid dress and it was too tight and I couldn't breathe but hallelujah now I'm free! I'm free!" I run back and forth in my underwear, fists victoriously in the air shouting "Freedom! Freedom!" Mom shakes her head and walks away.

I must have forgotten to lock the front door, as it suddenly opens. It's Alexei. Goddammit.

"Ummm, you left this in my car," he says, handing me my wallet with a semistunned look on his face.

"I uh— I was just . . ."

"You don't have to explain, Lele, I've pretty much figured out that you're a total nut job by now. It's part of why I like you. And I was going to see you in your underwear eventually anyway."

With a wink and a smile he's gone. I don't know if it's my boyfriend seeing me in my underwear for the first time or that sexy wink he just gave me or the fact that I haven't had a proper breath of air in a few hours, but a wave of dizziness comes on and I fall to the floor.

Everything goes black.

"I tried calling you a bunch last night, are you okay?" I answer the phone Sunday morning to Alexei acting all concerned and boyfriend-y.

"Yeah . . . actually, I sorta fainted last night."

"What do you mean you sorta fainted?"

"Okay, I did faint. I must have forgotten to eat or something."

"But you're okay? Why didn't you call me?"

"When I came to I just curled up in bed and fell back asleep and have been asleep until now. It was actually kind of cool, I had never fainted before!"

"Oh, Lele."

"Oh, Alexei."

"You should come over. I'm just babysitting Aya all day."

"Sure, I guess I could come over." I read somewhere once that you're not supposed to act overly excited when Bae asks you to hang out—you don't want him getting too comfortable in this relationship now, do you?

When I arrive, Alexei and Aya are on the couch watching *Adventure Time*. She's curled up with a pink bunny-spotted blanket and a Barbie doll, total angel.

"Hey, Lele, come watch with us." Alexei waves me over. "You'll love this show, it's completely bizarre."

From what I can gather coming in midepisode, this show is about a boy named Finn and his dog, Jake, who live in some sort of alternate universe where there's an evil king who shoots ice from his hands and kidnaps princesses in his spare time, forcing them to be his wife. Seems a little dark to be a show for kids, but I appreciate the outrageous direction cartoons have been going in lately.

"I'm going to get something to drink. Lele, want a Coke?"

"I want a Coke," says Aya, fluttering her eyelashes.

"You can have a Sprite, silly billy."

"Ok Alexei-y!" Aww, Alexei-y.

"I'll take a Sprite too, actually, can I help you get them?"

"No, no, relax. Enjoy the show. Be right back!"

Then I'm alone with Aya and the Ice King's pet penguin, Gunter, is using a set of icy stalagmites as a xylophone.

"So, is this your favorite show?" I ask. She turns to me and with a chilling calmness starts to speak. The look in her eyes says she isn't the sweet little girl she was a second ago.

"I have to tell you something," she says, "I like you, but if you make my big brother sad . . ." She takes the Barbie's head and deftly pops it off its body. I gulp for dramatic effect.

"Are you trying to tell me that if I do anything to hurt Alexei you are going to cut my head off?"

"Mm-hmm." She lowers her voice to the creepiest whisper I've ever heard and turns her eyes up at me like a demon. "And you won't be able to hide from me. I will always find you." Jeez, where is this coming from?

Alexei comes back into the room with our Sprites and sits down in between us.

"I think your sister just threatened me," I say, keeping my eyes on her.

"Oh yeah? What'd this little monster say?" Behind his back so only I can see, she runs one finger across her neck like a razor. What kind of freaky gangster movies have they been letting this four-year-old watch?

"Oh, nothing, we were just goofing around." I backtrack. She nods in agreement, drinks her Sprite.

"Aww, glad you girls got to talk. Isn't she just the cutest?"

"Yeah," I say. "Real cute."

I get out of there as fast as I can. I tell Alexei I'm really tired and should go nap, which actually isn't a lie. I feel a laziness growing in my bones and muscles that I desperately want to give in to.

At home I barely make it to my room before collapsing. I lie down on my floor, sprawled out like a starfish. I notice that when I let myself dramatically fall to the floor, my phone went skittering a few feet. I try to reach for it but my arm isn't long enough and I just don't have it in me to get up and move.

"It's okay," I say to my phone. "Go on without me. Save yourself. I'll see you on the other side."

This exhaustion gives me a great idea for a Vine but I'm too weak to look for pen and paper. Note to self: Vine where girl is too tired to do anything. We see a montage of her trying to reach for her phone, eating food right at the foot of the fridge, she falls asleep while walking her dog, lies facedown in a pool, falls asleep on top of a stranger who is forced to drag her around town. In the end, she finds peace sleeping in a mattress store, but is tragically woken up by a disgruntled employee.

I just hope I remember it when I wake up. Zzzzzz.

41

What You Wanna Do When You See Your Bae Cheating / How to Make an Exit with the Hewlett-Packard x360

(8,511,356 FOLLOWERS)

*F*or a lazy Saturday activity, Darcy and I buy bags of candy from Sweet Factory at the mall and eat them on the kiddie rides. You know, the rides you put quarters into that go like one mile an hour? We live life on the wild side, undoubtedly.

I'm chewing the head off a gummy worm when something catches my eye. My blood boils, my heart drops: it's Alexei . . . WITH ANOTHER GIRL.

"Lele? You look like you just saw a ghost," Darcy says, bobbing up and down on a bright yellow rodeo horse.

"I—I uh—" I stammer. The blood has drained from my head so that forming sentences feels impossible. I feel my body kick into fight-or-flight mode. "Be right back!" I say without an explanation, then dart off after Alexei and the girl.

Oh, when I get my hands on his skinny little neck I'm going to strangle the life right out of him—but not before I make him get naked and write "I'm sorry, Lele" one thousand times on a chalkboard. In front of the whole school. My cheeks get hot and I feel like I'm going to vomit, the tense pain of betrayal in the pit of my stomach. I'd start crying on the spot but I'm too stunned.

I slip through the crowd, past Claire's and Panda Express, turning the corner at Wetzel's Pretzels until I've sneakily caught up enough to see that . . . it's not Alexei.

Just a doppelgänger—same hair and style, less sex appeal. "Oh, thank the good Lord," I say, a little too loudly.

"Hm?" The couple turns around, thinking I'm speaking to them.

"Nothing, sorry. I thought you were someone else."

"Hey, are you that girl from Vine?" the girl says. She's super pretty; if it had been Alexei that she was with I would have had to kill her too.

"Me? Oh, yeah, I am. But ignore me. Pretend I'm not here. Have a lovely day, good citizens." I bow in their direction, then turn on my heels and get the hell out of there. Why do I have to turn into such a psycho in awkward social situations?

"What the hell was that about?" Darcy has moved onto the choo-choo train by the time I return. Who are we? What are we doing with our lives?

"I thought I saw Alexei with another girl," I pant. "So I chased them down."

"Oh my God! Are you serious? What did you say?"

"Turns out it wasn't him. But I did have a lovely conversation with what turned out to be two complete strangers."

"That makes sense. Alexei wouldn't cheat on you."

"Thank you. You're right. He's a good guy and he likes me."

"And if he did he certainly wouldn't be stupid enough to do it in a mall." I glare at her, throw a peanut M&M at her head, but she ducks and it sails past.

"I really lost it for a second back there," I say. "I'll tell you what, Darcy, if I ever do catch him with another girl I swear to God I'll make a voodoo doll of him and stick millions of pins in it. I'll flail it all about so that he acts totally insane and out of control, and after days of torture I'll throw the doll off a bridge."

"Why would you throw it off a bridge? Won't it just be gone then?"

"No, if I throw it off a bridge, Alexei will throw himself off a bridge. That's how it works."

"I don't think that's how it works."

"Oh yeah? Since when do you know so much about voodoo dolls?"

"I don't really, I'm just saying that— Look, he's not going to cheat on you. But maybe you should look at why you're so worked up about it."

"What do you mean?"

"It sounds like you're feeling insecure in the relationship. Maybe you should talk to him about it. I mean, that's what couples do, isn't it?"

Ugh, Darcy, what a know-it-all.

Later that day I'm in Alexei's room dwelling obsessively over what Darcy said. I have my head in his lap and he's stroking my hair, which sounds nice, but his fingers keep getting tangled and pulling at my scalp. Ouch. The energy in the room is off, everything feels out of sync.

"Hey, so, something funny happened earlier today at the mall," I say, after about an hour of deliberating whether I should or shouldn't.

"Oh yeah?"

"So I was with Darcy, and all of a sudden I could have sworn I saw you hanging out with another girl."

"What? That's ridiculous. I was at home with Aya all morning. Wait, are you saying I'm cheating on you?"

"No, no! It's just a funny coincidence. I followed them and saw that it wasn't you!"

"You followed them? So then you did think I was maybe cheating on you."

"No, it's not that. Darcy thinks maybe I'm just insecure in the relationship still. You know, because it's so new. Do you think that's normal? I don't think you'd cheat on me, but you never really know, do you?"

"No, I guess not." He lets his guard down a little bit. "The beginnings of relationships are always a little shaky, it does take some time to build trust."

"Exactly."

"But you should really know, I would never hang out with another girl without telling you about it first."

"What? You would want to hang out with another girl?"

"Well, of course, I have friends who are girls."

"Oh really? Name one."

"I mean, Darcy and Yvette are my friends, aren't they?"

"Neither of them would ever want to hang out with you without me around."

"Are you saying I'm not fun to hang out with?"

"No, I'm saying that my friends are loyal to me and wouldn't want to spend time with my boyfriend if I wasn't around because they know that's shady."

"How is it shady if I explicitly run it by you first?"

"It doesn't matter if you run it by me a hundred times, the answer is always going to be no."

"As in, no I can't hang out with other girls?"

"Correct."

"Like, literally any other girls, whether they're your friend or not?"

"That's correct."

"You're never going to let me hang out with other girls, even in a completely nonromantic, nonsexual scenario? From now on I can only hang out with guys?"

"Yes. Guys or me. I'm your friend, why do you need other friends who are girls?!"

"It's different now, you're not my pal the way you used to be. You're my girlfriend now, I feel like we can't goof around the way we used to."

"Why do you feel that way?"

"I don't know—you're not wacky around me the way you used to be. You try to hide that side of yourself, I can tell. Like the other day out at the movies you were so well behaved and . . . basic, but then when you got home you went wild. I miss that Lele."

"Oh," I say. "I didn't realize. Thank you for telling me that."

"I just want you to be you. And you have no reason to be worried about other girls, I'm not even a little bit interested in any of them!"

"Really?"

"Really."

"Okay, I believe you." We hug and he kisses the top of my head. Wow, I always thought having a boyfriend would be a dream come true, I never realized it would be the beginning of a whole new world of problems. I got ninety-nine problems and a boy is pretty much all of them.

We decide to take a nap and I fall into an intense, feverish sleep. I dream that I'm at a park with my great-grandmother Camilla who I've never met in real life, and we see Jackie and John F. Kennedy drive by in a long black car with big open windows. I never think about my great-grandmother, I don't even know much about her, but I guess she's in my subconscious somewhere . . . sometimes the human brain is too weird for me to handle.

When I wake up, Alexei isn't in bed anymore, so I go downstairs to look for him. He's at the kitchen table on his laptop working on an e-mail. I approach him from behind so I can put my hands over his eyes and surprise him, but before I can do that I glance over his shoulder and see that the e-mail is to somebody named Staci. I'm pretty sure it's a scientific fact that nine out of ten times somebody named Staci is always a person your man is cheating on you with.

"Who the hell is Staci?" I snap. He turns around, more startled than surprised.

"She's nobody! It's nothing, Lele, calm down." He tries to grab my wrists to subdue me, like I'm some kind of rabid horse.

"No! I will not calm down. I knew you were into other girls and this just proves it." I tear free from his hands. "I'll be taking this with me, jerk." I slam the computer closed and hold it to my chest, then run and jump out the kitchen window as it bursts into flames, *Mission Impossible*–style.

"You're always so dramatic!" Alexei calls after me, going down with his house in a fiery blaze.

I wake up in a cold sweat mumbling, "No, no!" Arms flailing.

"What is it? Are you okay?" Alexei is looking down at me, concerned and confused.

"Oh." I blink, try to reorient myself in the room, in reality. "Oh, it was just a dream. Thank God, it was just a dream."

Wow, I really need to get it together before I do something terrible.

42

That Friend Who Always Wants to Be Fashionably Late / When Someone Says Your Name Wrong

(9,000,000 FOLLOWERS)

*O*kay, so I'm not the most emotionally stable young lady, but I am internet famous and in this day and age that means something. It means that whether I'm sane or crazy, people wanna hang with me. And, as it turns out, not just any people, but Nickelodeon people. That's right, I've been invited to a Nickelodeon party in South Beach and it's such an exclusive party that I don't even get a plus one! Either it's exclusive or I'm just not as important in real life as I am in my own head. Either way, Lele flies solo tonight.

Now, I've always been a big Nickelodeon girl. Growing up in the 2000s you had to pick a side: Team Nick or Team Disney, and I was always the former. Don't get me wrong, I loved the Disney Channel original movies, *Lizzie McGuire,* and *That's So Raven,* but nothing on Disney could compete with *Hey Arnold!, Rugrats, All That, The Amanda Show, Drake & Josh, Doug,* and, don't forget, *SpongeBob,* whom I adore. If you're a Gen Z kid you remember when Disney got ahold of Nickelodeon's *Doug* and made it totally weird. Doug's pants got baggier and Roger went from poor to rich and Connie got skinny and Skeeter got a new shirt and the opening sequence was all different! Okay, if you're not from Gen Z it may not sound that horrible, but trust me, it was traumatic.

Being a nineties kid *and* a Nickelodeon girl, it is crucial that I look 100 percent amaze at this party tonight. Because I know you love listening to me ramble on, and because maybe you too might be in my position one day, here are the fifteen simple steps for getting yourself on fleek for a fancy Nickelodeon party.

1. Forty-minute workout. (Get your arms and abs looking fit.)
2. Shower thoroughly. (Scrub your entire body down with, you guessed it, body scrub, to make your skin look soft and radiant.)
3. Shave. (Take your time shaving every bit of unwanted hair off your body. Go slowly and act carefully, because even the smallest nick will be a huge black mark against your fleekness level. And you certainly can't use Band-Aids tonight.)
4. Blow-dry your hair. (Turn those tangled locks into smooth, steamed strands of gold.)
5. Straighten your hair. (Iron out any kinks. Be merciless.)
6. Curl your hair. (Why did you just straighten your hair if now you're going to curl it? If you even have to ask then there is nothing I can do for you.)
7. Spray a *very light* mist of hair spray. (Keep those loose though gorgeously buoyant curls in place.)
8. Apply a layer of liquid foundation over your entire face. (Smooth out any bumps or redness, anything that might give away the fact that you are a human being.)
9. Apply eyeliner. (And smudge it for a smoky effect.)
10. Apply bronze eye shadow on your lids. (Gradate it so that it's lighter closer to your nose and gets darker going out. DO NOT SKIP THIS STEP OR YOU'LL BE SORRY.)

11. Apply mascara. (Your eyelashes are much shorter than they're supposed to be, trust me. You want your lashes to look like spiders are stuck in your skull and are struggling to get out.)
12. Apply red lipstick.
13. Wipe the red lipstick off so that it doesn't look like you've put lipstick on. (It looks like your lips are naturally rosy, or like you've spent your day eating cherries.)
14. Choose an outfit. (This is by far the hardest step. You must choose something classy yet fun, sexy but sophisticated, flawless but also effortless. It is customary to spend more time looking for the right outfit than you spend at the actual party.)
15. Take a selfie. (This is for Instagram so that everyone knows how fabulous your night was. If you don't post it to Instagram, how are they going to feel like you're better than they are? This photo has to be just right, so you'll want to take a couple dozen before choosing the right one and filtering the hell out of it, and don't forget the Snapchat too!)

That's it, you did it! You are Nickelodeon-party ready! Or maybe you're not, but I definitely am.

Unfortunately, after all that prepping, quite a few hours have gone by, and by the time my Uber drops me off and I take an elevator to the penthouse, the party is *over*. Can you believe it? I spent so much time getting ready for a Nickelodeon party that I actually *missed* the Nickelodeon party. Note to self and readers: pick five out of the fifteen steps and just stick with those.

The penthouse is in Brickell Key and overlooks the whole city, which sparkles wildly below. I walk through the house admiring the marble and silver and carved lion heads as people filter out, leaving a field of bottles and cigarettes and glitter behind. Looks like it was quite the party—I wonder why everyone left.

"Hey, are you Lee Lee Pons?" someone calls as I'm making my way back to the front door. I turn around and guess who I see: Josh Peck from Nickelodeon's *Drake & Josh*! I'm so starstruck that I almost forget to be mad at him for mispronouncing my name. Almost.

"Actually," I say. "It's Lele . . . Drake." For a second he's stunned, then he laughs.

"Are you trying to insult me by pretending you don't know the difference between me and Drake Bell?"

"Maybe."

"You're ridiculous!" He seems impressed. "Enjoy the party?"

"Yeah. I mean, no, because I got here too late."

"Too bad. It was dope."

"Hey, why'd it end so soon? It's only like eleven thirty. I thought this is when parties start."

"It is when parties start. This was sort of a pre-party, we're all headed to the Mondrian now."

"Ohhhhh. Okay, I get it."

"You should come."

"Yeah? Yeah, okay."

"All right, Lele, let's go."

By the rooftop pool at the Mondrian I get a text from Darcy:

Hey, you comin over?

Dammit, I forgot I said I'd come hang with her after the party. I text back:

At a dope after party at the Mondrian, come!

Then I slip my phone into my navy-blue Givenchy fold-over purse and order a club soda with cranberry juice from the bar.

"Been here before?" Josh asks, drinking a Corona. I don't know if it was the harsh Nickelodeon lighting or the fact that I watched *Drake & Josh* before I hit puberty, but it's not until right now that I notice Josh is kinda cute.

"No, uh— I don't go to a lot of parties that aren't, like, high school parties. I guess."

"Well, you do now," he says. "Cheers." We clink glasses and I look out onto the crystal-blue pool, black letters spelling out "Mondrian" projected onto the surface—black, rippling light. *Well, I do now,* I think to myself. Wait, is this my life now? Is this how it's going to be? Mansions and luxury hotels and Nickelodeon stars calling me out at parties?

For the first time the reality of it all starts to sink in. My new life is thrilling and glamorous, but what about my old life? Is it gone forever? I can't help but feel scared, like I'm on a bus and it's racing uncontrollably toward a cliff. Snap out of it, I tell myself, look where you are! You better start being grateful, otherwise you won't have to be on a bus going off a cliff because I will throw you off a cliff. I'll throw you off this balcony right now if I have to, so get it together!

Whoa, the voice in my head is kind of a bitch.

43

When Bae Mistakes Your Name with Someone Else's/ *The Notebook*

(9,000,230 FOLLOWERS)

*T*hings aren't getting any less weird with Alexei either. After the Mondrian I take an Uber to his place and he drops a rope ladder so I can climb up to his room. He puts on some Dashboard Confessional and we start making out. I get super into it and I almost think tonight could be the night until . . .

"I love you, Nina." NINA? Who the F— oh, that's right, his EX-GIRLFRIEND.

"Nina?! Are you serious right now?" I'm beyond annoyed.

"No! I mean Lele, you know I didn't mean it. Old habits. I was with her for three years."

"Yeah, that's right. That's a long time to be with someone, Alexei. And you probably still do love her."

"I don't know . . . I hadn't thought about it."

"I'm going home." I put my jacket back on. "I want to be alone."

"What the hell are you talking about, Lele? You're the one who's been at a party with another guy all night. How do you think that makes me feel?"

"I don't have feelings for any other guys and when I'm making out

with someone I put in the effort to make sure I know their name."
And with that, I climb back down the rope ladder. I know this
sounds dramatic, but you have to understand, if I would have stayed
things would have only taken a turn for the worse. If anything you
should be proud of me that I'm learning how to control myself.

For one sweet second I'm finally cozy and snug in my own bed after
a long night, but once I'm asleep the nightmares start again:

I'm hanging off a bridge with white, raging waters gurgling vio-
lently beneath me. The only thing saving me is Alexei's hand, which
I cling to for dear life.

"I don't wanna die, I don't wanna die!" I scream, looking down at
the water that now seems to be hundreds of miles away.

"Don't worry, Nina, I'll never let you go." Niiinaaaaa, Niiinnaaa,
Niiiinnaaa. The name echoes over and over, blending into the
sound of the rushing water.

"Nina?" I scowl at him. "Oh hell no." And with those words, like
a magic spell, our places are reversed: he's hanging off the bridge,
clinging to my hands.

"I didn't mean it!" he pleads. "You know I only love you!"

"It's too late for that now," I say, letting go of him.

"Lele, no!!!!!!!!" He falls and falls and falls and falls. The sight of
him falling breaks my heart—I wish I could get him back but, just
like I said, it's too late for that now.

The scene shifts in the way that dreams do—swiftly and hazily
so that I don't know where one setting ends and the other begins.
Now, Alexei and I are standing on a dock in the pouring rain—it's
just like *The Notebook*, except contemporary, almost sci-fi.

"I waited for you for seven minutes!" I cry out, soaking wet from
head to toe.

"I tweeted you five times!"

"You tweeted me?"

"It wasn't over!" he laments, fists clenched.

Relieved, exhausted, I lean in to kiss him. Just one kiss and all this chaos and heartbreak will be over.

"It wasn't over," he repeats. "But now it is." He steps away at the last second and instead of kissing him I fall face-first into the frozen lake.

When I wake up my heart is pounding and I feel sick to my stomach. Something is seriously off in my mind, I've never been this anxious in my entire life.

44

How You Fight with Your Best Friend

(9,400,000 FOLLOWERS)

*I*n English on Monday, Alexei is distant and a little chilly; he greets me with what you could call a cheek-kiss, although I don't think it even counts as that. But at least he acknowledges me—Darcy, on the other hand, does not.

"Hey, Darcy, what's going on?" She darts out as soon as the bell rings but I manage to catch up to her.

"I don't know, Lele, you tell me." She walks ahead.

"Slow down, slow down. Where are you so eager to get to?"

"Class. Second period. I believe you should be on your way too."

"Stop walking so fast, I want to talk to you! Why are you being like this?"

"Fine, you wanna talk about it?" She stops in her tracks. "You totally ditched me on Friday."

"What are you talking about? No, I didn't." Did I? Friday at the Mondrian was a blur, it's hard to be certain what went down.

"We had plans to hang out after your VIP party, remember? You just never showed up. You didn't even have the decency to tell me you were ditching me, you flat-out stood me up. I texted you to make sure everything was okay and you didn't even respond!"

"Wait, that's not true," I say, remembering. "I did text you back. I told you to come to the Mondrian. That's where I was. But then you didn't text me back."

"I never got a text from you," she says coolly.

"Wait." I take my phone out and open up the text exchange with Darcy.

"Look!" I show her. "I tried to text you but it didn't send! Look, right here, proof!"

"Great, well next time make sure to hit Send. It's kind of a crucial part of sending a text." She turns and keeps walking.

"You're still mad at me? I tried seeing you, I'm sorry it didn't work out."

"You really don't get it, do you? We had plans. And you just dropped them because you got invited to do something better. Sorry I'm not as exciting as a bunch of has-been Nickelodeon celebrities, but you don't treat friends like that. I know you think now that you're famous life is just gonna be a ball, but you still have to keep your commitments, you're still a human, you know, you're not invincible and you can't go around doing whatever you want just because you have money now."

"Whoa, that is so unfair, you're way out of line. This was a mistake that happened one time and you're totally attacking me for it. Give me a break, it's not my fault you feel uncool and unexciting. And you're not being such a good friend either, how about instead of being jealous and bitter you try being happy for me, because that's what a good friend would do."

"You are seriously so self-obsessed, you honestly can't see how what you did was messed-up. Fame has gone straight to your head and I don't recognize you anymore."

"So I was supposed to be a loser my whole life?"

"Oh, so now people who aren't famous are losers?"

"Ugh, no, I didn't mean that. You're seriously overreacting!"

"I tell you how I feel and you tell me I'm overreacting?! Go to hell, Lele."

"Bitch!" We look like we've just slapped each other. With a huff and a scowl we turn away and walk in opposite directions.

What a crazy bitch, I think to myself as I anger-walk to second-period history. She thinks she has a right to try and hold me back from having fun and living my life? She's not the boss of me. She's not my mom: I don't have to check in with her; I don't owe her an explanation. And the way she just attacked me like that! She didn't even give me a chance to explain! It's not fair, this is the most exciting time in my life and she's trying to make me feel bad about it! Right? This is a really great time in my life, isn't it?

During history I stare out the window and think about the party Friday night and how scared I felt. I've been catapulted into a new world and in some ways I'm having to leave my old life behind. But I don't want to, I don't want it to be like that—it feels so lonely. And it must feel lonely to be in Darcy's shoes too, having a friend get famous. If I were in that position I would be totally afraid that my friend was going to move on and leave me behind. Is that how Darcy feels? Is that why she overreacted? Did she even overreact? If I'm being totally honest with myself, I probably would have acted the same way. Agh, I should have been more sensitive to her feelings. If people got mad at me every time I "overreacted" there'd be nobody left in my life.

In third-period calculus Darcy pretends like I don't exist. She takes out her notebook and blue sparkly pencil and scribbles away attentively as if she doesn't even care we're in a fight—no, worse, it's as if she doesn't even remember she ever had a friend named Lele. Are we in an alternate version of reality where Darcy and I never met?

"Darcy," I whisper over her shoulder. "I'm really sorry. I know I'm the one in the wrong here. Let me make it up to you."

"Shh." She turns around, glaring. "I'm trying to focus. I need these notes."

"But can we talk after class?"

"No. I'm not ditching school to deal with your drama. Unlike you, I actually need good grades if I want to have a bright future."

Ouch! Burn! Cold! I don't know how it could be a burn and also be cold, but it is! It's a freeze burn! *Fine, Darcy, I don't need you, I have other friends.* I try to reassure myself, but I know if I lose Darcy it will be my first real failure as a human being. Gulp.

After calculus I skip lunch and gym. I'm too embarrassed to show my face, so I go around to the back of the language building, where there's a hole in the chain-link fence big enough to climb through and sneak down the block to Starbucks, where I drink down a few caramel Frappuccinos to numb the pain. Is there any way I don't have to ever go back? Go into the wild and live with wolves? Please, God, anything to forget what a lousy friend I've been and how self-centered I've become. Oh, I know—I'll become a nun, repent for my sins. I can't help wondering how things got so out of hand. I'm pushing Alexei away; I'm neglecting my friendship with Darcy—everything is a mess and it's all my fault. Maybe fame really is changing me; it's turning me into someone I don't like. I don't want to be the type of girl who lets fame get to her head, I just wanna be Lele from the block!

As soon as the clock strikes 12:58, I hurry back into campus to find Darcy. By the time I get there I'm out of breath and sweaty, my hair is a mess but I don't care: I know if I'm going to fix this, I'm going to have to make a big gesture—I'm going to need to put my dramatic disposition to good use.

"Darcy," I pant, grabbing her arm like I'm the walking dead. "I'm so sorry. This is all my fault. You're right, you're right about everything. Being famous is stupid; I don't think I even want it. Especially if it's going to get in the way of our friendship. Thank you for making me realize I've been acting weird; I've definitely been feeling weird, but I'm still the same old me. See, I'll prove it!" I pull out a black marker from my backpack.

"Lele, no, what are you doing?"

"I'm showing you how I'm still the same old me and how I don't care about fame or about being cool." I take the marker and draw a circle around one of my eyes. For a second she seems like she's going to try and stop me, but then she just stares, speechless, motionless, as I color in the circle until I have a scribbly, lopsided black eye. "See?" Darcy laughs.

"Are you out of your mind?"

"Yes! That's the point."

"Why a black circle though? Is that supposed to represent something?" Oh, intellectual Darcy, always looking for symbolism.

"I'm a pirate! Remember? Like on the first day of school when I got a black eye and everyone made fun of me all day? Because I looked like a pirate?"

"I vaguely remember."

"Really? I thought that was like a big important day that everyone remembered. Hm, maybe I really am self-obsessed."

"You're not that bad."

"Does that mean you forgive me?!"

"Yes."

"Yay!" I jump up and down and squeeze her until she says that she can't breathe.

"Wanna go to the bathroom and I'll help you get that ink off your face?"

"No, I'm good."

"Seriously?"

"Yeah, I'm leaving it on for the day."

"To prove that you don't care about being cool?"

"To prove that I'm not cool."

"Well, I think you are," she says.

"Aaaawww, I think you are too! Now stop before I get emotional."

"Nick Kowel's parents are out of town and he's having a party tomorrow night, wanna go with me? Mingle with the little people?"

"I'd love to."

Okay, I wouldn't love to, but it will be nice to spend some quality time with Darcy after all we've been through.

45

How Kids Partied Then Versus Now

(9,400,202 FOLLOWERS)

"Hey, Mom, what's up?" I spring into the living room where she's reading *People*. "How's your evening so far?"

"All right, Lele, what do you want?" She sets down her magazine and raises an eyebrow at me.

"Want? Nothing, I don't want anything!"

"Great, so I can keep reading my magazine?"

"Okay, fine. I want to go to a party with Darcy tonight."

"So? You go to parties all the time. I thought we—no, I thought you decided you don't have to ask us for permission?"

"I know, I know, but I was thinking. I'm sorry I've been so . . . reluctant to let you be parents lately. I just don't want to let anything get in the way of my career, but I need to step back and realize that I really am still a kid, and my parents are still my parents. I have my whole life to be a grown-up."

"Oh, Lele." She jumps up and wraps her arms around me. "Thank goodness you have such a strong head on your shoulders. We're not worried about you; you've always done things differently. You're still that spirited little girl from Venezuela, making your own rules. We're proud of you for that."

"Does that mean I don't have to go to college?"

"It means we trust you to make the decisions that are smartest for *you,* and not for anyone else."

"Okay, now pretend like I have to ask permission to go to the party."

"What? Why? Crazy girl."

"So that I can live like a regular kid!"

"Lele"—she makes her voice really stern—"did you think you could go out without asking?"

"No, I swear I was going to ask first! Mom! Can I please go to a party with Darcy? I'll be home early!"

"Fine." Fake sigh. "All right. Have fun and be safe."

"Thanks, Mom, you're the best!"

"You're the best." She winks. We both laugh and I go upstairs to change, a significant weight lifted from my shoulders.

Darcy picks me up around eight and we head over to Nick Kowel's house in a highly suburban part of town. I consider texting Alexei to invite him, but I don't have the energy to risk another dramatic scene. Spending time with him used to be so fun and carefree, now it requires so much effort just to keep our conversations from going off the rails!

When we show up, a bunch of jocks and sorority-types are gathered around a Ping-Pong table covered in red cups filled with beer arranged in the shape of a triangle. Oh no, it's beer pong. The dreaded beer pong. I hate to be judgmental, but my general findings are that if you like to play beer pong, you don't have much going on upstairs. Yvette and the Cliques (ugh, we still haven't come up with a permanent name for them) are in the corner taking selfies, reapplying lip gloss in between shots.

Is this really all there is to high school parties these days? I mean, not that the Mondrian event was much more spectacular. Maybe for Generation Z all parties are just a variation on a theme, the theme being "looking cute while letting loose!"

It's disappointing. Growing up I always got the idea from movies that parties were the one thing about growing up to really look forward to. The Prohibition Era parties of the Roaring Twenties celebrated excess and rebellion, the disco parties of the seventies celebrated modernity and inner rhythm—what are we celebrating now? Anything?

Parties of today seem to be about nothing other than denying mortality. Or embracing it? It's hard to tell. See, everyone drinks to excess and acts recklessly (jumping off stuff, hooking up with strangers, experimenting with anonymous pills from God knows where) as if they're invincible, but all the while they claim to be doing it in the name of "only living once." I hear a lot of "party like it's your last night on earth," but surely kids wouldn't behave so recklessly if they actually considered that it could kill them.

Sorry to get so dark, but I'm just trying to understand the limited minds of my peers. I guess at the end of the day, living like you'll never die and living like you'll die tomorrow actually look very similar. Long story short: of all the generations, I'm stuck with the one that's all about beer pong. And what's with the furry, neon-colored boots all the girls are wearing? It makes them look like Sully from *Monsters, Inc.*

"Lele, hey!" My depressing reverie is interrupted by Alexei sidling up next to me and pinching my hip. "I didn't know you were coming to this, I figured you were busy."

"No, uh, didn't have any plans and Darcy convinced me to stop by so . . . here I am."

"Awesome. Was starting to think I'd never see you again." Ha, very funny.

"Hey, Alexei." It's Yvette calling from her little selfie corner. "That shirt looks really sexy on you. But of course— Oh my God, Lele, I didn't see you there, I'm so sorry. My bad!" She laughs and brushes it off like it's just a cute little mistake. Like, whoops.

Alexei is white as a ghost, probably thinking I'm going to scold him. But it's not his fault that she's such a backstabbing flirt. And what's weird is I don't really care—I don't know if it's that I'm exhausted or that I've grown up in the past day and a half, but I suddenly understand that everyone is who they are, I know I can't change anyone, and that's okay.

As a great, wise woman once said, shake it off, shake it off.

True poetry, if I do say so myself. And I do.

46

When You Realize You Miss the Old Disney Channel

(9,550,202 FOLLOWERS)

*O*n the Uber ride home Alexei keeps glancing over at me nervously like he thinks I might be about to attack him. If I didn't know any better I would think he was riding in a car with a ticking time bomb. Jeez, what's he so scared of, it's not like I've given him any reason to think I'm a dangerously dramatic psycho girlfriend or anything. Heh. Okay, so maybe I haven't been the chillest lately, but he doesn't know that I'm super mature and enlightened now! Once again, I am a whole new Lele . . . dare I say, Lele 10.0?

"Alexei, I'm not mad that Yvette was flirting with you, you can stop looking at me like that."

"Like what? I wasn't . . ."

"Like you think I'm going to yell at you. It's not your fault she's a flirt. I know what she's like and I know I can't change her. And I can't change you either, sorry if I've been trying to."

"I don't feel like you've been trying to change me. I just feel like you're constantly expecting our relationship to implode. You don't have any faith in us, and that ends up making me feel . . . disheartened." Sound the alarms: it's time for emotions! Being a girl, and a dramatic one at that, you'd think I'd be well versed in the art of emotional expression, but the truth is it terrifies me. I've never known how to honestly say how I feel without crying. And once I start crying it's almost impossible for me to stop, so I try to avoid the whole thing altogether. I take a deep breath.

"Well, listen—" The driver senses the seriousness of the situation and turns on the radio. In the days of taxis he would be able to just slide the partition in the window, but Uber drivers don't have that luxury (LOL, as if I know anything about the days of taxis). He also puts on the radio, and of all the stations it's RADIO DISNEY. There couldn't possibly be a less appropriate station for the mood of this car right now. But God bless this Uber driver, because this is exactly what I needed. After all my talk about being a Nickelodeon girl, there is a very special place in my heart for all things Disney Channel. The theme song from *That's So Raven* comes on and I pause, lift my head so I can soak in the lyrics as if they're gospel— this is no doubt a religious experience. I don't want Alexei to see me like this, but I have no choice, the spirit has taken over. I sing the whole theme song.

> *That's so Raven—it's the future I can see.*
> *That's so Raven—it's so mysterious to me.*

Amen. A-men! Like, really, can I get an amen? Alexei stares, perplexed—maybe a little worried?

By the end of the song I have tears streaming down my face. Having to face getting raw and honest with Alexei plus the reminder of simpler days really puts me over the edge. And on top of all that, Raven has such a way with words! She tries to save the situations but always ends up misbehaving . . . oh man, I feel you girl, I feel you.

I haven't heard this song since I was eleven years old. It triggers a wave of memories: eating vanilla ice cream with rainbow sprinkles down by the beach, shopping for back-to-school clothes at Limited Too, looking forward to Disney World and then getting to Disney World and finding that it's even more magical than I could have ever imagined. . . .

The wave of nostalgia becomes a wave of sadness. The carefree part of my life is over and I'll never get to go back to a time without boyfriends and mean girls and fame and pressure, now I can only go forward, fighting the uphill battle of life forever. Or until I die or whatever. Well, this got bleak. I apologize, but you have to understand, the moment you realize your childhood is over is never a happy one.

I thought getting a boyfriend was the most exciting thing to ever happen to me—and the fact that it was a boy I wanted for so long made it even better. But maybe I'm just not ready. Maybe all of this is happening too fast. Yvette was my enemy and then she was my friend and now she's a frenemy, which is basically a friend who you can't trust and secretly hate. Do I want that in my life? Is that the type of person I want to be close to me? This school year raced forward and upward, dragging me with it, pushing me into new roles and experiences so quickly I didn't have time to think any of it over. Everything that happened this year chose me, I didn't choose it. I think I might need to slow it down, regain control of my life, reevaluate what I want and who I am and who I want to become. I can't be a kid again, but that doesn't mean I have to grow up right away.

"I'm sorry I've made you feel disheartened," I say as the Uber pulls up to my house. "I've never doubted our friendship. Not for one second."

47

Queen Bully

(9,661,000 FOLLOWERS)

*R*emember at the end of *Mean Girls* when Lindsey Lohan's character talks about the next generation of mean girls? The freshmen mean girls in training who will inevitably grow up to be junior and senior mean girls? Well, she wasn't making that up. Mean girls in training are not just a myth, they are a reality, and now I know it for sure.

It's Monday (again. Ugh, why is Monday always coming back? Monday is like a disease you can't get rid of. Just when you think you're in the clear, there it is again.) and I'm strolling leisurely in between third and fourth periods. Strolling leisurely is a part of my new plan to take it slow, smell the roses, live life on my own terms etc. As I pass through the main quad I see a group of freshmen girls—all with impeccably straightened hair and wearing various shades of skintight pink—gathered around a table like a gaggle of baby prostitutes (yet another *Mean Girls* reference, get with the program).

"Like, really though," one of them is saying, obviously the queen bee with her golden hair and espadrille wedges sitting on the tabletop. "Who still wears glasses in this day and age? I mean come on, get yourself some contacts! Make the effort, have some self-respect!

I'm telling you guys, Morgan Blanchard is seriously the biggest loser at this school." The other girls giggle, nodding along. Ew. Where does this cruelty even come from? I walk by and the gaggle goes quiet.

"Oh my God, Lele, wait up," Queen Bee says, hopping off the table to follow me. "You're Lele Pons, right?"

"Yep."

"I just have to tell you, you're literally my hero, I can't tell you how much I love your videos. I can't believe you go to my school!" I'm about to just thank her and be on my way, but then I have another idea.

"Yeah? What's your name?"

"It's Brooklyn," she chirps. "Brooklyn Miller."

"Of course it is. Listen, Brooklyn, if you look up to me you should know I would never talk badly about someone behind their back. What you were just doing to Morgan, saying she's a loser, that's really mean. Not everyone has to be preppy and pretty and rich like you and your friends; when people are different, it doesn't mean you have a right to try to put them down. If anything, that just shows your weaknesses and insecurities. If you felt good about yourself, you wouldn't have to pick on other people. Not so long ago I was a 'loser' like Morgan. Kids here were mean to me, constantly, and it was really hurtful. I'm kind of famous now or whatever, so people here respect me, but I haven't changed, and I wouldn't want to. I'm dorky, I'm seriously awkward, and I'd rather be friends with the nerdy outcast girl than the girls making fun behind her back. Those girls are the real losers, and I think you're better than that."

Brooklyn is stunned; she presses her lips together until they disappear into a thin line. Her girl-squad looks terrified, staring at her intently to see how she'll react, what she'll do next. I didn't mean to embarrass her in front of her friends, but girls really need to hear this.

"I uh— Wow, I never thought of it that way."

"Well, just something to think about," I say. Then, channeling Darcy: "I have to get to class. And you probably should too."

Yvette keeps her face practically buried in her locker as she gets dressed. Anything to avoid talking to me.

"Yvette, you're my tennis partner, you won't be able to avoid me forever."

"I'm not trying to avoid you, don't be so self-involved."

"Okay, then let's talk."

"I didn't realize there was anything to talk about."

"You were blatantly flirting with my boyfriend."

"Just because he's your boyfriend doesn't mean you own him."

"Are you serious? You're my friend, you can't hit on my boyfriend!"

"You don't own me either."

"So that's how you want it to be? You want to go back to us hating each other?"

"Ugh." Yvette sighs deeply. "No. No, that's not what I want. Look, I'm sorry. The truth is I've liked Alexei for a long time, since before you and I were friends. I could always tell he had a little thing for you and that's what made me so jealous. Well, that and it was clear from day one that you're the coolest girl in school. So—"

"But you didn't think I was cool, you thought I was such a loser, you made fun of me for being so lame, don't you remember? You taunted me and called me a pirate!"

"Yes, yes, I remember, and I'm sorry for that. But it wasn't because I thought you were lame, it was because I thought you were independent and free-spirited and unique. I knew you weren't going to follow me around like the other girls did, if anything you were going to take over as queen bee, and that threatened me. Yeah you were dorky, but you had that unshakable confidence, and that counts for everything, even I know that."

"Wow. That's so insightful . . . and so big of you to admit."

"Thanks."

"So now what were you saying about liking my boyfriend?"

"Oh. Yeah. That. Look, I've always kind of had feelings for Alexei, but I knew you two liked each other, so I stayed out of it. Every now and then I thought maybe you weren't going to happen, so I would try again, but he's never been into me. Ever since you got together with him I've backed off, I promise. And I've tried to move on. But at Nick's party the other day I had like six beers and was actually embarrassingly drunk. I got out of hand. But you don't have to worry because he would never cheat on you. If anything all you have to worry about is me not being a very good friend. At least when I'm drunk."

"No, hey, look, it was a good-friend thing to do to be able to say all this. I think you're strong for admitting this to me; I actually admire you for it. I'm not great with honesty and, like, emotions or whatever. It takes strength. The fact that you can be honest about what matters is a sign that you're a real friend. Friendship isn't perfect, there are always going to be problems, it's just about how you deal with those problems. And I think you're dealing with them amazingly right now."

"Oh. Thank you, Lele."

"And I'm sorry you've liked Alexei for so long. I never thought we were going to happen; I always thought he liked you, actually—he's always talking about you and about how funny you are. In a way I sometimes think he still does. I'm actually always a little bit worried he's going to leave me for you. I don't know if that's rational or just totally insane, but it's one of the many, MANY reasons that our relationship is kind of falling apart. I'm starting to think we were better off friends. So hey, he might be available soon."

"No! I would never date him after this! Hoes before bros, right?"

"Yeah," I say. "Hoes before bros."

• • •

I ditch gym and sneak off campus through a gap in the chain-link fence behind the language building, skip the rest of the day. I need to be alone, to get back in touch with myself. I walk down Fourth Street all the way to the beach, buy a vanilla ice-cream cone with extra rainbow sprinkles. I take off my shoes and turn off my phone and walk down to the water, savoring the feeling of ocean air on my face and cool sand between my toes and the crystalized sugar of rainbow sprinkles melting on my tongue. It feels nice to be alone. This school year I've been so preoccupied with becoming my best self and then proving to everyone that I'm still me that I forgot that I'm human, just like everyone else. And that means being flawed, it means trying your best but making mistakes, then waking up and trying your best all over again. I guess what I'm trying to say is being human means having to say you're sorry . . . and sometimes it's to yourself. So, I'm sorry, Lele, for being so obsessed with you that I ironically ended up neglecting you. No, I'm not crazy, I'm just trying to find a little peace of mind.

I sit down right at the edge of the water and trail a finger through the damp sand. It feels good to be alone; no Alexei, no Yvette, dare I say no Vine? It's only me and the ocean and, like, countless sailors and mermaids before me, I feel free.

48

I'm Not Good with Breakups / When You Don't Know How to Break Up With Someone

(9,700,000 FOLLOWERS)

I have a distinct memory from when I was a kid where my mom's friend Jill slept on our couch for a week because she was "going through a breakup." I was about five and didn't know what a breakup was, and so my mom explained that it's when a boyfriend and girl-friend decide not to be together anymore. Being five and believing that boys not only had cooties but that they were also flat-out evil, I decided to be happy for Jill, as she was finally free. In addition, the week she spent on our couch seemed like the most fun way imagin-able to live life. She had people to cook and clean for her, people who felt bad for her and loved her and wanted to make her happy all the time. My mom baked her cookies and kept a steady stream of weepy romantic comedies on the TV and brought her fuzzy blankets and kept her stocked in tissues and rubbed her feet and listened to her talk and cry for literally hours. I made her bracelets from my lanyard kit and put on dance shows in the living room to entertain her. Even my dad put in an effort to make her laugh.

"I can't wait until one day I go through a breakup," I said to my mom one night at dinner.

"Why?" She laughed. "What a silly thing to say."

"Well, just because it seems so fun! Everyone treats you special and you get to have lots of sleepovers with your friends."

"Oh, honey"—she was amused—"it doesn't quite work like that. People have to be extra nice to you because you're going through so much pain. A breakup can be one of the most painful and difficult things in the world."

Aaanndddd she was right. I've decided things will be better with Alexei as my friend and not my boyfriend, but I can't help but feel the sadness of failure and loss. Plus, how the hell are you supposed to break up with someone? Do you pass them a note in class that reads, *Do you think we should break up? Check YES or NO. (PS, I personally think we should)* . . . ? Ugh, no, that's not right. I take out a pen and paper and get down to brainstorming.

Ways to break up with someone when you just don't know what you're doing

Take a sick day to think it over. Decide you need a week of sick days. Keep taking sick days until he assumes you're dead or forgets you exist altogether.

Hire his little sister to do it for you, even if she's evil. He can't get mad at her for that, so in the end everyone wins because nobody gets yelled at.

Go into the witness protection program: change your name and hair color, flee the country, never return.

You don't do anything: you know that you've broken up and that's all that really matters. Right? Heh.

You hire your friend to kiss him so that you can "catch him cheating," then use this as an excuse to break up with him.

You bake him a cake with frosting letters that spell out "It's Over." By the time he reads it you'll be long gone.

Skywriting?

Did I already say leave the country?

Hire a hit man? (Too dark?)

Be a mature, decent human being and have a conversation with him, no matter how hard it is for you to do.

Dammit. Why do I gotta have this intuition to do the right thing?

After sixth period I have a powerful urge to book it, run home and hide under my covers for the next twenty to thirty years, but I force myself over to Alexei's locker, where I know he'll be waiting for me. At first he isn't there, and I think I've caught a lucky break—maybe *he* has fled the country and I'm totally off the hook—but I make myself wait it out just to be sure, and sure enough he does show up, looking effortlessly cute as always. *Are you sure you want to do this?* The lovesick voice in my head always has to get its two cents in. Yes, I'm sure. If I want Alexei as a friend, if I want things to go back to the way they were, if I want to get back in touch with myself, this is what has to happen.

"Hey, girl," he says, his eyes already melancholy, predicting what's to come.

"Hey. I think we need to talk."

"You're probably right." He nods, hunching his shoulders. Suddenly he looks more like a cartoon drawing of an emo kid than an actual human being. Awwww.

We walk to my house, taking the same path we took the very first time he walked me home about nine months ago—several million followers ago. I joke that if we had had sex back on that day, then by today I could be giving birth to our baby, but he doesn't think it's funny. Men, am I right?

"So what do you think we need to talk about?" he asks.

"Okay, listen, I've been thinking about this all day and I still don't know the right way to say it, if there even is a right way. But I guess the bottom line is, do you ever feel like we were happier when we were just friends?"

"Yes! I do!"

"Whoa, really? That's such a relief. I think so too."

"I didn't know how to say it either. I didn't want to hurt your feelings."

"I didn't want to hurt your feelings!"

"Well, this is perfect then," he tells me.

"So perfect."

"Do you, uh . . . do you think we can go back though? To just being friends?" he asks.

"I don't know, I hadn't really thought about that. We were friends before . . . and if you think about it we've kind of just been friends throughout all of this, the only real difference is that I've turned into a melodramatic monster with an apparent hormone imbalance." I frown.

"That's a good point. I mean, not the part about the hormone imbalance, I actually think it's great that you're so . . . intense. Well, don't get me wrong, it's not the most fun to be in a romantic relationship with someone so . . . never mind, that's not what I'm trying to say. What I'm trying to say is that I think you're right that we've stayed friends throughout being boyfriend and girlfriend. I think for us being 'more than friends' meant being friends with romance and drama. So yeah, maybe we could just take away the romance and drama and go back to 'just friends.'"

"Yeah . . ."

"What's wrong?" He makes a concerned face.

"I dunno. It's just that 'just friends' sounds like such a down-grade."

"But it won't be. I think maybe in our case less really is more."

"I feel like that's one of those sayings that doesn't actually mean anything but people say it to sound smart and it only sounds smart because it is actually nonsense and no one is brave enough to stand up and say, 'Hey, I think this is nonsense,'" I say.

"First of all, you are hilarious. Second of all, that's not true. It means sometimes taking less can be a more rewarding experience. It means being 'just friends' means so much more than what it sounds like."

"Ohhhh. I see! Yes, very profound."

"Now the only question is, do we still have romantic feelings for each other?"

"I dunno." I shrug, trying to play it cool.

"Okay, well I definitely do."

"Fine, I do too."

"So then will we be able to let each other date? I mean, won't we get jealous?"

"Yeah, we'll get jealous," I say. "But I'll be an adult about it. The jealousy will be worth it if I can have my friend back."

"So what you're saying is you won't try to sabotage my wedding like Julia Roberts in *My Best Friend's Wedding*? Because I sort of think you will."

"You're getting way ahead of yourself, no one is ever going to want to marry you."

"Why you gotta be so rude?" He punches my arm lightly and I shove him into some hedges. It's like we're just a pair of kindergartners trying to figure life out. It's perfect.

May and June fly by, an exciting tangle of countdowns to summer and weekend beach days and Vines upon Vines upon Vines. There's

always something oddly unsettling about the last week of school—
the sun is high and perfectly positioned for beach parties, and yet
you're still indoors. The teachers have run out of assignments to
give you, and yet they insist on keeping you as prisoners. There's
this tension between how much fun you could be having and how
much fun you are not actually having.

So, we spend all day signing yearbooks, despite the fact that we
are all going to see each other again in two months, and then on the
last day they always have some sad activity you have to participate
in, like boys versus girls softball or capture the flag. This year for
the juniors it's a relay race involving water balloons and trivia from
the year's curriculum. Alexei and Darcy and I play one round before
we can't handle the anticipation of summer anymore, and decide to
just make a run for it.

"Hey! Get back here!" Coach Washington calls after us. "Eh,
never mind, it's summer. Just go." Awwww, I like to think summer
vacation brings out the very best in people.

#HIGHSCHOOLSURVIVOR

Three Months Later

49

Meeting Your Ex's New Bae

(10,000,000 FOLLOWERS)

*W*hen I tell Alexei about my ten brainstormed ways to break up with somebody, he thinks it's hilarious and insists we adapt them into our six-second masterpieces. Yvette and Darcy are kind enough to join our crew and help turn the visions into realities. Even Yvette's crew wanted to pitch in! What's best is Darcy and I finally came up with a name for them: They're the Whatevers, because seriously, whatever, they're not important enough in our lives to warrant thought or attention.

Summer comes full of freedom and possibility, everything is bright and beautiful and I've never felt so optimistic. There is one tiny itsy-bitsy little glitch in the perfection that is summer, and it happens sometime around July. Okay, fine, it happens on July 1 at 3:47 p.m., but who's keeping track? Not me, that's for sure.

So, like I was saying, it's 3:47 p.m. on July 1 and I'm lying like a beached whale on my bed without a single care in the world, when I get a phone call from Alexei.

"Hey, loser," I say.

"Hey! How are you?"

"Fine, chillaxing. What's up?"

"I just wanted to . . . I guess I just wanted to tell you this before you heard it from anyone else. I met someone, her name's Lila and, well, she's pretty much my girlfriend now." HOLD THE PHONE. Wait, I'm already holding the phone. What do you say in this situation when you are already holding a phone?

"Wow, that was . . . fast." A gray rain cloud drifts over the spectacularity (Lele Vocab Trademark) that is this summer.

"I know, this is probably super uncomfortable for you; I didn't mean to meet someone so fast but—"

"Uncomfortable? Please! Who's uncomfortable? I think it's awesome. Good for you, buddy. Happy for you." I chew on a cuticle until it bleeds.

"Really? I was worried that—"

"No need to be worried about anything, I'm fine with it. Why wouldn't I be? You're my best friend and you met someone you really like so— Hey! I think we should all go out to dinner together, I'd love to meet her!"

"Really? Well, okay, just the three of us?"

"No, of course not. Us three and uh . . . Bryce."

"Who's Bryce?"

"Just this guy I've been seeing. Casually. He's not my boyfriend or anything, but we've been hanging out." Actually Bryce is a guy who has been relentlessly trying to get me to go out with him who I have up to now not given the time of day.

"I see. Well, yeah, okay. Why not?"

"*Exactly*," I say. "Why the hell not?"

Lila. Hmpf. Sounds like a mutilated version of Lele if you ask me, but NO ONE IS ASKING ME I GUESS.

Me and my big mouth. Why'd I have to suggest dinner? Now I have to find the absolute perfect outfit and act like the absolute perfect version of myself throughout an ENTIRE MEAL. Plus, I have to spend an entire evening with Bryce, who I really have had no intention of getting to know. Getting yourself on fleek in order to meet your ex-boyfriend's new girlfriend is one of the most involved processes of all time. This is how you do it.

Start early. Go to the spa for massages, soaks, scrubs, and, of course, a full mani-pedi. Spare no expense!

Go shopping. Sure you could look through your closet for the perfect outfit, but everything you own has been done before. If you really want to present yourself as the unique butterfly that you truly are, you will need a brand-new outfit. Again, spare no expense—your appearance is more important on this occasion than any other time. If you show up and the new girl looks more magnificent than you, your self-esteem could be seriously damaged. The outfit should be casual but sharp—jeans and kitten heels, a tight-fitting black T-shirt and leather jacket, for example.

Unwind, get relaxed. You don't want to show up tense and anxious, so take an hour or so to profoundly chill out. Watch mindless TV, take a bath, take a nap, go swimming, whatever helps you get into your cool-girl headspace. Cool-girl headspace is basically just being so relaxed and laid back that nothing can shock or upset you. You're above it all, floating on a cloud.

Find a date. This should be someone who likes you more than you like him, someone who will make you look good and contribute to your cool-girl vibe, instead of detract from it. So, you know, someone cute to show you're a catch!

Last, but not least, follow steps one through fourteen of "How to get yourself on fleek for a fancy Nickelodeon party" (see page 215). Remember how on fleek you wanted to look for that? You should look and feel at least three times more on fleek tonight.

If you think these steps seem harsh or intense, it's only because I'm trying to look out for you. And myself. Following these steps will put you (and hopefully me) in a position to feel good about the night. God save us all.

Bryce picks me up around seven in a metallic blue BMW from 2006. He's wearing a polo shirt that is practically the exact same shade of blue and a backward baseball cap that says Yankees or Dodgers or whatever, who cares, it's a sports team no doubt and that is all you need to know. The blue polo is something I can live with, the baseball cap is not, so I make him take it off and put it in the backseat where I can't see it. Crisis averted. For whatever reason, Alexei has chosen the nearest Olive Garden as our meeting place, which is a crisis that simply cannot be averted. On the bright side, they do have a killer virgin watermelon margarita. You always gotta look on the bright side.

When we show up, Alexei and Lila are already sitting in a booth. They're not speaking to each other, or touching—instead they are scouring the menu as if on a treasure hunt, examining the contents intently with squinted eyes.

"I'll save you the trouble," I say. "You won't find anything you actually want to eat." I scan Lila from head to . . . where the table cuts her off: long blond hair, green eyes, edgy leather jacket. Okay, okay, so she's a less cute version of me. If I started this year as Lele 1.0, she's Lele 0.5 (but remember, by now I am basically Lele 10.0, especially with all the emotional growth I've done).

"What?" Alexei looks up. "Oh, ha-ha. Yeah," Alexei says. "It's not so bad."

"I know, I'm kidding." He stands up and so Lila stands up and I just keep thinking, *What am I supposed to do now? What am I supposed to do now?* in a loop over and over again.

"Lele, this is Lila. Lila, Lele."

"Hi!" she says. She's smiling hugely and idiotically, so I match it with a huge and idiotic smile of my own. "I've literally heard so much about you." Literally? *So much* doesn't need to be qualified with a *literally*. It's too vague to even be a close estimate of an amount let alone a literal amount. Ugh. Then she opens her arms and I guess I'm supposed to hug her?

We wrap our arms around each other in an embrace that is more intimate and constricted than I would have ever wanted it to be. She hugs me tightly, as if to say, "I'm cool with you!," so I hug her back even tighter, as if to say, "I'm even cooler with you!" How long has she been hugging me? Why won't this girl let go? She's so thin and fit and smells like Herbal Essences and Marc Jacobs perfume and the last thing I need is her pressing all of that perfection up against me—it's like she's literally rubbing it in. The combination of jealousy and irritation is too much for me to handle and suddenly I just snap: I squeeze my arms around her neck tighter and tighter until I hear a distinct snap and she falls to the floor, dead.

Okay, *fine*, that's not what happened. But do I always have to tell it as it really happened? Sometimes the truth isn't interesting enough . . . and that's where Vine comes in. On Vine I can rewrite history to make it the way I want it to be, I can re-create reality to match the vision in my mind, the version of reality that transcends the mundane. It's my playground, my laboratory, my escape, and my sanctuary.

"So, how did you two meet?" Unfortunately Alexei and I ask this at the exact same moment and have to spend a few seconds untangling and deliberating on who will answer first. I insist that he does.

"We met at a party. Well—that might be a little misleading. Our sisters are friends, and they were at a party. Lila was picking up her sister when I was picking up Aya." *Aya. I knew you'd be the death of me.*

"That's adorable," says Bryce, ripping off a piece of bread with his teeth.

In my head I have smiled and said something charming, but apparently I haven't because then Alexei goes, "Lele? You all right?"

"Yeah, why, what's up?"

"You were just staring blankly past my head."

"Oh was I? No, I'm fine. I'm great. I was just looking at that uh . . . erm . . . that painting back there. It's . . . pretty." They turn around to look at the painting, which is just a pixelated image of a wineglass.

"That one?" Alexei asks.

"Yeah, don't worry about it. Anyway, so you met at a kiddie party, that's awesome."

"Yeah!" Lila chirps. "It was so funny because the last thing I would have expected was to meet a cute guy at a four-year-old's birthday, right?"

"Riigghtt."

"So how did you two meet?"

"Well," Bryce volunteers. "I was a big fan of Lele's videos and—"

"Oh yeah! You're like really big on YouTube, right?" Lila says, turning to me.

"Vine, actually. But yeah, kinda big. Like over ten million followers. It's no big deal though," I tell her.

"It's a huge deal, actually," Alexei says. "It's very impressive."

"Well, yeah." I feign modesty, but in an obvious way, so that it's clear I actually do know how awesome I am, but just don't like to brag about it.

"Okay, cool, so then what?" Alexei asks.

"Well, I knew someone who knew someone who knew her, so I was able to get her e-mail address, and so I e-mailed her telling her I thought she was cool and . . . the rest is history." Agh, I could murder him. First of all he skipped the part where I ignored him for three months, second of all he made himself sound like the creepiest stalker of all time, and third of all, why does he have to start literally every sentence with "well"?!

"Should we order now?" I say. "I feel like we should order."

The meal goes by painlessly enough. Just kidding, it was excruciating—an unbearable combination of boring and emotionally straining. By the time it's over my face and butt are sore from all the clenching. On our way out, Lila goes to the bathroom and Bryce gets a phone call, so it's just Alexei and me standing outside Olive Garden, shifting back and forth on the soles of our shoes.

"She seems sweet," I say, hoping it came out genuine and not as totally forced as it actually was.

"Yeah. She's simple," he says. "I mean, in a good way. It's . . . pleasant."

"Yikes."

"What?"

"I don't know. *Pleasant* isn't a very exciting word."

"Yeah, I think I need a break from exciting."

"That's fair."

"Bryce seems cool."

"He's okay, it's not a real thing though. Maybe we'll go on a few dates. We'll see."

"Yep, there's lots to be revealed. Are you all right? You seem sad."

"I guess I am a little. When we broke up I knew you'd end up dating someone else, I just didn't think it would be so soon."

WAIT, was I just honest about my emotions? Without screaming or crying or causing a scene? What is this? Am I dying?

"I was worried you might feel weird about it." He sighs. "But listen, if it's too uncomfortable for you I can stay single for a little bit. You know, until us dating other people feels more natural."

"Alexei, that is seriously so sweet, but you're my best friend and I want you to be happy. If you're not happy I won't be happy."

"You sure?"

"Yes, moron, shut up."

"So, to get our friendship back to normal, do you think we should hang out less or more?"

"More," I say, "Definitely more. More is more."

Darcy comes over and we paint each other's nails while watching vintage *Beverly Hills, 90210* and laugh at the outfits. I start to complain about Lila but then quickly give up.

"You know what, never mind," I say. "She's a perfectly fine girl. Let them eat cake."

"I don't think that expression totally fits here but—"

"Ugh, Darcy, the point is I am growing up and learning to accept life for how it is. You should be really proud of me."

"I am proud of you," she says, glaring. "And I never tire of having a friend who tells me how I should feel."

"That's right. Because you accept me for who I am."

"Sure." More glaring.

"But really, though, I know I've put you through a lot this year, and to make up for it, you know what I'm gonna do?"

"Do I want to know?"

"I'm going to give you the prettiest fingernails anyone has ever seen in their whole lives."

"Oh, really?"

"Yes. Just watch."

"I think I'm fine with this basic purple."

"That basic purple is exactly that: basic. Please, please, please! Let me make them fabulous!"

"Fine."

I spend the next hour working on her nails like they're a bomb

I'm trying to defuse, like they're the only thing that exists. On top of a purple base I paint thin pinstripes in gold, then cross them diagonally with silver. I glue tiny rhinestones and studs onto the empty diamond-shape spaces and then top it all off with a layer of clear polish.

The final product is sparkly and regal and dope and on fleek and everything you would want in a manicure—until I lose balance and fall into Darcy, knocking her to the floor where all the work on her entire right hand smudges on the carpet. For a moment we freeze, stunned, speechless. Then we burst into hysterics and I let myself fall to the floor and we lie on our backs giggling and gasping for breath, giving into life and the wacky twists and turns it takes.

"We have to turn this into a Vine," I say. "'When Your Best Friend Is the Clumsiest Human Alive.'"

"Dope," she says. "Do you think we can get it in six seconds?"

"Let's find out!"

Not a lot can happen in six seconds, there's not much you can do. You can't write a song or read a book or pass a test or complete a manicure or clean your room. You can't cook a meal or make a plan or learn to drive or write a letter or save the world. But this year I've learned what you can do: You can wake up, become alive, send a text, take a shot, make a friend, fall in love, fall into place, save a life, make a change, make a first impression, get a second chance . . . and, most important, you can tell a story. I need only six seconds to tell a story, and as long as I have that, I know I'll be just fine.

EPILOGUE

Beware of the Psycho Girlfriends ("Blank Space"–style)

(10,100,000 FOLLOWERS)

"*N*ice to meet you, where you been? / I could show you incredible things." "Blank Space" by Taylor Swift starts to play as I make my way down the stairs in an elegant, strapless black dress. And there he is waiting for me, my knight in shining armor—a handsome man with stunning eyes ready to take me out for a night on the town. Taylor sings, "You look like my next mistake" as Alexei pops up behind me. I can see his reflection in the window above the front door trying to warn "my knight in shining armor." He makes an X with his arms, he raises a finger to his ear and spirals it around, the universal pantomime for "she's crazy!"

He thinks he's being discreet, that I can't see him, but I can. Trying to scare off new suitors? I don't think so. With one swift motion I swing my arm back and punch him in the face. He falls to the ground, and I continue to float effortlessly down the stairs.

Zoom out: Alexei and me IRL watching our latest Vine "Beware the Psycho Ex-Girlfriend," laughing our asses off on his bedroom floor.

As it turns out, Alexei has a thing for drama queens: Lila quickly went from innocent sweet pea to phone-snooping, revenge-wanting psycho. Just like me! I'm not saying all girls are like this, but Lila and I definitely aren't alone.

So, once again he's single, and things are starting to feel stable between us. In the course of a year we went from strangers to secret admirers to friends to "lovers" and back to friends again, and it's been awkward every step of the way. Maybe it will always be awkward, but that's just who we are, and maybe we're just building a new type of relationship, something that you haven't seen before. We do tend to be quite innovative.

At the end of the day this year wasn't a total epic fail. I made friends, fell in love, got famous, found myself, lost myself, and found myself again.

Best of all, I survived.

See you next year, Miami High. I'll be back.

ACKNOWLEDGMENTS

Lele:

$\mathcal{I}$ would like to thank everyone who has been a part of this amazing opportunity. I would like to thank Melissa for her dedication and patience in collaborating with me on this incredible book; without her this could not have been possible. I would like to thank Mark Schulman and Richard Abate for believing in this project and making it happen, and Natasha Simons for her amazing job as our editor. I would also like to thank Natalie Novak and Jordan Berkus for their support, and Luke and Logan for always being there for me, and of course my parents for their unconditional love and support. Thank you all for helping me fulfill one of my biggest dreams!! It has been an honor working together with all of you.

Melissa:

$\mathcal{I}$ would like to thank my team: Richard Abate, Rachel Kim, Zahra Lipson, and everyone at 3 Arts and Spilled Ink; Natasha Simons, our genius editor at Simon & Schuster; my friends Margie Stohl and Rafi Simon, for every mental-health day; my family—my ever-patient

and tireless husband, Mike Johnston, and especially my daughter,
Mattie, who watched Lele's Vines with me over and over again and
became Lele's biggest fan and was the reason I was so glad I did
this project. Thanks especially to Team Lele: Luis Pons and Anna
Maronese, Mark Shulman, and Lele herself for being so much fun
to work with!